APPLE CIDER SLAYING

APPLE CIDER SLAYING

JULIE ANNE LINDSEY

WHEELER PUBLISHING
A part of Gale, a Cengage Company

GALE
A Cengage Company

GALE
A Cengage Company

LIBRARY OF CONGRESS CIP DATA ON FILE.
CATALOGUING IN PUBLICATION FOR THIS BOOK
IS AVAILABLE FROM THE LIBRARY OF CONGRESS

ISBN-13: 978-1-4328-8098-9 (softcover alk. paper)

Published in 2020 by arrangement with Kensington Books, an imprint of Kensington Publishing Corp.

Printed in the United States of America
1 2 3 4 5   24 23 22 21 20

To my sweet daddy who has
West Virginia in his soul

CHAPTER ONE

"Welcome to Smythe Orchard," I said, smiling brightly at a group of holiday shoppers stepping off a shuttle bus. "I'm Winona Mae Montgomery, but you can call me Winnie. I live here on the farm with my granny, who you all know as Granny Smythe."

The small crowd chuckled as they arranged themselves before me.

"Not coincidentally," I continued, "we have a fantastic harvest of apples this year, including Granny Smith." I led the group from the parking area, through the beautiful late November morning and beneath our arching orchard gates, lined in fresh green pine boughs and twinkle lights. The broad vinyl banner stretching overhead announced FIRST ANNUAL CHRISTMAS AT THE ORCHARD. I turned to walk backward a few beats, enjoying their faces as they took it all in.

Autumn in the Blue Ridge Mountains was

breathtaking, and views from my family orchard were no exception. Granny's little strip of land was darn close to paradise this time of year, nestled neatly between two richly colored mountains in a valley so pretty the angels might've painted it themselves. "Granny and Grampy Smythe bought this land forty-seven years ago with money from their wedding," I explained, turning back to stay on schedule. "This was all just a fledgling orchard then, but they saw opportunity where the seller had seen failure, and Granny and Grampy set down roots. Thanks to their vision, love, and dedication, Smythe Orchard is now twenty-five acres of the finest fruits in northern West Virginia. In addition to apples, we harvest blackberries, blueberries, peaches, and cherries."

I stopped at the large white tent with a strategic cross section of Smythe Orchard products showcased beneath. "This," I said dramatically, "is the fruit stand." In keeping with my new theme, I'd generously sprayed canned snow over every crate, barrel, and display in sight. And despite the unseasonably warm temperatures, I thought the place looked rather festive.

Granny parked a wheelbarrow of leftover gourds and pumpkins from last weekend's harvest festival, a festival that normally signified the end of our business season, beside the register and headed our way. She hadn't quite bought the idea that her orchard could be a popular Black Friday alternative for those who didn't want to shop retail or fight the crowds, but she'd agreed to give it a try. She'd even worn her nice red wool coat with matching hat and muck boots in case I was right.

"Here she is now," I told our guests. "The amazing woman who turns fresh, home-grown fruits into all the delicious holiday products you see here. My Granny Smythe."

I did a soft clap then shook the jingle bell bracelet on my wrist. Christmas at the Orchard was a sales ploy created very recently by me. It was a last-ditch effort to make some extra cash before the orchard went dormant for the winter, along with Granny's income. She was undeniably the heart of the place, but Grampy had been the business-minded one. It was no secret that sales had slumped after we lost him unexpectedly about three years back, but it wasn't until a few weeks ago, when Granny came to me with a stack of unpaid bills and a nearly depleted savings account, that I'd realized the orchard was in serious financial trouble. We had to turn things around fast

9

and drumming up Christmas sales seemed like a solid start.

Lucky for us, I'd been taking business classes at the local community college every Saturday since high school graduation, and, if I kept it up, I'd have my bachelor's degree before my next birthday. Earning a four-year degree in just shy of a decade didn't seem like much to brag about, but taking things slow had made it possible for me to pay cash as I went. So, unlike a lot of folks I knew, I'd be debt free when I finished next spring, and that was something I was proud of. I even had a little nest egg to show for my patience and some big ideas on how to help Granny make money from her harvest all year long — assuming I could get the local banker on my side. Luckily, I had another week of Thanksgiving break from classes to get things in motion.

"Come on in," Granny said, waving the guests closer and enchanting them with her smile. Her heart-shaped face and thick brown bangs made her look deceptively younger. Her narrow, youthful figure didn't hurt. She'd been mistaken for my mother more times than I could count over the years, and it was probably the most accurate mistake ever made.

I'd gotten my dark hair and eyes from

Granny, my wide cheekbones and pointy chin too. My go-getter attitude and big mouth came straight from Grampy. He'd taught me to speak up and state my mind because ladies didn't always get the respect they deserved in farm endeavors. I'd loved the empowerment in those lessons. Sometimes a little too much and to Granny's chagrin.

I stood back as Granny shook a few hands and smiled warmly, the only way she knew how. "Thank you so much for joining us. I know the popular notion for Black Friday is to crowd into a mall and fight your way to deals, but I think you'll go home feeling much more satisfied after spending a day in the fresh air and sunshine. And it couldn't be a more beautiful morning," she said. "It seems as if these old hills have put on the dog just for you, showing off all those brilliant colors in a grand West Virginia welcome. If that's not enough, Winnie and I have plans to spoil you too." She shot me a wink and a grin. "We'll start with a proper hayride and farm tour, then move on to a fantastic sampler buffet around noon. So if you see anything you'd like to try while we're out exploring, chances are you'll get a little taste of it soon."

The tour group's faces lit up at the mention of free food.

"First," Granny said, clasping her hands in front of her, "Where are y'all from?"

A woman dressed like a stewardess lifted her lanyard and smiled. The plastic badge on the end identified her as the tour guide for Ohio Senior Trips. "Cleveland," she said.

It was our third tour group of the morning and our second from Ohio. The first had arrived from Columbus with the sun, and the group in between had been from Pittsburgh.

Granny grinned. "Well, we're sure glad to have you." She opened her arms and corralled the group toward her waiting tractor and flatbed wagon with safety rails. "Let's start with a little ride around the property. We'll visit the buildings where we sort and wash apples the same way today that we did forty years ago. You're going to love it." She herded the bulk of the Senior Trip people onto the wagon. When every hay bale seat was full, she locked the gate behind them.

A few stragglers looked confused, stuck between the fruit stand and wagon.

"You're welcome to wait here," Granny said. "Browse the selection, walk the grounds, or sample some cider, and I'll be back around in a bit to pick you up for the tour. Until then, Winnie will take good care of you."

Granny climbed aboard the big green tractor, and the stragglers headed in my direction. An elderly man in cargo pants and a fanny pack stopped to eyeball a festive display of cider dispensers near the register. I'd stenciled holly leaves and berries on a sign encouraging customers to help themselves to samples. He filled a tiny paper cup and swigged. "That's good."

"Thank you." I'd heard the sentiment before, and quite often, but it never stopped puffing my chest with pride. "It's a personal recipe of mine."

He nodded approvingly, then refilled the cup and pointed it at the piles of fresh picked apples opposite us. "How much for a bushel?"

"Fifteen dollars," I said. I couldn't help wondering how many apples he could carry on his person with all those pockets.

The man turned back to the cider dispensers and sampled the next flavor while he considered his apple options. "Do you have Gala?"

"Yes, sir," I assured. "We have nine fantastic varieties, including Gravenstein, Gala, Honeycrisp, Cortland, Jonathan, Red and Golden Delicious, Granny Smith, and Pink Lady. The Honeycrisps are especially juicy this year."

He cast his gaze around the fruit market, sunglasses hooked in the collar of his John Denver T-shirt. The words *Almost Heaven* were scripted over a backdrop of trees and a river. "What do you put in your cider? This is exceptional."

"The first sample you tried has cinnamon sticks and a little nutmeg. Simple. Traditional. The one you have there is blended with cranberry juice and a dash of lemon. Fresher. Crisp."

He sipped. "Delicious."

"Thank you."

"Do you sell your ciders by the gallon?" He went back to sample from the third dispenser.

"Yes, sir," I told him, gaze locked on his as he lifted the cup to his lips once more. "That flavor is something new I'm trying. It's best served warm with chai spices and a little milk."

He handed me a pair of twenty-dollar bills and selected a basket of Galas. "I'm going exploring. Mind if I pick these up when I come back?"

"No, sir," I said.

"I'll take a gallon of all three ciders too."

I beamed. "Excellent. The chai blend won't come with milk. You'll add that to taste once you warm it to serve."

"Perfect." He finished the last dregs of his sample before tossing the little cup into the wastebasket.

I made his change and wrote up a receipt. "I'll transfer your apples into something better suited for traveling when you return, and I'll pull the ciders from the cooler while you're gone."

"Much obliged." He tucked the change and receipt into one of his many pockets and headed across the grass for a look around.

I climbed onto my stool at the edge of the tent and popped my collar against a chilly breeze nipping at my neck. Hopefully the man I'd just waited on had a jacket in the tour bus. He'd regret the decision to wear nothing but a T-shirt once the deceptively warm day gave way to a seasonably cold night and the sun set before dinner.

Beside me, the stack of papers I'd left weighted with a rock began to protest the wind. I gathered the pages into my hand, unwilling to let them get away. The business proposal had taken me two weeks to write, and convincing Mr. Sherman, the banker, to come out for a visit had taken even longer.

It had been my lifelong dream to open a

cider shop at the orchard, and given Granny's financial situation, the time was now or never. But I needed a small business loan to get started. I'd painstakingly prepared the proposal and included a few sketches illustrating my vision for the space. I'd been doodling and daydreaming about my cider shop for years, especially during my breaks at the Sip N Sup where I waitressed most nights. With a little luck, I wouldn't be serving for someone else much longer because I'd soon be running the show.

I organized the pages and tapped them against my thigh. A cider shop at Smythe Orchard had limitless potential. We could bring in money year-round with this kind of creative addition. The space could be rented for events like weddings and baby showers or used to host local bands for concerts. It would be amazing. I just hoped I could convince Mr. Sherman.

I'd strategically scheduled multiple bus tours to be on the grounds during his visit today. The volume of shoppers should give him the impression business was booming and, therefore, granting me a small business loan would be a low risk, basically brilliant financial move on his part. Unfortunately, in a town as small as Blossom Valley, he probably already knew about the orchard's money troubles, and convincing him to pour more cash into the place would be tougher than it should.

"Winona Mae!" A familiar voice cracked the silence and pulled my shoulders to my ears. Granny's nemesis, Nadine Cooper, stomped into view, hips swinging with each step of her hot pink platform shoes. Her black pedal pushers and white fitted blouse were straight out of the 1960s, but the bulge between blouse buttons was new. "Where is your granny?" she asked as she came to a stop. "I need to talk to her right now."

I settled my dark sunglasses over my eyes and lowered the papers onto my lap. "Hello, Mrs. Cooper," I said, staring upward toward her grouchy face and the bright morning sun. "It's nice to see you."

"Yeah, yeah." She scanned the area, chomping fluorescent green gum at fifty miles an hour and locking no-nonsense hands over her hips. "Is she in the house?"

"No, ma'am. She just left with a wagon-load of guests," I said, thankful for that truth. The last thing I needed was for Mrs. Cooper to be hanging around causing a stink when Mr. Sherman arrived in an hour. "They're taking a tractor tour, but they'll be back in a bit. Would you like some cider while you wait?"

"I can't wait," she said, crossing her arms and further testing the integrity of her blouse buttons. Had she overstuffed her bra? "I'll be back. You tell her we need to talk ASAP, and this is important. I'm mad as a wet hen, and she needs to hear about it."

"Yes, ma'am," I said. "I'll send her your way as soon as she can get there."

Granny didn't have a cell phone, so she couldn't call until she went back to the house, and she probably wouldn't do that until the gates were locked for the night. That didn't matter because Nadine was the closest neighbor, and she and Granny just marched back and forth to fight instead of wasting time with a telephone. According to my calculations, they'd been at it forty-three years. Granny said Nadine bought the adjacent parcel out from under her and Grampy when they'd hoped to expand. Nadine had responded with something like, "So what?" And the battle was on.

Mrs. Cooper wiggled her way back across the lawn and into the trees separating our land from hers. Whatever new grievance had her all worked up would have to wait a few hours. Meanwhile, I went back to practicing my speech for the banker.

■ ■ ■ ■

Mr. Sherman was late, but he showed up, and I counted that as my first victory.

I hobbled along to greet him on three-inch pumps, which might as well have been stilts since the tallest heel I'd worn this side of prom night was on my tennis shoes. I'd made a quick trip to my place in the remodeled building across the field from Granny's house between bus arrivals. I'd traded my jeans and knockoff Nikes for a dress without pockets and shoes that hurt my feet. Now, unlike the man I'd met earlier, I had zero places to keep anything, and I was forced to stack my paperwork, drawings, and cell phone onto a clipboard that my shaking hands were sure to drop.

"Hello, Mr. Sherman." I met the banker with a hearty handshake and a smile.

"Miss Montgomery," he said, seeming a bit confused by my outfit despite the fact he was in a three-piece suit.

"Thank you so much for coming." I led him through the gates and stopped, strategically, near the crowded fruit market. "I won't keep you long. As you can see, business has really picked up, and Granny needs my help."

Mr. Sherman gave the visitors a long look. "I see." Mr. Sherman was tall and fancy with his bank job, shiny shoes, and little satin pocket square. He had dark hair with shocks of gray above the ears and cheeks so smooth my legs were ashamed of themselves.

"I thought we could take a walk along the tree line to get a feel for the property, then go right to the old Mail Pouch barn where I want to open the shop. What do you say?"

He lifted a palm, looking less than interested, and indicating I should lead the way.

"As you know, folks come from far and wide to buy my cider and Granny's apples. We sell a substantial amount of pies and preserves as well," I said, my heels stabbing holes into the ground behind me, "but only when the weather allows. Our numbers are strong from late spring to early fall, but from November until March, the income is typically almost nil. We rarely have warm days or traffic like we do today so late into November, and you want to know the worst part?" I paused briefly for dramatic effect. "We have the capability to produce the same organic, high-quality cider, jams, jellies and pastries all year long. We just need a proper place to sell them."

Mr. Sherman slowed to a stop beside me.

"You want a storefront."

"I want more than a storefront."

His gaze slid away from mine and latched onto something over my head.

"Something wrong?" I asked, pivoting in search of whatever had caught his attention and hating the fact my pitch had been disrupted before I'd really gotten going.

He cocked his head and stared at the leaves on one tree. "What's wrong with this one?"

"Nothing." I stepped closer to confirm the obvious truth, except once I did I wasn't so sure. The leaves of the tree in question were slightly discolored and brittle-looking on the ends, but it wasn't the result of a normal seasonal shift, so I changed my answer. "I'm not sure." I moved around the trunk, examining the leaves on other branches and noticing a frightening pattern.

Mr. Sherman followed my lead, scrutinizing adjacent trees. "I see it here too," he said. "Are they sick?"

"No. I don't think so."

"Will this impact the fruit's quality? The annual yield?"

"Mr. Sherman," I said, cutting him off and feeling heat rise to my cheeks. "I walk these trees every day, and this is the first I'm seeing this. I don't know what it is, but

I will find out."

Mr. Sherman pulled a small pad of paper from his inside jacket pocket. He clicked a pen to life and made a note.

Suddenly every word I'd planned to say went right out of my head. Familiar feelings of dread and panic tightened my throat and constricted my lungs. I needed this loan, needed his approval. Things couldn't go like this or Smythe Orchard would be no more.

Focus, Winnie, I demanded internally. *Tighten up before you blow it and Granny loses everything.* My ears rang as I forced the panic away. I hugged the clipboard and its burden to my chest, hoping to still my pounding heart. "A year-round cider shop," I croaked through a suddenly dry mouth and parched throat, "would be a great addition, not just to the orchard, but to the community. It would be so much more than a storefront, though we could certainly have a display area where Smythe Orchard's fruit, produce, or prepackaged treats could be served."

Mr. Sherman gave me a small, sad smile. "You might not be aware, Miss Montgomery, but this orchard is in serious financial trouble, and there are clearly bigger problems here than you realize." He shot a pointed look at the strange yellowed leaves.

"You're wrong." I bristled, hating the condescension in his tone. I'd put up with shades of disdain all my life. For being young. For being a woman. For attending a community college instead of some big university. For being from Blossom Valley, West Virginia, a small farming community, instead of someplace people had heard of. "I know all about our financial troubles, Mr. Sherman," I said. "That's why I asked you to come here, and I know more than most people about how this orchard operates. I know the obstacles in front of me, and I know all about the labor-intensive, knuckle-busting, back-breaking hours given to the harvest and production of our products. I know the blood, sweat, and tears it takes to maintain a property like this one because my granny and I have been doing it, on our own, for three years." I blinked through the stinging reminder that Grampy was gone. What we had left was this orchard and each other. I wasn't letting either go without a fight. "And I also know the payoff," I said. "The fruits of our labor, if you will."

Mr. Sherman listened quietly to my rant without making a move to leave.

I rushed on before I lost his attention or

my nerve again. "*You* might not know, Mr. Sherman," I said, playing his words back to him and enjoying how it felt, "but Smythe Orchard provides things that the bulk of this community needs at prices they can afford. As a banker, you must be aware half our town struggles to make ends meet sometimes. Did you know those folks count on Granny's fruits and jams for their kids' lunches and for their dinner tables because she lets those families set the price?" I squared my shoulders and lifted my chin. "With this cider shop, we could do so much more. We would make more and we could give more."

Mr. Sherman nodded. "All right," he said softly. "May I see the proposed business location?"

I puffed a breath of relief. "Thank you." I hurried past him, returning to my sales pitch as we made our way toward the Mail Pouch barn at the corner of Granny's property. "Did you know that our Mail Pouch barn is a registered landmark?" I asked. "People have come here all my life just for the opportunity to take pictures of it. I've met photographers from Anchorage to Los Angeles and as far away as Sweden. These barns are more than iconic. They're a much sought-after piece of American culture and history. There are government grants and loans available for their maintenance and upkeep. Grampy always took advantage, and the barn stands as strong today as the day it was built."

Mr. Sherman was silent behind me.

I checked to be sure he hadn't turned tail and run.

"The Bloch brothers were the first to paint this barn," I said, beaming with pride as we approached the apple sorter and press building. "The Bloch brothers were from Wheeling and they made popular flavored chewing tobacco but couldn't afford to advertise, so they, like me, used their heads and made a plan. They utilized what they had, which was time and elbow grease, to get what they wanted, which was exposure. They offered to paint barns for free, as long as they could put their ad on one side. Simple. Effective. Legendary." I said. "Which makes our barn the perfect venue for my cider shop."

I held up a finger as we reached the building. The apple press was normally a tourist favorite, but someone had closed the door. I doubted anyone would be forward enough to walk inside if I didn't prop it back open. I climbed the three wooden steps and curled my hand around the knob. "Just one second," I said. "I'm not sure why this door is closed, but I don't want the next group coming by to think it's off-limits."

Sure enough, a group of onlookers saw me at the building and headed our way. I swung the door open and stepped aside. "Go on in," I said, cheerfully, "have yourselves a look around. This is where the magic happens."

They picked up their pace across the short strip of ground.

Mr. Sherman made a strangled noise, his skin suddenly pale as the moon.

"Mr. Sherman?"

He lifted the end of his tie to cover his lips.

I followed his horrified gaze into the building.

A pair of black pedal pushers and two hot pink platform sandals came into view, hanging over the side of the metal tray table beneath the apple press. Slowly, my brain processed the rest of Mrs. Cooper's body. Her unseeing eyes stared through me as blood slid over her cheek from an angry wound at the top of her head.

The shrill scream that rattled the roof was mine.

CHAPTER TWO

"Miss Montgomery?" A slow southern drawl poured under the closed door with such assured authority I nearly wept. "This is Sheriff Colton Wise. I'm going to need you to open up."

I nodded, though no one could see me. I wasn't sure how much time had passed since I'd first seen Mrs. Cooper in the cider press, but *forever* seemed roughly accurate. I'd slammed the door against the cluster of tourists headed my way when I saw the body and locked myself inside.

I'd shut the door in Mr. Sherman's face.

The knot in my stomach tightened.

When Grampy installed the new locks to protect his equipment five years ago, I'd thought he was bonkers. Who would want to steal apple sorting or pressing machinery and paraphernalia? He'd said that I would understand some day, but I'd never dreamed I'd need the lock to protect tourists from seeing Nadine Cooper's dead body.

I flipped the deadbolt and moved out of the way.

The door opened slowly, and a lean man with broad shoulders and kind eyes slipped inside. He wore jeans and boots with his sheriff's jacket. His big hat was in his hands and pressed to his chest. "Winona Mae Montgomery?"

I nodded, my dry and swollen tongue stuck to the roof of my mouth.

"Have you touched anything in here?" he asked, throwing a pointed look at Mrs. Cooper.

I shook my head and tried uselessly to swallow the constricting lump in my throat. I'd seen the new sheriff a time or two since his election last fall, but we'd never officially met.

"Have you been right here since you locked the door?"

"Yes," I managed to say.

The sheriff offered a small but compassionate smile. "Do you know this woman?" he asked, glancing again at Mrs. Cooper.

"Yes." I willed myself to elaborate, but my thoughts moved too quickly for my sticky mouth, and I wasn't convinced I wouldn't throw up if I parted my lips longer than necessary.

A rap came at the door, and Sheriff Wise pulled it open. He held it wide with his boot.

The blast of sunlight brought tears to my eyes.

"There." He tipped his head toward the cider press, and a pair of EMTs charged in that direction with a yellow backboard and matching medical kits. Behind them, an elderly man shuffled along. The back of his black jacket had seven white block letters: *CORONER.* A woman with a toolbox fell into step at his side.

"Winnie!" Granny's frantic voice echoed through the open door, laced with fear and worry. I hated the sound of it; I never wanted her to be alone or scared.

"I'm okay!" I yelled back. "I'm coming!"

The sheriff swung his face in my direction. "Just a minute now. Can you tell me what happened in here?"

"No. I opened the door, and Mrs. Cooper was there," I said, finally finding my voice. "I was showing Mr. Sherman the property, and when I saw the door was closed, I opened it." My heart pinched as a new thought emerged. *Mr. Sherman will never give a small business loan to a failing orchard with a dead woman in the apple press.*

I hated myself immediately for the selfish

thought. Against my will, more awful notions followed. *Could the press even be cleaned after this?* No way, right? *We'd have to buy a new one, and presses cost a fortune.* We couldn't afford it. *Maybe I could offset the cost of a new press by selling this one on eBay?* I pressed my palms to the sides of my head and hoped lightning didn't strike me on the spot.

"Miss Montgomery," the sheriff said, sharp blue eyes scanning the beads of sweat gathered on my forehead. "Would you like to step outside?"

I flicked my gaze to the coroner poking and prodding Mrs. Cooper. The woman with the toolbox scraped a stick under Mrs. Cooper's fingernails, and my stomach flopped. "Yes."

Sheriff Wise held the door while I scurried into the sunlight, sucking in deep lungfuls of fresh air after far too many shallow breaths inside the crowded barn. A deputy stood between Granny and an ambulance. A pair of cruisers were angled several yards away as a makeshift barrier.

"Baby!" Granny wrapped me in her arms. "I'm so sorry you had to see something like that. Mr. Sherman told me what happened, and I headed right over here, but when I saw the guests outside the locked door, I knew I had to gather everyone back at the fruit stand before the authorities arrived." Deep lines creased her brow. "By the time I did all that, and the deputies questioned me as well, I couldn't get away again until now." She wiped her shirtsleeve over her puffy eyes. "I just can't believe any of this." Her bottom lip quivered as she pressed my cheeks between her soft palms. "I'm so sorry I wasn't here for you."

My stomach rolled as I stepped out of her embrace. The heels of my uncomfortable shoes sunk into the earth. "I hadn't even thought about the visitors," I whispered. "None of those companies will ever book with us again, and it's my fault that so many were here. I wanted the orchard to be busy when Mr. Sherman came so I would get my loan." I rolled my eyes skyward and wrapped myself in a hug. *He left before I had a chance to finish my pitch and show him the Mail Pouch barn.* Now, he was never going to agree to that loan, and this day officially couldn't get any worse.

"Miss Montgomery," Sheriff Wise began again. "Do you have any idea who might've wanted to hurt Nadine Cooper?"

I turned my eyes to him, then they flickered traitorously toward Granny.

He raised his brows and looked at her too.

"Mrs. Smythe?"

I cringed. He was sure to find out about Granny and Mrs. Cooper's relationship. If we didn't tell him, would it make us look guilty? What if Mrs. Cooper had run into Granny on her way home and the two had fought? I hadn't spoken to Granny since Mrs. Cooper left. I had no idea what had happened next, and the orchard was crowded today. Someone could've heard them argue before Mrs. Cooper was killed. "Mrs. Cooper came looking for Granny today, but I haven't had a chance to tell her until now."

"What did she want?" he asked.

"I'm not sure. She wanted to talk to Granny as soon as she could."

The sheriff crossed his arms and focused on Granny. "Any idea what that was about Mrs. Smythe?"

"None," she said. "I haven't seen Nadine in two days."

He nodded, maintaining eye contact and tipping his head over one shoulder. "Were the two of you close?" he asked.

I shut my eyes so I couldn't give anything else away. The world seemed to spin faster.

"We weren't friends, if that's what you mean," Granny said.

"I see," he said. "How would you describe

your relationship with the victim?"

"I suppose I'd say we're neighbors, and we tend to bump heads more than shake hands."

"Did you like Nadine Cooper, Mrs. Smythe?"

My eyes popped open. Maybe I was wrong. The day could definitely get worse.

"Of course," Granny blurted. "I liked her just fine."

"Really? Because a lot of folks have the idea you two were enemies."

I turned to face the sheriff directly. "Why would you say that?" I asked. "My granny likes everyone."

He hiked an eyebrow, then let his features settle into a frown. "The way I hear it, your grandma's relationship with Nadine Cooper was as tumultuous as the New River rapids."

Granny sighed. "You're not wrong. I've known Nadine for forty-three years, and we've never had a conversation that didn't end in someone's ruffled feathers. Nadine and I weren't friends, but we're part of this community and that made us family. Does that make sense?"

"No." The sheriff widened his stance and continued to look Granny and me over with keen, judging eyes. "I think Nadine Cooper was practically your sworn enemy. So, I can't understand why she was over here looking for you today."

"I don't know," Granny repeated.

They both looked at me.

I lifted my shoulders and palms. I'd already told them everything I knew. "She was mad again, and she wanted to talk to you ASAP. She didn't say why."

Granny frowned. "She rarely does. That's how she keeps the upper hand, by making me walk into her little ambushes." Granny's ruddy cheeks went pale and her lips formed a tiny O. She slapped a palm over her mouth. "Gracious! I didn't mean to be so disrespectful. I just can't believe this is happening."

I slipped an arm around her waist and tugged her against my side.

The press building's door opened once more and the coroner stepped into the frame. "Sheriff?"

Sheriff Wise stared at us another long beat before turning and walking away.

I released a shuddered breath and leaned my head on Granny's shoulder, letting my tears flow free. "Who would do something like this?"

Granny rubbed my back in big comforting circles. "The sheriff will figure it out. Don't worry."

I wiped my eyes to stop the tears as she pressed a kiss to my head.

A heavy shadow stretched over us a moment later, blocking the sun and sending a chill across my skin. Granny's hand stilled on my back.

I turned to find Sheriff Wise evaluating us once more. He frowned down his nose from the eight or so inches he had on my shrimpy five-foot-four frame. His big hat was stuffed back on his head, and the shadow it threw across his face was utterly intimidating. "Mrs. Smythe. Where were you at noon today?"

"Bringing the tractor back from the tour," Granny said.

"Alone?"

"Of course. I dropped a group off at the pavilion to sample our wares, then I took the tractor over to the house for a quick sandwich and bathroom break. After that, I headed back up front to collect the next bunch of riders."

"So, no one can vouch for where you were, what you were doing, or who you were with between noon and one o'clock this afternoon. Is that correct?"

Granny puckered her lips and brow. "Well, I suppose someone must've seen me driving back to the fruit stand. I was on a big green

35

tractor."

I gripped Granny's hand in mine and squeezed. "I think you should stop talking," I said softly. "I think Sheriff Wise is implying something he shouldn't be."

The sheriff narrowed his eyes. "The last call Mrs. Cooper received on her cell phone was from you, Mrs. Smythe."

Granny's eyes widened. "That's right," she said, "I forgot. There was a message on the machine from Nadine when I stopped home for lunch, so I returned her call. She didn't answer."

I folded my arms and glared back at him, suddenly more angry than frightened. "What exactly are you suggesting, Sheriff?"

"Just that the body of your granny's longtime enemy was found in a building belonging to your granny, after receiving a call from your granny, at a time that no one can confirm her whereabouts or activities," he said. "It's interesting, yeah?"

Granny's knees buckled slightly, and I held her tighter.

"No," I said. "It's not interesting at all. You're just restating the fact that someone left a dead body on our property while Granny was busy working elsewhere. You can twist and manipulate that statement any way you'd like, but it won't change the fact

36

Granny was nowhere near this building today until thirty minutes ago. Now, are you arresting her, or can we go?" I asked.

The sheriff's frown deepened. "You're free to go, but I'd consider getting a good lawyer." He handed us each a business card with his contact information on it. "I'll be in touch."

He tipped his hat and headed back to the crime scene.

I would've kicked stones behind him, but my heels were buried three inches in the ground.

CHAPTER THREE

I hurried into the Sip N Sup diner for my shift at 7:00 p.m. sharp. Trucks were lined up in front of the long plate-glass windows and around both sides of the building on our main street through town. The after-dinner crowd had arrived, and I was about to catch hell from my boss, Mr. Kress, for showing up last minute. Mr. Kress thought we should be on the floor when our shifts started, not punching in.

I tied my apron as I ran for the time clock behind the kitchen.

" 'Bout time," Mr. Kress called from his office, feet up on his desk, door open so he could yell about something every few minutes and make sure no one enjoyed their job any more than absolutely necessary.

"Sorry!" I yelled back, shoving my time card into the machine. I held my breath as the stamp of judgment thumped down, then peeked at it with one eye closed. "Seven!" I said, turning the card to face Mr. Kress's open office door. I wasn't early, but I wasn't late. Thank goodness for the little victories.

He frowned, then went back to scowling at the paperwork splayed across his desk.

I headed for the dining area in my traditional baby blue waitress uniform, complete with A-line, knee-length skirt, structured top, and tennis shoes. Some of the other waitresses thought the uniforms were degrading or misogynistic, but I was just thankful I never had to think about what to wear. Though, I supposed, a uniform of jeans and logoed T-shirts would have been a lot better.

The Sip N Sup was packed with patrons, happy voices, and the gentle clink of silverware on plates. It continuously smelled like mouthwatering joy because thirty years of grease, salt, and melted cheese had permeated the walls. We sold burgers, fries, and salads faster than the cooks could make them, and our fair share of coffee and pie as well. Occasionally someone would ask to see a menu, but that was almost always a tourist. The nearby national forest, New River, and endless West Virginia beauty brought birders, hikers, and outdoor enthusiasts to Blossom Valley in droves from May to November. Only the few who were brave enough to eat with the locals instead of at the chain establishments up the road, needed menus.

"Order up!" the cook called as I passed.

I grabbed the tray and the ticket, then delivered it to its final destination and went back for another.

Reese McFee, the pretty blonde waitress sharing my shift, stood near the pickup window when I returned. Her jaw nearly unhinged at the sight of me. "Winnie! What on earth are you doing here? I thought for sure you'd call out tonight. What are you thinking? How's your Granny doing?"

I did my best to process the questions as quickly as she spouted them out, but Reese talked faster than most people could think, and at the moment, I was struggling. "Granny's okay," I said, deciding that was the only real question in the bunch. "I guess everyone's heard about what happened?"

Her wide-eyed expression said that was true. "It's awful."

"Yeah," I agreed.

"So what *are* you doing here?" she asked. "Shouldn't you be with your granny? Or maybe a therapist? I heard you were the one who found the body." She whispered the last two words, an unwritten custom when it came to speaking of distasteful things.

"Granny wanted to rest," I said. "It was a long day, but I was too jittery to sit still, so I thought a busy night at work might help take my mind off things."

Her bottom lip jutted out and she pulled me in for a hug. "Bless your heart."

I forced a small smile and tried to swallow the guilt and shame creeping up my throat. I didn't like to lie, and I really was jittery, but confessing the whole truth would've made me seem nosy, and no one liked a snoop.

I had planned to call out. Then it occurred to me that I had the busy shift tonight, and I'd probably see a lot of folks who'd heard all kinds of stories about what had happened at the orchard today. One of those people might even know something I didn't, having heard it from an actual witness, through the grapevine, or even from the murderer without realizing. That was when I'd pulled on my figurative big girl pants and donned my uniform. I'd hated the fear in Granny's eyes when Sheriff Wise looked at her as if she could be a killer. So, I'd rushed right to work hoping to pick up and pass on some information that could help the sheriff get his handcuffs on the right person and his sights off my granny.

I took the next order to its intended guest,

then kept on moving. Before long I had a corner set of my own tables to care for and a smile on my face. There was something about the busyness of a full diner that made me feel like I was moving mountains instead of wading in quicksand, which was how I felt whenever I wasn't in motion. I liked setting goals and reaching them. Every cleared table was another victory. Every newly seated guest was a fresh challenge. Classic country music on the jukebox was just a blessing.

"Miss Montgomery," a young girl called. She and her friends were working on their second shared basket of fries and individual Diet Cokes.

I stopped at their table with a smile. "Refills?"

She shook her head, then turned on the red vinyl seat to face me. "We were wondering if the rumors are true."

"Well, that depends on what you heard," I hedged.

The girl across from her leaned in on her elbows. Her long brown hair dusted the table. "We heard that Nadine Cooper was murdered at your granny's orchard today."

"And you found her," the third teen whispered from her place nearest the window. She shot her friend an ugly look, presumably for forgetting to whisper her blunt accusation.

I nodded. "It's true." Flashes of poor Mrs. Cooper's slack face burst through my vision, and I tried hard to erase them.

"Who do you think did it?" the first girl asked, a bit more quietly this time.

The friends scooted in my direction, matching looks of mischief in their wide eyes, and I realized they were testing me.

"I don't know," I said. "I wish I did. Have you heard anything else?"

"We heard your granny did it," the first girl said, speaking for the group once more. "I heard my mama telling my daddy after she came home from getting her nails done."

I shook my head. "Your mama is wrong, and you shouldn't be spreading rumors like that. It's awful."

"I don't spread rumors," she snapped back, shoulders squared and chin high. "Mama heard it straight from her best friend who is the receptionist at the police station. The sheriff himself told someone to look into Granny Smythe. Why would he do that if she isn't guilty?"

I pursed my lips and gritted my teeth. "I'm sure I don't know."

The long-haired girl gave a smug smile. "At least if she gets life in prison, the sentence won't be that long," she joked. " 'Cause she's old."

"Let me know if you need anything else," I said, spinning away before I unleashed my tongue on the extremely rude group of teens.

Had I been such a punk when I was that age? No. I'd been the one who toed the line. Worked hard. Kept her nose clean. And I'd never spoken to anyone over twenty without a *yes ma'am.* It was basic respect, wasn't it?

My head swam as I cleared tables and sat the next round of guests. Had the gossip girl's mom or the loose-lipped police station receptionist told others the sheriff was looking into Granny?

I slunk into a back booth at break time and tipped my head against the wall. Diners at nearby tables gave me sideways looks and lowered their voices. Maybe coming to work had been a bad idea after all.

Freddie, the cook, slid onto the bench across from me with two Cokes. "I thought you could use this," he said in his usual fatherly way. Freddie was barely forty, but he had two girls at home, and he looked out for everyone as if it was his job.

I poked a straw into the tall plastic cup and paddled the ice cubes before taking a long cold drink.

"I heard what happened," he said. His sweaty red hair clung to his forehead and temples. "I'm real sorry about what you've been through today."

"Thanks," I said, unsure where to go from there. "I appreciate it."

"Be sure your granny knows my Margaret sends her love. She didn't think you'd be at work tonight after she heard what happened. She was down at the bank and ran into some friends who passed the news along. It's a shame. Hard to believe there was a murder in Blossom Valley."

I rolled my shoulders forward, leaning over the table between us. A lump rose in my throat, but I needed to say something out loud to try to process it. "The sheriff thinks Granny did it." The knot in my throat moved to my chest. "She didn't. She wouldn't."

"We know," he said. "Margaret and I know. Which means other folks know too. You've got to give them some time to work it out for themselves. Right now people are riding the excitement train, gobbling up the thrill and mystery." He looked at his hands folded on the table, maybe considering his next words. "Some people have to make more out of everything than what it is. Like Margaret's friend, Paula, at the bank. You

45

know her?"

"The teller?" I guessed. "Not really." A groan rocked loose as I wondered how news had traveled all the way to the bank. Then, I remembered Mr. Sherman. He'd probably told everyone at the bank about how I'd invited him out to the farm to ask for money and wound up part of a murder investigation.

"Paula's a conspiracy theorist," Freddie said. "Before the news about Mrs. Cooper hit, Paula was caught up on Farmer Bentley. Apparently, he's been buying up farmland all over town for months now, but he's not doing anything with it."

I waited, but that seemed to be the end of the story. "And?"

He shrugged and smiled. "That's it. So, Paula's been obsessed, trying to figure out what it means and what he's really up to." He shook his head. "Some folks are just like that. Always looking for something to talk about. Hearing a beloved member of our community killed her arch nemesis in an apple press is some pretty juicy fodder." He gave me a sad smile. "No pun intended."

I groaned.

"Don't worry though. This will pass. The novelty will wear off, and the same vipers who slander your granny today will be the first ones to organize the protest rallies if she's arrested, and they'll do both for the same reason."

"Excitement." I flopped back and took my Coke with me. I didn't want Granny to be arrested.

Mr. Kress hollered from his office, and Freddie left.

The card club was seated in my section when I returned from break. I tucked a fallen mass of hair behind my ear and improved my posture. "Evening, ladies," I said. "What can I get you started with?"

"Coffee," several women answered in near unison.

"And keep it coming," Birdie Wilks added with a wink and a smile. "We're playing poker all night, or at least until I'm broke."

I smiled back. "I can promise to keep the coffee coming until eleven." I didn't have any plans, but I sure wasn't staying after closing time to watch them play cards.

"Deal," she said. "We want to get home in time for the news anyhow." Her smile fell, and her eyes widened. "Oh, Winnie. I'm so sorry. I wasn't thinking, sweetie." She caught my hand in hers and gave it a quick squeeze before setting me free. "How are you doing?"

"I'll be okay," I said.

"And your granny?"

"Sleeping. She barely made it to supper."

The ladies nodded.

"A shock like that can knock a person off their feet," Birdie said. "The good news is I heard all sorts of bragging about our new sheriff when he was elected last year, so let's hope even half of it is true. If so, he ought to have this mess wrapped up in a jiff."

I felt the lump wedge back in my throat. "He thinks . . ." I started but couldn't say it aloud again.

"We know, sweetie," she said. "but once he starts digging, he'll see Nadine argued with more people than your granny. I imagine she probably had a few skeletons in her tight-fitting wardrobe as well."

"I wouldn't mind the sheriff digging in my wardrobe a while," one of the other ladies added. Several members of the card club joined her in a hearty round of giggles.

Birdie shot them a reproving look.

I stared openmouthed at both notions. For starters, the sheriff was borderline rude and one hundred percent presumptuous. No woman should want him anywhere near her wardrobe. For seconds, I hadn't given Mrs. Cooper's life outside of provoking Granny any thought at all. What did she do with her time when she wasn't fussing over the tractor noise or the number of bees around our apple trees? I worked my mouth shut and cleared my throat. "Do you know if Nadine fought with someone else recently?"

Birdie peered down the long table at her girls. "Anyone?"

Mary Beth Hesson raised her hand and gave the group a sheepish look. "I heard she had a big fight with the trail master of her hiking club this week."

"Why?" I asked.

Mary Beth shrugged. "Hard to tell."

A man seated at the counter spun his stool in our direction. "Are you talking about Nadine Cooper?"

The card club answered in a jumble of nods and yeses.

"Have you heard anything?" Birdie asked, batting long lashes his way.

The man adjusted his trucker hat and stroked his beard. "I heard she was seeing a married man over in Winchester."

"Winchester, Virginia?" I asked. That was across the state line and about a forty-minute drive from Blossom Valley. Probably far enough to keep a relationship quiet, if that's what Nadine had wanted, and I supposed most women dating married men weren't shouting it from the rooftops.

The ladies began to trade stories about

other folks in town, so I skipped out before I could be accused of gossiping. I wasn't sure what asking about Mrs. Cooper made me, but I had no intention of passing the stories along to anyone other than Sheriff Wise.

By ten o'clock, the card club was going strong, but business had otherwise thinned to couples on dates who didn't need much attention from me to satisfy them.

I waited at the door when I saw my favorite white Jeep pull up out front.

Dorothy Summers, aka, Dot, my very best friend since preschool, climbed down from the driver's seat in full forest ranger uniform, looking like she could use some coffee, fast. Dot had been rescuing and protecting animals all her life, and after high school, she'd made a career of it. These days, she had a menagerie at her place to rival Old MacDonald.

"Hey." I wrapped her in a hug and fought back the tears that always came when I was hurt and she was there to fix things. "How was work?"

"Please," she said, shoving me toward the nearest empty booth. "I came right here as soon as my shift ended. Tell me everything, then tell me what I can do."

I did a quick scan of cups and plates to be

sure no one would need me for a few minutes, then took a seat across from Dot. I unloaded the entire story from start to finish, leaving nothing out, including my selfish internal thoughts about selling our murder press to an unsuspecting shopper on eBay. "I would never," I said, "but it crossed my mind. What is wrong with me?"

"You were in shock. People get irrational in times of severe trauma. It's only human." Dot unfurled her tightly wound bun and pulled the elastic band from her hair, letting the thick auburn waves fall over her shoulders. She rubbed her scalp, and her heavy eyelids drooped. "Is there anything I can do?"

"Not really," I admitted. "I'm hoping to learn something that will put Sheriff Wise on a path that leads him away from Granny as a suspect, but other than that? No."

"This is really awful timing, but I have something I need to tell you and it's going to make your bad day worse."

I frowned. "Hit me."

"Hank's sister is having a big birthday party out at the park pavilion this week," she said.

The sound of his name coiled my stomach. "I know," I said. "Granny and I were invited, but we're not going." After five long years of dating, Hank Donovan had dumped me for an executive position at a big oil company last Christmas and moved to Ohio two weeks later. I'd been expecting a marriage proposal and had gotten a broken heart instead. That was a year ago, but I was still working on my residual anger. "If I never see that guy again, it will be too soon."

"Hank will be here for the party."

"What? How do you know?"

"I ran into his mama at the gas station. She said he's staying a week." Dot's sympathetic tone dulled the blow, but only slightly.

Sweat prickled across my chest and forehead. "He can't stay here a week!" I blurted. "Not now!" I had too many other awful things to deal with already.

She nodded slowly. "I'm so sorry. I know you're still getting past all that, and you've already had the worst day, but I had to make sure you weren't blindsided by him."

I dropped my forehead onto the cool Formica tabletop with a thud. "Ow."

"I kind of figured this might be your reaction." She rubbed my shoulder across the table. "You okay?"

"No." I dragged myself upright.

Dot's gaze lifted to my forehead where a large red spot had undoubtedly formed.

It was probably impossible to avoid anyone

for a week in Blossom Valley, but I was willing to try.

"Now that I got the ugly news out of the way, guess what?" Dot asked, unzipping her jacket. "You'll never believe what I found in the forest today."

"Gee." I smiled. "Was it by any chance an injured or needy animal?"

She managed to look surprised. "It was! I found an injured cat laid out near a tree. It was barely breathing, and it looked as if something had attacked it. When I picked the poor thing up to take her to the rescue center, I found four babies underneath. Tiny ones."

"Aww," I said, half brokenhearted already. "Did they live?"

"Not the mama," she said with a grim shake of her head. "I think she did all she could to protect the little guys, then stayed with them until the end. Two of the kittens were already gone when I found her. The other two are survivors though and pretty as a pair of peaches, but they're going to need a lot of care."

"What's wrong with them?" I asked, fully drawn into the story of a mother's love.

Dot grinned. "I'm glad you asked." She unzipped her jacket and opened one side to reveal a tiny pair of orange tabbies curled in her inside pocket. "Kenny Rogers and I need a favor."

I made a sour face. "You can't name every animal you find Kenny Rogers."

Dot's love for the singer went back to middle school when we nearly wore out her grandma's copy of his *Greatest Hits* album, and it surpassed all understanding. It was almost as extreme as her dedication to animal rescues.

"I can," she said, "and I do. It keeps me from getting overly attached while I find them forever homes or release them after rehabilitation. Plus, I call one name, and everyone comes, so it's a timesaver, and Kenny Rogers is basically the perfect name. Anyway, these Kennys and I were talking on our way over here, and they're going to need someone to look after them, and also bottle feed every few hours. Trouble is, I can't take them to work with me."

I saw where this was going and leaned away shaking my head. "I'm terrible with animals, maybe even worse than you are with kids."

"Yeah, but come on," she said, "look at these faces. They're already at least five weeks old. Maybe six. They can start eating regular kitten food once they're weaned from the bottle. They have an appointment with Doc Austin in a couple days. I've already called and set it up."

The kitties mewed, and I jumped, suddenly remembering where we were.

"Shh," I said. "You can't have cats in here. I'll get fired." My gaze fell back on the two little fluffballs inside Dot's coat, and I felt my heartstrings tighten. "Are they boys or girls?" I'd learned long ago not to let the name, Kenny, fool me.

"One of each, but I can't tell them apart yet."

"Then how do you know?" I asked, genuinely interested again. "I thought kittens had to be a little older for that."

Dot rubbed their little heads with one finger, stroking the fuzzy orange hair between their big blue eyes. "I took them to the rehabilitation center for advice, and the vet on duty made the call. Orange cats are usually male, but the business end of one of them said otherwise."

"Gotcha," I said. "It's too bad she's got a boy name when there are so many nice girl names."

"Why don't you name her?" Dot suggested. "In fact, name them both. I'm sure they'll make excellent barn cats one day or a set of mascots for your cider shop, or even your personal cheerleaders." She took one of their small paws between her fingertips and waved it. "Go, Winnie, Go!"

My eager heart thunked hard and something stung my eyes. "Fine," I said, "Meet me around back. I'll get a box."

By midnight, I was in my jammies and pacing the floor of my little home until I thought I might wear a groove in the floorboards. Grampy had renovated the former storage structure across the field from their farmhouse into a simple dorm-style apartment after I finished high school. I was the envy of all my friends that summer, until most of them scattered across the country for college. When I'd turned twenty-five, Grampy hired a crew of local handymen to expand and revamp my little apartment into the respectable 1,100-square-foot home I knew and loved today. My place had everything a lady could want. From a small master bedroom and attached bath to an open living space and kitchen with an island bar. I even had a mudroom with stackable washer and dryer and front and back porches where I could enjoy the peaceful country views from my rocker. I still ached to hug him every time I stepped through the door.

My decorating style hovered somewhere

between country chic and sentimental hoarder. I stockpiled memories and used the vast number of things I'd collected throughout my life to liven up the rooms. Collages of framed photos covered my walls. Most were images of my loved ones and me, sharing precious moments and trapped in time. I also had Grampy's military photos and black and whites of him and Granny as children and newlyweds. Paintings and knickknacks I'd bought at flea markets and craft fairs stood proudly on shelves and side tables. Apple crates filled with books or blankets nestled in the corners of every room, looking as decorative as they were functional, and completely appropriate considering they'd once been used for orchard storage in this very building. My hand-me-down furniture was covered with quilts and throws made by relatives and locals. Mismatched pillows lined the sofa and chairs. The result was my perfect oasis, a nest where I normally found myself at ease. At the moment, however, my foggy head needed some fresh air.

Kenny Rogers and his sister, who I'd tentatively named Dolly, were snoring soundly in their box and not due for another feeding until dawn. I, on the other hand, had no chance of falling asleep until I ordered my thoughts, and that wouldn't happen while I was cooped up inside.

I tiptoed to the back door and threaded my arms through the sleeves of one of Grampy's old flannel jackets, then stuffed my bare feet into tennis shoes and slipped into the night. I breathed easier immediately, lifting the soft fabric of his sleeve to my nose and imagining I could still smell the pipe tobacco in the threads.

I puttered around the property on autopilot, nostalgic for better times, desperate to erase the events of the day from reality. I still couldn't believe Nadine Cooper was gone. I'd taken a peek at her Facebook page after work to confirm that her friends and family had been notified. The page had been updated by her forty-year-old son in Nashville. He'd announced his mother's untimely death with the emotion of a newspaper headline. She was dead. He was flying her body home to be buried with family once the coroner released it following the autopsy. Period. Not exactly a tear-jerking tribute, though he had signed the post with his title and a link to his real estate development firm. His callousness was nearly as shocking as the fact she'd had a son. Or that she was from Tennessee. The question, How well do you really know your neighbors, popped into my head. Not very well, I guessed. And it begged the question, How well did I really know anyone? I made a loop through the stately trees, lit by an enormous full moon and billions of stars, then turned back, knowing exactly where I needed to go.

The big pole barn beside Granny's house was home to Grampy's classic cars. Three vintage Mustangs, and an old Ford truck. Grampy left the barn's contents to me and everything else to Granny when he passed. She'd never understood our fascination with cars, but it was never really about the cars to me. I just loved spending time with Grampy. He would have known what to do about Mrs. Cooper's death and the sheriff's accusing looks. Sitting behind the wheel of one of his cars might help me think. Maybe inhaling the scents of leather upholstery and recalling the timbre of his voice was what I needed to come up with a plan to fix my suddenly crumbling future.

I slowed outside the press building where Mrs. Cooper's body was found. A smear of light bled under the closed door. The officials combing the crime scene earlier must've forgotten to turn the light off when they left. I hung my head and blew out a sigh. Granny was a stickler about wasting electricity, and right now, we didn't have the money to blow on a single extra watt. I climbed the short flight of steps to the door. *It would've been nice,* I thought to myself, *if the sheriff and his minions were a little more considerate. Then I wouldn't have to face the murder building alone after dark.*

I shored up my nerve and decided on a course of action. I'd stick one arm inside the building, hit the light switch, then run. I would not, however, under any circumstance look at the cider press, and if I was lucky, the door would be locked, and I could forget about it because I didn't have my keys with me.

Satisfied with the cowardly plan, I hurried to the door. The knob turned smoothly under my hand. "Great," I muttered, then steadied myself to reach inside. I forced ridiculous images of Mrs. Cooper's ghost dragging me in and pressing me to death out of my head. *One, two, three . . .* I shoved the door open, but before I could reach for the light switch, the door banged shut, slamming hard against my face and sending me onto my backside.

"Oof," I grunted as air expelled from my lungs in a massive gust.

A figure in head-to-toe black reopened the door then barreled over me. His toe caught on my flailing legs and he pitched forward as I toppled down the wooden steps.

The trespasser scrambled to his feet in the grass before disappearing into the shadows on quick, quiet feet.

I rolled onto my side and dug my cell phone from my coat pocket, attempting to take inventory of all my aching body parts and collect my marbles at the same time.

A headlight flashed on nearby, temporarily blinding me before an ATV roared to life and barreled out of sight.

I dialed 911, then pushed onto my hands and knees and shuffled toward Granny's house as I answered the dispatch officer's questions and formed a few horrific follow-ups of my own. Like, was it a coincidence that our first intruder ever had come on the same night, to the same place, where Mrs. Cooper's body had been found?

Or had I just come face-to-face with a killer?

CHAPTER FOUR

I ran straight to Granny's home once I found my bearings. She'd seen me coming and pulled the door open before I had the chance to knock. Apparently I wasn't the only one who couldn't sleep after the awful day we'd had. A sob broke on my lips as she dragged me inside.

"Are you okay?" she whispered before locking the door. "Did you see the four-wheeler?"

Hot tears burned a path over my cheek as I nodded. "Someone was in the press building," I croaked. "The light was on, and I went to turn it off."

"Oh, dear." Granny's eyes widened as she scanned me head to toe. "Tell me everything that happened."

I pulled in a few deep breaths, assessing my aches and pains. Adrenaline had propelled me to safety, but now everything seemed to hurt double. "I called the police.

Someone's on the way."

Her gaze flickered to the shotgun leaning against the wall beside the door. "Have a seat. Breathe. I'll get you something to nibble on. It will help with the shock."

I hobbled to the table where I'd routinely nursed heartaches for nearly three decades. Over coffee. Over pie. Over breakfast or dinner. Always with Granny. I dropped onto the chair and set my hands onto the tabletop. The extent of visible damage to myself and Grampy's jacket came swiftly into view. I wiggled free from the button up, then dragged it onto my lap for inspection. My hands and fingers were covered in scrapes and scratches, but the long tear in Grampy's coat sleeve somehow hurt worse.

"I can mend that," Granny said, hanging the coat on the back of my chair and patting my cheek before turning to the cupboard.

I pulled my knees up to my chest on the same kitchen chair I'd escaped to all my life and caught my heels on the seat's edge. My body curled forward on instinct, arms locking around my legs, cheek resting on my knees. Everything hurt. The tumble I'd taken down the steps had rattled me to the core. I could only imagine the welts and bruises I'd find in the morning.

Granny poured two cups of coffee, loaded her shotgun, then checked my scrapes and bruises before handing me two aspirin and a dish towel filled with ice.

I wasn't sure where to put the ice. I needed about ten more dish towels full.

"How about some pie? I've got at least ten kinds left over."

It was hard to believe Granny's kitchen had been crowded with extended family and friends just two short days ago, all stopping in to wish her a happy Thanksgiving or share the enormous feast she'd prepared. I unfurled myself to reach for the coffee. My toes found the grooves in the floorboards where I'd swung my feet for years before they could be planted firmly. I balanced the homemade compress on my throbbing shoulder as I sipped. "Thank you."

The hundred-year-old kitchen hadn't changed much over time, save for the necessary plumbing and electrical updates and the increasing number of family photos on the walls. The cabinets were original beneath a dozen layers of paint. The knotty pine floors were smooth from wear and the leaded glass windows reflected light as majestically as any cathedral. Between the enduring beauty of the room and the size of my granny's love, it was no wonder my heart had healed so many times with so few scars. I hoped tonight would be no different.

Sheriff Wise arrived midway through my second slice of pie. Granny let him inside, then bolted the front door behind him and returned her loaded shotgun to its place against the wall. "Coffee?" she asked.

Sheriff Wise accepted the mug, already filled from a fresh-brewed pot. "Thank you." His sheriff's jacket hung open over an untucked thermal shirt and jeans. His sandy hair was dark and mussed. Damp from a recent shower, I suspected. The scents of his shampoo and soap still clung to his skin and hair. Clearly, we had dragged him away from home. He studied Granny and me before letting his sharp gaze flicker over everything else in sight, including the shotgun set behind him. "That thing loaded?"

"Bet your whiskers," Granny said. "I've been shooting that gun since it was tall as me. I'm a crack shot and everyone around here knows it. Winnie too," she bragged. "She was the Young Annie Oakley four years running. I taught her everything I know."

I let my eyes fall shut and pressed my palms against them. Not exactly the kind of information I would've chosen to offer a man who'd all but accused Granny of murder a few hours ago. At least Nadine hadn't been shot. I cringed again at the selfish thought. The poor woman was dead and all I could think about was myself. I lifted my face and found Sheriff Wise watching me.

"I've heard," he said. "Folks around here love to talk, and they seem especially inclined to discuss you, Miss Montgomery. You've made quite an impression. Did you know?"

"No," I said, mystified. I looked to Granny for understanding.

She beamed. She and Grampy had raised me, so whatever the town thought of me, it started with them. They'd blamed themselves when my too-young mother had run off to marry her high school sweetheart before he joined the military. I'd been the result of their torrid teenage love affair, so I'd been whisked away with them. Temporarily. A year later, Mom hauled me home to Granny and Grampy, then left again, without me that time, in search of a divorce attorney and a better adventure than "teenage single mom."

I squared my shoulders and met the sheriff's measured stare. "Would you like to see the building where I found the intruder?"

He watched me another moment, jaw working side to side, as if he might be mulling something over. I braced myself for what he might say next.

"I would," he finally answered and headed for the door.

I wrenched upward with the grace of a ninety-year-old woman and tried not to whimper audibly from the pain.

Granny freed Grampy's flannel coat from the back of my chair and helped me put it on. "Do you want me to come along?" she offered.

"No," I said, buttoning all the way to my chin. "You should try to rest. I'm sure the sheriff will see me home safely before he goes."

Granny pressed her lips into a thin white line. "All right. But you call if you need anything. I'm only a stone's throw away, and I've got two spare rooms upstairs, plus Bessy. You don't have to be alone or afraid."

"How about I come by for breakfast?" I suggested. Then I could introduce her to Kenny Rogers and Dolly.

Granny nodded. "All right." She swung her gaze to the man at my side. "Take care of my granddaughter."

He tipped a finger to the brim of his hat, then opened the front door to let me pass.

I paused on the porch steps when he didn't follow.

He waited for the soft snick of the sliding deadbolt before motioning me onward. "Who's Bessy?"

"The shotgun." I gave the hem of Grampy's jacket a tug, hoping to cover most of the script on my rear and kept moving. My unfortunate pajamas had a smiling brown bear face on the shirt and a little embroidered tail on my backside underlined with the words: *Bear Bottom.*

It had seemed funnier at the store.

"Are you badly hurt?" the sheriff asked, moving to my side. "I'd be happy to take you to the hospital for a proper exam."

"I'm fine," I said. "I'm not a fan of hospitals, and I've been in worse shape." A dozen painful, but still fond, memories returned to me. Stitches after falling from one of our trees and catching my thigh on a branch. Dislocating an elbow while performing a daredevil rope swing maneuver into the swimming hole. Bruised ribs from falling off my first pony.

"The life of a country girl," he said.

I slid my eyes his way, wondering if he'd somehow read my mind. "Yeah."

I admired the white lights twinkling around us thanks to my Christmas at the

Orchard efforts. Granny's home was outlined in them, as were the gates, perimeter fence, and a cluster of nonfruit-bearing trees near the front of the property.

"Did you get a look at the intruder?" Sheriff Wise asked.

"No." I wet my lips, feeling my heart rate rise at the mention of the man. "He was dressed in all black with a ski mask. He was practically a shadow out here." *A shadow made of bricks.*

"Did you see which way he went?"

"No," I said again and shook my head. "He took off on a four-wheeler, and the trees swallowed him up."

Sheriff Wise grunted.

I tipped my head back, taking in the sky full of stars. No smog. No skyscrapers. Nothing to interrupt or inhibit the view. "I keep thinking this can't be real," I said to myself as much as to the man at my side. "How can something so ugly have happened here, in a place so full of peace and beauty." It was a senseless thing to say, of course bad things happened everywhere, but I couldn't recall another horror of this magnitude ever happening in Blossom Valley. It pained me, selfishly again, to know the violence had happened on Granny's land. A place that held a lifetime of my happiest memories.

I looked to Sheriff Wise and found him appraising me once more.

"Tell me again about what happened tonight," he said. "You might want to start with the reason you were out walking alone at this hour."

I narrowed my eyes at him. "You say that as if I had some reason not to. I've lived here all my life, and I've never had a single reason to be afraid on this land or anywhere else in town. I had no reason to think tonight was any different."

"Except the fact that a woman you knew was murdered here yesterday," he said flatly. "Didn't that concern you?"

I wrinkled my nose. "Death isn't contagious, Sheriff. What happened to Mrs. Cooper is unthinkable, but it had nothing to do with me or this farm."

"Any particular reason you happened to walk past that particular building?"

I didn't like his tone, so I worked to better control mine. "I was on my way to the barn beside Granny's house."

"Why?"

"To sit in one of Grampy's cars and think. Get some fresh air on the way."

Sheriff Wise bobbed his head. "You're referring to your late grandfather's classic

Mustangs?"

"Yes." I rolled my eyes and kept moving. "Inheriting them is probably the most interesting thing about me."

"I doubt that," he said softly, casting a quick look in my direction. "Folks love to talk about those cars though." By the little grin on his face, I suspected he would probably like them too.

When he smiled, I could almost see what Birdie Wilks's card club had been talking about. I normally didn't go for the unshaven, testosterone-oozing alpha types or anyone with an unreasonably square jawline and standoffish disposition, but under different circumstances, I supposed the term "ruggedly handsome" might have come to mind.

My tummy tightened with a new selfish fear. The sheriff had been asking about me, and it seemed people had plenty to say. I couldn't help wondering what they'd mentioned besides Grampy's cars and my old Annie Oakley title.

Sheriff Wise stopped outside the press building and turned to me. "Aren't you thinking about what else folks said about you today?"

"No," I lied, considering for the second time that he might be able to read my mind.

71

"Interesting." He turned his blue eyes to the door where the intruder had emerged, then slid a pair of gloves over his hands before climbing the steps. "Looks like the door was pried open." He ran his fingers along the splintered jamb. *So much for new locks to keep bad guys away.* He flipped the light switch and motioned me inside. "Can you tell if anything is missing?" he asked.

The room looked the same to me. There wasn't anything to steal besides the press and related materials, which would've required something much larger than a four-wheeler for transportation. "I don't think so." I crossed my arms to hide the growing tremor in my frame.

Sheriff Wise circled the room. "How did you manage to cross paths with the intruder?"

"I saw the light was on and assumed one of your people had forgotten to turn it off when they left. The door was unlocked when I tried the knob. I pushed it open, but he slammed it back at me." My fingers moved to touch the tender spot on my forehead. "I fell onto the porch, then he bowled right over me." The stings and aches of my injuries flared in response to the story.

"Any idea who the man might've been?"

"Yeah. Mrs. Cooper's killer," I said. "Who

is obviously not Granny."

The sheriff paused his examination of the space and turned his attention back on me. "Why do you assume it was the killer?"

"Who else would sneak into a crime scene?" I asked. Then a more interesting question formed in my mind. "Why?" I whispered, turning my gaze around the room again, more carefully this time. Why would the killer risk returning? Especially so soon?

"Why, indeed," the sheriff echoed, crouching to snap photos of the splintered door jamb.

"What if the killer was looking for something and I interrupted him?" I asked, beginning to search the floorboards.

Sheriff Wise stretched upright and dropped his hands to his sides. "Don't do that."

"Do what?" I nudged a hunk of mud with my toe. Just some dirt off one of the authority's shoes. Not a smoking gun.

"Don't hypothesize," Sheriff Wise said. "I'll handle the investigation. If you want to help, then you need to find out where your granny was at the time of the murder. See if there's anyone who might've seen her at home having lunch like she claims because without an alibi, she's the obvious prime suspect."

My jaw tightened. "Granny didn't do this."

"That's what you keep saying."

"Because it keeps being true," I snapped. "You're wasting time looking at her when the killer is still out there." I hugged my middle a little tighter and gritted my teeth against a flood of emotions. "If Granny hurt Mrs. Cooper, then who broke in here tonight and why? I think this proves her innocence."

Sheriff Wise swept his gaze over my hot cheeks and locked in on my eyes. "I think that sounds like a mighty convenient theory."

I wrinkled my nose. "What?"

"I don't like theories. Theories are just speculation that alters the investigation. People with theories conveniently begin to find evidence to support the idea they've already cemented in their heads. It's no good. I follow facts."

"I like theories," I said, stubbornly.

He frowned. "How about this one? I think you could have easily splintered this door jamb and made the call to my department in an effort to prove your granny's innocence and move my focus onto some mysterious unidentifiable male?"

I could only gape at him in surprise.

"That's right," he said, looking exactly like the infuriating man I'd met earlier. "Theories cause trouble. I won't dismiss your granny as a possible suspect until the evidence leads me elsewhere, and frankly, your desperation to prove her innocence is keeping my eyes on you as well." He pulled a flashlight from his pocket and headed outside, swinging the beam across the ground between apple trees. "Which way did you say the four-wheeler went?"

Fire burned in my gut as I stormed out behind him. "I was the victim tonight," I seethed, careful to keep my voice low and my temper in check. "I don't appreciate being treated like a suspect." I turned on my heel and marched back in the direction we'd come.

"Where are you going?" he called after me.

"Home." I moved as quickly as possible without limping. "Don't bother following me."

"Well, I can't agree to that," he said, his voice growing nearer. "I'm going to need a formal report."

"Not tonight," I said, fighting a rush of emotion. Tonight I needed a hot shower and about ten hours of sleep.

Sheriff Wise didn't speak again, but I felt him follow me all the way to my door. I jumped inside and locked up without a goodbye. Had he really suggested I'd faked the break-in to distract him from arresting Granny?

Ridiculous!

I'd been hoping to help the sheriff get to the bottom of Nadine's murder, but clearly I was on my own. Two investigations were probably better than one anyway. We'd cover more ground and clear Granny's name sooner.

I woke to the sounds of desperate mewing and tiny paws on my face. I'd slept straight through my alarm and missed the kittens' morning feeding by an hour. "Ugh." I grunted upright on my couch and wished I'd taken the kittens and their box to my bedroom instead of falling asleep in the living room.

My head pounded. My neck, back, and legs ached. The scrapes on my hands and knees were puffy, red, and partially scabbed.

I shuffled to the kitchen to prepare the kittens' bottles. The sheriff's face flashed back into my mind and I frowned. I didn't like rude or bossy men, and he was by far the worst I'd ever dealt with. Accusatory too. His soulful blue eyes and unreasonably engaging smile probably got him what he wanted most of the time, but it wouldn't be that simple with me. Not where the fate of Granny and Grampy's orchard was concerned or the good name of my family. And why did it seem like every question he asked had a secondary purpose? Who was he anyway? The county sheriff or opposing legal counsel? And where had he come from? Why did he get to march around town asking everyone about me when I knew nothing personal about him?

I toted the bottles back to the couch and arranged the kittens on my lap, balancing everything so that I had one free hand to perform an internet search on my phone. First stop, the local sheriff's department website for the scoop on our good Sheriff Wise. "What do you think, kitties?" I asked. "What's this guy's story?"

They chugged their formula, tugging at the nipples and kneading my legs with their tiny paws.

When the web page finally loaded, I went straight to the biographies.

Sheriff Colton Wise began his career in service at the age of eighteen when he enlisted with the US Marine Corps, I read flatly, determined not to be impressed. *Nine years and three tours of duty later, he returned to his hometown of Clarksburg, West Virginia, where he joined ranks with local law enforcement and continued to serve with the National Guard. Wise quickly became the youngest detective at the Clarksburg PD.* I stopped to process the accomplishments and readjusted the kittens' bottles. *So he's an overachiever. So what?* I read on.

From there, Sheriff Wise assisted local federal agents on a Joint Terrorism Task Force . . .

I scoffed. "Well, that's just ridiculous. How old is he?" I asked the kittens, trying to figure his age on the fingers of my free hand. "Can one guy even do all these things since turning eighteen?"

The kittens didn't have any answers.

I forced myself to keep reading. *A Joint Terrorism Task Force that resulted in more than thirty arrests and stopped a known terrorist cell from mobilizing in the state.* I threw my palms up. "That's it. I don't care. Irrelevant information."

I set the kittens in their litter box and went to clean out their empty bottles. If Sheriff Wise was such a great lawman, then why was he stubbornly looking at Granny as if she could be a killer?

I took my time getting ready, planning my

day and organizing my thoughts. I might've also performed two more searches for *Colton Wise* and *Clarksburg, West Virginia.*

An hour later, I arrived at Granny's door with the kittens in a box and dissatisfaction in my chest. Colton Wise was thirty-three, a full five years older than me, with two lifetimes' worth of achievements. I'd also learned that he had a big family, retired parents, a school teacher and a coal miner, and three siblings. One sister and two brothers, all grown. They attended church, participated in fund-raisers and seemed to adore Colton. Thanks to his family's dedication to Facebook, I had all the lovely details that made up Colton Wise. And they irked me.

The details, not his family.

"Morning, Granny," I said, setting the box on the floor near a small rug covered in cast-off shoes and muck boots. "Were you able to sleep?"

"Nope." She dropped her cross-stitching on the table and came to see the kittens. "Who are these precious sweeties?"

"Kenny Rogers," I said, shooting her a droll look, "and Dolly."

Granny smiled. "Dot finally got you."

"She preyed on me in my weakened state. Plus look at them. It was a lot easier saying no to the three-legged pygmy goat and the

79

flogging rooster."

Granny gathered the kittens into her arms. "Help yourself to coffee."

I upturned a mug from the drying rack and filled it to the top. "Thanks." I fell onto the chair across from hers and groaned. "The sheriff said you need an alibi. Then he told me he's watching me too."

Granny puckered her brows. "Well, that's not good."

"Nope." I sipped my bitter pick-me-up and contemplated everything that had happened in the past twenty-four hours. None of it seemed real. Certainly not Mrs. Cooper's untimely death or the sheriff's misdirected ideas about Granny. I still wasn't sure how I'd wound up with two kittens who still needed to be bottle fed. And I hadn't forgotten my ex, Hank, was coming back to town today. I needed a major distraction, and I had a good idea for one. "What are you working on?" I asked, dragging the corner of her unfinished cross-stitch in my direction.

A delicate framework of purple and blue flowers worked their ways around the canvas in a fancy border. Large navy-blue letters in the center instructed: TAKE A SHOWER, YOU DIRTY HIPPIE.

"It's for Kimmy Thorton's grandsons,"

she explained. "She's going to hang it in their Jack and Jill bathroom. What do you think?"

It took me a minute to respond. "Lovely stitching?"

"Thank you. What do you think about the saying?"

"Clever?"

She sighed, releasing the kittens onto the floor. "It's rude, isn't it?" she asked. "I've been getting more and more requests for things like this, and I'm not sure what to do about it. Last week I finished a five-by-seven for a friend's kitchen that read, DON'T MAKE ME POISON YOUR FOOD. I know where I won't ever be eating again."

I laughed.

She stared at the red mark on my forehead. "I hope you're planning to rest today."

"Actually, I have something else in mind. Would you consider watching the kittens for a while?" I asked. "I'm thinking of visiting Mrs. Cooper's hiking club this morning, and these two need a bottle every few hours until I can convince them to eat kibble. I'll pick up some on the way home. Dot says they're ready to transition. Getting them to *want* to might be a whole other story."

Granny attempted to kiss Kenny and

Dolly while they attacked the ends of her hair. "I'd love to keep the kittens, but why are you hiking? You hate hiking."

"I don't hate hiking." I just wasn't a fan of heights after the spill I'd taken from an apple tree in elementary school, and local hiking clubs spent too much time climbing mountains in my opinion. Plus, I was a little out of shape. "I heard that Mrs. Cooper argued with the trail master, and I thought I'd ask her group what that had been about. Maybe one of them knows something that will help me figure out what really happened to her."

Granny's smile spread slowly until it reached her eyes. "I've invited my stitching crew for cider," she said. "I'm hoping that once they're here, the topic of Nadine's death will come up. Then I can see what they know."

I tapped my mug to hers, impressed. "We make a good team," I said.

"True. Plus, in my experience, good old-fashioned hospitality solves most things. Might as well start there."

Good old-fashioned hospitality hadn't helped mend fences between Granny and Mrs. Cooper for four decades, but there was probably no point in mentioning that.

At least we both had a plan. "Between the

two of us, we should know more by dinner, then we can meet up and exchange notes," I suggested. "Just be careful not to let the sheriff know what you're up to. He'll assume we're trying to cover our tracks or some other nonsense. That man really gets my goat." I froze, mug midway to my lips as someone began to knock on the door. "Are you expecting anyone?"

"No." Granny stood and shuffled toward the sound. She pushed the frilly lace curtain aside and Sheriff Wise's stern face came into view.

I made a stink face. "Speak of the devil."

"Mm-hmm."

I waited while Granny unlocked the door and invited Sheriff Wise inside.

"Mrs. Smythe," he said in greeting, "Miss Montgomery." He removed his sheriff's hat and made an apologetic face. "I'm here to ask you not to open the orchard for business today. I hope you'll understand. I'd like time to search the grounds, and I've brought a team to help. We'll be professional. Keep things quiet and respectful for you. We focused solely on the crime scene while we were here yesterday, but especially given last night's events, I'd like to broaden our search."

I fought against the urge to remind him

that he thought I'd falsified the entire set of events. I wanted them to look. Needed them to find something that would lead them to the real killer, but I didn't want Granny to have to close for the day. The bad press was bad enough and we needed the business.

"All right," Granny said.

The sheriff nodded humbly.

I pressed the heels of my hands against my temples. "It's not all right," I said. "No guests means no customers. No sales. No income. That's not fair. We haven't done anything wrong."

"It's just for today," he assured, "unless we find something that would cause us to need more time."

Basically, he could shut us down for as long as he needed to investigate the murder, and the longer that took, the more negative attention and fewer sales would come with it. "Super."

He locked those cool eyes on mine, always evaluating.

"I'd better get going," I said. "Busy. Busy. Busy." I kissed Granny's cheek. "Good luck," I whispered.

"Where are you going?" the sheriff asked, an echo from last night's departure. "You don't work until seven."

I tented my brows. "You checked my work

schedule?"

He didn't answer, but I thought I saw a flash of something in his eyes. Amusement, I guessed. He had a shiny badge that granted him access to all sorts of information.

Well, I had his mother's Facebook page.

I forced a tight smile. "I'm going to take a hike," I told him, and stopped myself short of suggesting he take one as well.

Granny squeezed me goodbye, and I strutted into the day fizzing with renewed purpose. Smythe Orchard couldn't afford to be closed longer than absolutely necessary. It was already mid-November. Winter was coming, and I hadn't secured a loan to open my cider shop.

I needed to get Mr. Sherman back out to see the Mail Pouch barn, and that was going to be hard enough after what happened yesterday. It would be downright impossible to convince him this was the perfect business location for my shop if the orchard was closed.

I resolved to learn something useful from Mrs. Cooper's hiking club if it killed me.

I just hoped it wouldn't.

CHAPTER FIVE

I hustled to the cars, ponytail swinging. I'd dressed in a red long-sleeve T-shirt with gray yoga pants and a hoodie, then paired that with my most comfortable sneakers. It seemed like a sensible outfit for hiking and was also not my favorite, in case I took a tumble and ruined them. I'd dropped a water bottle in a drawstring backpack on my way out this morning and tucked a ball cap inside as well.

I let myself into the massive forty-by-sixty-foot pole barn where the vehicles were kept and flipped on the lights. Grampy's garage and workshop smelled of oil and old cigars. He'd been gone three years, but his favorite scents had long ago permeated the metal walls. The ceiling was high, at least twelve feet at the peak with exposed rafters and the occasional abandoned bird's nest. His old cassette player still sat on the workbench beside a stack of Johnny Cash tapes. His tacklebox and fishing pole still poised at the ready, in case anyone stopped by wondering if the bass were biting.

The Mustangs took center stage. A red, white, and blue collection of previously junked vintage Fords that Grampy had nurtured back to greatness. Each car had required untold hours of love, work, and dedication, but Grampy had seen beyond that, and now each car turned heads. I liked to think the junked vehicles had just needed someone to believe in them, and he had. He'd taken his time, years even, working on them in the moments between running a growing orchard, raising a wild daughter — then, a needy granddaughter — and loving his devoted wife. Eventually, he'd brought out the best in the cars the way he'd brought out the best in me. Maybe that was another reason I loved the Mustangs so much. I could identify with them.

I unearthed the ball cap from my bag and tugged it over my hair, threading the ponytail through the little hole in the back. Then, I plucked a set of keys from the peg on the bench and smiled.

Grampy had three beloved, restored treasures and one sturdy and reliable work truck. The truck was great in bad weather, but today was expected to be one of the prettiest days of the year, despite the fact we were closer to Christmas than Independence Day. So, the decision was easy. I'd drive Sally, my favorite Mustang. Sally was a 1968 1/2 Ford Mustang 428 Cobra Jet in Wimbledon White. I'd learned to drive in Sally, went to the prom in Sally, and Grandpa had driven me to my high school graduation in Sally. It was supposed to be my college graduation gift one day, and I wished more than anything that he'd lived to see me earn that degree. Sally's sisters included a 1964 1/2 Ford Mustang in Nightmist Blue with a white top and a 1984 Ford Mustang SVO in Bright Red, but Sally was the one that sang to me.

I dropped behind the wheel and tossed my bag onto the passenger seat, then donned my sunglasses, opened the garage door, and eased Sally outside. A crew of men in Blossom Valley Sheriff's Department T-shirts peppered the area, peeping under apple trees and kicking their boots through weeds in search of clues to the identity of Mrs. Cooper's attacker. Or maybe, I thought, they were just looking for proof Granny was a cold-blooded killer. Either way, I had work of my own to do.

The sheriff spotted me as I approached the front gate, and he pushed it open for me. I gave him a little wave, and he watched intently as I passed, his gaze warming my cheek. Would he stand guard at the closed gate all day turning customers away? What would folks say? It could only be interpreted one way. *Badly.* I dared a look in my rear-view mirror before making a left onto the quiet country road at the end of the drive. He hadn't moved, still staring, eyes trained on my departure. I half-expected him to make a run for his cruiser and follow me. I wondered idly if he could catch me if he tried.

I cracked my window open as I put some distance between Sheriff Wise and me. It was currently 8:15 a.m. and forty-nine degrees, still chilly from a cold night, but the sun was up and fast burning dew off the land. The weather report predicted a high near seventy, and I couldn't wait. A gentle morning breeze wiggled trees along the roadside, tossing a rainbow of autumn leaves into the air. The scarlet and gold confetti cartwheeled and careened around me. I tipped my nose toward the window and inhaled the crisp cool breeze as it blustered over the glass and through the space inside my car. The scents were heady and nostalgic. Decaying leaves, dampened earth. The telltale tinge of chimney smoke from homes fighting the seasonal chill with fire.

I took another left onto the county road through town and passed a dozen silent businesses that would open promptly at nine and close again at five. The Sip N Sup, situated on Oak and Main, wasn't one of them. The diner's parking lot there was already full and probably had been since dawn. Sally would be among the parked cars tonight. With the orchard closed and the sheriff's department scouring the grounds, there was bound to be plenty of gossip for me to consider. Maybe even something that would help me clear Granny.

The road widened outside the downtown area, and the speed limit increased. I pressed the gas pedal with a little more purpose, floating around curves and over hills toward the national park entrance where Mrs. Cooper's hiking club met weekly before taking to the trails.

I slowed at every trail head, peering into the parking lots and reading the signs until I found one marked WILDCAT TRAIL. Seven vehicles and ten people filled the space. Walking sticks and water bottles leaned against a short wooden fence beside a dark green portable potty. Several women performed a variety of stretches in the nearby grass. "This looks like the place," I told Sally and angled her into the first open spot.

The group turned to look as I hopped out to join them. "Hey, y'all," I said with my brightest smile in place. "Are you the Sole Sisters?"

A willowy brunette cut through the line of onlookers and gave me a quick hug. "Winnie Montgomery, what are you doing here?"

I pulled back and felt my smile turn genuine. "Jenny Mencer," I said, relieved to know at least one of the Sole Sisters before I began asking my questions. I'd known Jenny most of my life. Her wide brown eyes, dark wavy hair, and model-like figure had always reminded me of the contestants on beauty pageants, but she could shoot, rope, and ride with the best of them, which had made her my hero through middle school. Jenny was a few years older than me, and that had kept us from running in the same circles, but she'd played the role of my babysitter a number of times. "I didn't know you were a part of this hiking club. How are you?"

"Better," she winked. "About one hundred seventy pounds lighter."

A little snort of laughter burst from my nose. Jenny had publicly dumped her ex-husband after a local football game last fall, and everyone had had front row tickets to the show. Whatever he'd done that night had apparently been the last straw, and she'd exposed him for the controlling, manipulative snake he was via the band director's borrowed microphone. Folks had talked about it for weeks, months even. Her ex would never get a date in our town again, which was probably why he'd moved, and she'd become an unintentional beacon for all mistreated and unappreciated Blossom Valley women.

"I was just talking to my mama about you," she said. "It's just terrible what's been going on over at your Granny's farm. How are you holding up?"

"Okay," I said. "The sheriff's there now. Hunting for clues. He thinks Granny is a suspect because she and Mrs. Cooper fought all the time. That's why I'm here. He can waste his time searching our orchard if he wants, but I'm trying to find something that can move this horse forward."

"Good for you," she said. "How can I help?"

"I didn't really know Mrs. Cooper outside her arguments with Granny, so I thought it would help if I talked to folks who did."

Jenny nodded solemnly. "Of course. What would you like to know?"

I scanned the curious faces around me. "You all knew her?" I asked.

"Hiked with her once a week for years," a short redhead in gauchos said.

I nodded, considering the fact. I wasn't sure how much talking happened while hiking, but this group had clearly spent more time with Mrs. Cooper than I had. Surely someone could provide insight into her life and the heated argument she'd allegedly had with their trail master.

A plump middle-aged blonde moved to stand with Jenny. Her face was screwed into a knot. "Nadine told me that hiking was how she stayed so fit. I joined this group a year ago and it still ain't helping."

"Oh, Alice," Jenny smiled, "I think you look great, and I've heard you say you sleep better and have more energy."

The woman rolled her eyes. "Talk to me when I can button my pants."

Jenny snickered. "Alice is the funny one," she told me. "You should ask her about her pie shop sometime."

I looked to Alice. "I will," I said, but meanwhile, I was on a mission. "I only knew Mrs. Cooper through Granny," I began.

The collective moan that followed said everyone present was up to speed on what that meant.

"Every time I saw her she was all wound up," I continued. "The version of her I knew was formed through personal bias of her relationship with Granny. I'd love to know what she was like when she wasn't mad."

The group looked at their neighbors. No one spoke.

A man in cargo pants and a fitted olive-green T-shirt marched in our direction. He stuffed a cell phone into his pocket with one hand and smashed a fishing hat onto his head with the other. "Let's move!" he called, bypassing us completely for the narrow dirt trail into the woods.

The group dispersed immediately, grabbing their water bottles and walking sticks with a hop to their steps. They fell in line behind the man and quieted like a row of children on a field trip.

Jenny nudged me and smiled. "Ready?" she asked. "It's a beautiful day for a hike, and this is one of my favorite trails. It's rigorous and Oscar leads at a brisk pace, but the workout is fantastic, and we'll go right under the Emerald Falls eventually. The mist feels like heaven once when we get there."

My tummy clenched. "We're climbing to the falls?" I pried my swelling tongue off the roof of my mouth. "That's really high and the path down to it is nothing but water-slicked stones."

"Mm-hmm," she said and beamed. "It's a perfect fall adventure, and on a sunny day like this, that mist will have the whole sky painted in rainbows."

I looked over my shoulder at Sally, nestled safely in the shaded, level parking lot and wondered if waiting with her for the group to return was a smarter move.

"Come on," Jenny called, already several yards ahead of me and quickly catching the tail end of the group.

I reminded myself this was for Granny and fell into step behind Jenny.

A canopy of trees arched over us, shading the morning sunlight and dimming the rocky terrain. I tried not to twist my ankle on loose stones or exposed roots while racking my brain for a line of useful questions. I had a captive audience to quiz about Mrs. Cooper, but I wasn't sure what to ask.

A few minutes later, the quiet forest path turned toward the forking river. Trees fell away on my right, exposing the rushing water far below. The angry roar of a powerful current echoed through the mountains, amplifying the sound and rattling my waning calm. I tried not to imagine rolling over the hill and being carried to my death among the rapids.

"This," the trail master announced, "is Wildcat Ridge. Elevations here are some of the highest in the state. The path is one of the narrowest in the park, so take your time, watch your footing, and stay hydrated. We'll rest at the falls in about an hour."

An hour? My burning calves were already in need of a break, and we'd only been in motion fifteen minutes. Hiking was nothing like the hours I spent on my feet at Sip N Sup. I'd hoped my nightly cardio around the diner would translate to something useful this morning, but I was colossally mistaken. Burning calves aside, I wasn't sure I could remain upright and alive for an hour along the treacherous high-altitude path. A line of sweat formed on my brow and rolled over my temples.

"It's a beautiful view," Jenny said, walking easily at my side.

The others had fallen into single-file formation along the ridge but seemed to have plenty of room. Meanwhile, I walked a tightrope.

"I normally hike for the escape," Jenny said, "and I appreciate the exercise, but this sort of thing always clears my head. It's like running away for a while."

"Really?" I asked, thinking of a lot of

other, safer ways to escape the world for a couple hours, like curling under a tree with a good book or soaking in a tub with bath oil and lavender. Maybe even taking a long drive on a warm day in a convertible.

I considered the hikers ahead of us on the trail. Why did they hike? Why had Mrs. Cooper? I couldn't help wondering if there had been something she might've wanted to escape lately?

"Did you know Mrs. Cooper well?" I asked.

"No." Jenny made a sad face. "We were friendly, and she was nice enough most days, but that was the depth of it."

"Any idea what was on her mind while she hiked?"

Jenny wrinkled her brow. "She always had a lot of advice to offer."

The women ahead of us nearly choked on quiet laughter.

I made a mental note to ask them about it as soon as we stopped somewhere my life wasn't in imminent danger. "I heard she had a big argument with the trail master last week," I told Jenny. "Do you know what that was about?"

"No. You'd have to ask Oscar about that."

I strained for a look through the long string of hikers and spotted the ugly fishing hat as it bobbed up ahead. "I will," I said, putting Oscar on my mental chat list as well.

The path grew steeper, and I forced my screaming muscles to push on. I clung to the inside track, while Jenny walked carelessly along the gorge. She hummed softly, easily adjusting her strides to the incline, calmly trailing her fingertips over the too-short, utterly inadequate fence on her opposite side.

A few minutes later, I slowed to watch as the folks ahead of us moved around something in the path. Surely if it was a log, a rock, or a root they would've stepped over it. Wouldn't they? I couldn't bring myself to move any closer to the rickety fence and roaring river. So, if I couldn't get around whatever it was some other way, I'd have to return to the lot and wait for the group to come back. The shameless chicken in me hoped that would be the case.

No sooner had I made my decision to turn back if necessary, the blonde woman I'd met at the trailhead came into view. She was seated on the ground, drinking from her water bottle and dabbing sweat from her brow with one forearm. She smiled encouragingly as each hiker stepped past her.

I stopped. "Alice, right?"

Jenny waved as she went on. "See you at

the falls!"

Alice nodded, patting the ground in encouragement and welcome. "Winnie, yeah?"

"That's me." I lowered myself to the ground beside her. "Tough climb." My body sang in sweet relief as I pressed my back to the sturdy hillside behind me and let my aching legs flop across the path.

"Yeah." She panted between gulps of water. "Would you believe this is twice the distance I was able to go before stopping on my first trip with this crew?"

I smiled. "Wow."

"Yeah. I guess Nadine Cooper was right," she said solemnly. "Exercise helps. Maybe my pants don't button, but it's certainly not because of the hiking. Without the hiking, I might not be able to get them on." She finished her first bottle of water, then traded it for a spare in her backpack and waited while her breathing slowed. She gave me a long careful look. "Nadine was at least twenty years older than me, but she looked like someone I could've graduated with. She said her secret was communing with nature. All the fresh air and sunshine." She made a show of looking around at the beautiful scenery. "I figured those things are free and just about everywhere, so maybe I'd do what she did and start looking half my age too."

"And why not?" I said with a shrug. "It can't be bad for us."

She chuckled. "No, it's all fine and dandy until I have a stroke climbing this blessed mountain and Oscar has to call in Life Flight."

I laughed.

A woman with platinum blonde hair headed our way, one hand over her head as she moved back through the line of hikers. "Everything okay?"

Alice pushed onto her feet and dusted her backside with her palms. "Just a little break."

I extended my hand in greeting. "Hi. I'm Winnie. Did you know Nadine Cooper?"

"Libby," the woman said. She made a sour face and slid her eyes toward Alice before turning her attention back on me. "Well enough. We met at spin class."

"That's nice," I said, forcing a smile and wondering how much weekly exercise Mrs. Cooper had gotten.

"Nadine introduced herself with her age tacked to the end, as if it was part of her name," Libby said, her words dripping with disdain. "I wasn't sure what to say, so I complimented her on her appearance and asked her if she'd found a fountain of youth

I could visit. She told me to spend more time outdoors."

"See," Alice said, "That's what she told anyone who asked her how she did it. She was always fishing for compliments, then blowing us off when we wanted her secret."

Libby fussed with the cuff of her sweat-shirt. "I don't get it. I watch everything I eat, drink a gallon of water every day, and hike weekly with this club. Sometimes I use the gym too. I still look exactly my age."

"Twenty-five?" I asked, hoping to score a smile.

Instead, she appraised me blankly. "Wait twenty years, you'll see."

The words *no thanks* came to mind.

I adjusted my ball cap and fell back into formation with the others, now significantly ahead of me. I'd never had a normal conver-sation with Mrs. Cooper, but she hadn't struck me as an outdoorswoman, a health nut, or someone who valued natural beauty in her high-end, too-tight apparel and bouf-fant hair. Clearly, this group knew things I would have never guessed about my former neighbor, and I wanted to know everything I could.

Forty harrowing minutes later, we arrived at the falls, and I slumped against the hillside sucking the dregs of water from my bottle. I waited while the trail master, Oscar, led the others down to the falls to bask in the cool spray of misting water. I'd taken enough chances already this morning. There was no way I was trusting my life to a hundred-year-old handrail and two dozen wet stone steps. When Oscar started back up, I waved him closer.

"Hi," I said as pertly as possible given my thoroughly exhausted and barely verbal condition. Sweat had plastered my clothes to my skin and glued strands of lifeless flyaway hair to my neck, cheeks, and forehead. "Do you mind if I ask you a few questions about Nadine Cooper?"

Oscar's brows knitted together. He crossed his arms and widened his stance before me. "What about her?"

An odd way to start, I thought. Not with any sign of grief or regret for her premature demise or even shock at the horrific way she'd gone. Just a defensive stance and gravelly retort. *What about her?*

I backpedaled mentally in search of the common ground between us, then gave him a small, understanding smile. "Mrs. Cooper loved to yell at Granny," I said. "Sometimes it seemed as if she enjoyed it. Her complaints about Granny's offenses were so constant that they might as well have been on her weekly to-do list." I plucked a long blade of grass between my thumb and finger, twirling it absently as I watched Oscar's shoulders relax. "I knew her as all fire. All the time. I hear that you got a little taste of that last week." I lifted my gaze to meet his. "Is it true the two of you argued?"

He didn't answer right away, but I could see the truth of it on his brow.

"What was that fight about?"

Oscar's grimace deepened. "It wasn't a fight. It wasn't even a disagreement. It was an ambush," he said.

That sounded like the Mrs. Cooper I knew. "How so?"

He released a small sigh, peered over the hill toward the other hikers, still gathered in the mist below, then took a seat beside me in the grass. "Nadine was usually all smiles and bubbles here, but it wasn't out of kindness," he said. "She was always bragging. Always boasting. Her life was always grand and great and perfect. It got on my nerves, and she rarely bothered with me. I'm sure it made the others nuts."

"Why?"

Oscar stared past me for a long beat, then plucked a blade of grass for himself. "Some of these folks come here to get away from their problems, their insecurities and disappointments. Nadine made it very difficult for any of us to find a moment of peace even out here in God's country." He took his hat off and scrubbed a heavy palm over sweaty hair. "She came all gussied up. Fancy exercise gear and shoes. Hair just right. Makeup on. It all looked very natural, but no one's skin is that taut and perfect at her age, and I know her age. She was the mother of a school friend of mine once a upon a time, and I'm forty-six years old. I swear she came here in search of worshippers. Looking for people to praise her." He screwed the hat back over his heavily lined forehead and slouched forward, pulling his knees closer to his chest and wrapping them in thin hairy arms. "I tried to ignore her. She usually focused her efforts on the ladies. Then, last week, out of nowhere, she sauntered up to me during our break and asked what was in my trail mix. I told her, then she started complaining about all the preservatives in my store-bought oats. I moved away from her, but she followed. She seemed repentant, then complimented my tan. She wanted to know how I was maintaining the color so late in the year, so I told her." He gave me a curious look. "You know the new spray tan place in the back of the bakery?"

"Sunny Buns?"

"Yeah. They're really good over there and the baker throws in a bag of pepperoni rolls every ten visits if you complete your punch card."

"Nice."

He nodded. "I think so. Nadine didn't. She flipped out, complaining about chemicals again. When I wouldn't let her convince me to stop tanning, she stormed off. It was the craziest thing I'd ever seen, and she left me there, holding the bag, so to say. Everyone was looking, wondering what I'd done to upset her." He shrugged. "I eat food from the Piggly Wiggly and get a tan at the bakery. Those are my crimes."

Oscar stretched back onto his feet and called the group together. It was time to head home.

The return trip was moderately less terrifying. I stayed close to the mountain again and kept my eyes on the ground to avoid stubbing my toe and rolling into the river, but I had to admit the experience had been surprisingly exhilarating.

I mentally replayed my conversation with Oscar all the way back to Sally. Mrs. Cooper had complained about the chemicals in his spray tan, and it bugged me. I couldn't quite put my finger on why until I said my goodbyes and tossed my backpack onto the passenger seat. The evergreen I'd parked in front of was totally brown, long dead but still standing and suddenly reminding me of the sickly yellow leaves Mr. Sherman had noticed on our walk through the orchard. Could the apple trees have been sabotaged with chemicals? I'd recently seen a documentary on the upsides and downfalls of using pesticides on crops, and a clear downside was that if not applied properly, pesticides could become a problem for the plants themselves.

But Granny didn't use pesticides.

"Miss Montgomery," Oscar called my name before I pulled the driver's side door shut behind me.

"Yes?" I turned with a smile and climbed back out to meet him.

He hurried away from a clutch of lingering hikers, a look of excitement in his eyes.

"There was one other thing," Oscar said, stopping near Sally's trunk. "Jenny says you're here because you want to find out what happened to Nadine." He shifted his gaze nervously. "It makes sense that you asked me about our argument, but I never saw Nadine again after that day. I don't want you to think we had some big blowout and I went looking for her days later to settle the score."

I lifted my eyebrows. Had I given him that impression?

"I watch television. I know how this works."

"Then, you're ahead of me," I said. "I'm just trying to gather information about who she was when she wasn't aggravating Granny. I didn't come here thinking you hurt her."

He pressed his lips tight, clearly on the fence now that I'd announced I didn't think he was a killer.

I squirmed under the scrutiny, hoping he wouldn't change his mind about whatever he'd come to tell me. "If there's anything else you can think of that might help point me in the right direction, I'd really appreciate it." I softened my smile and used my best *do the right thing* tone. "Any idea at all about who might've been angry enough to hurt her?" I let the notion float between us.

Oscar shoved his hands deep into his front pockets. "Maybe. I think she'd been upset with someone else the day she yelled at me."

"Really?" I asked. "Who?"

"I'm not sure, but I overheard her on a phone call before we got started. She was holding us up, so I went over to let her know we had to get started with or without her.

That's when I heard a snippet of the conversation. Completely unintentionally, of course."

"Of course," I agreed as sincerely as I could. "What did you hear?"

"I think she was breaking up with a boyfriend," he said. "She told whoever was on the line that it had been a tough choice, and they'd been together a while now, but she couldn't get past their disagreement, so she had to let him go. Then she flat out said she'd already started seeing someone else. I pretended not to hear, but she probably knew I had. I think that's why she picked that fight. She wanted to make me as mad as she was. I can't otherwise see why she'd care what I ate or how I got tan."

I nodded. "Thank you. I think that's going to be very helpful," I said. "Any specific ideas who she was on the phone with?"

"Not a clue," he said, "and that's all I know." Oscar raised both hands in a gesture of surrender and walked away.

I dropped behind Sally's wheel and smiled. If Oscar was telling the truth, a spurned boyfriend might have had reason to lash out at Nadine, and if Oscar was lying, I could only think of one reason for it. He knew I was looking for her killer, and he wanted to throw me off the trail. Either way,

I'd taken one hike and come back with two potential suspects, neither of which were Granny.

I called that success.

CHAPTER SIX

My mind raced all the way home. Had Mrs. Cooper been keeping a secret boyfriend? If so, it would fit with the gossip I'd heard at the diner. Hadn't someone accused her of seeing a married man in Winchester? Maybe that was true after all. Maybe she'd even dumped him for another man. It was all very juicy and suspect. As was most of the rumor mill's products. I longed to tell Sheriff Wise what I'd learned, but I couldn't go to him with unsubstantiated information. Could I? He'd told me not to interfere. Then again, I wasn't interfering. I was gathering information. I was helping. And now *I* needed help.

The sheriff had a better chance of getting to the bottom of an alleged love triangle than I did. A love triangle was definite grounds for heightened emotions. Two men, one woman. Three hearts. I'd seen it on Granny's soap operas a thousand times. The man she'd dumped was probably angry, but was he angry enough to lash out? Hurt her? Worse? I suppose that depended on the man. So, how could I know who this man was? In another town. In another state. Two more good reasons to let the sheriff take it from here. Except, I didn't want him scolding me again. Maybe I could call in an anonymous tip.

I repositioned my hands on the steering wheel and sailed around the next bend, anxious to get home. I wondered what Granny had learned while plying her stitching ladies with cider and sweets. I wondered if the man Mrs. Cooper had dumped the first guy for lived in Blossom Valley. If he did, it seemed the kind of thing someone around me would know. Surely one of them had told someone. A neighbor, family member, or friend. Someone must've seen them together. It was nearly impossible to do anything in Blossom Valley without someone taking notice. *Except commit murder,* I thought wryly.

I turned up the long gravel drive, enjoying the pine green and twinkle lights wrapping the fence on either side, and I slowed at the arching orchard gates. The sheriff had relented his position as guard dog since I'd left. I couldn't wait to ask Granny about him. How long had he and his deputies stayed today? What had they found? I recalled Sheriff Wise and his men, scouring the grounds of our orchard, literally looking up the wrong trees. I hoped Granny had gotten some new information today too. If she and I each found a little thread to pull, we could unravel this business in no time.

I parked Sally and hurried to Granny's place on weak noodle legs, rubbing the tender muscles in my neck and shoulders. I needed a shower worse than I needed oxygen, but curiosity drove me past my little house.

Movement in the trees caught my eye, and I stutter-stepped. A smattering of officers fanned through the rows of trees, most crouched on the ground, closely examining the dirt. Still looking for a smoking gun or maybe tire tracks. I watched for signs of Sheriff Wise. I was still mad at him for thinking Granny was a killer and implying I was an accomplice. I also didn't want him to see me looking like I'd gone over Emerald Falls head first without a barrel. Or a bar of soap. When I was sure the coast was clear, I darted up the steps and into Granny's kitchen.

I locked the door behind me and checked

the front window to be sure I wasn't followed.

"Winnie?" Granny called from the living room. "Is that you?"

"Yeah." I poured a glass of ice water and wrenched the hat and elastic band from my hair. "I had to hike all the way to the falls, but you wouldn't believe what I found out about Mrs. Cooper," I said, raking sweaty fingers through ratty, matted hair. I looked at my reflection in the window above the sink and tried to fluff the flattened mess to no avail. The unruly mass responded by standing in a big grubby halo around my sticky face and neck. I sighed and gave up, refocusing on what was most important. "According to the trail master, Mrs. Cooper had a secret b—" I stopped short as the sheriff's reflection appeared over my shoulder in the window glass.

I spun around, one hand on my constricting chest.

He scanned my tragic appearance with a hint of humor on his lips. "Go on," he said. "I didn't mean to interrupt. You were saying Mrs. Cooper had a secret what?"

I blinked. *Where had he come from? Why was he here? Where was Granny?* "I . . ." I started, unsure where to go from there.

Granny eased into view, a look of apology

113

on her face. She carried two empty mugs to the sink. "We were just having some cider," she said, her voice sugary sweet. "Sheriff Wise noticed I had some company earlier, and he came to chase them off."

"I didn't come to chase them off," he countered, equally sweet. "I asked that the orchard be closed today for a reason. When I saw six trucks in the parking lot and my deputy said the drivers and passengers were all in here, I came to ask why."

"They're my stitching crew," Granny answered in an unusually labored tone. Clearly it wasn't the first time she'd explained this. "The orchard is closed. Just like you asked, but you never said I wasn't allowed company. Why would you? A terrible thing happened here, and we wanted to console one another."

His eyebrow ticked up. "They came to console you over the loss of an enemy?"

"Yes." Granny pressed her lips into a thin line. "It's like I've already said. It doesn't matter who's feuding with whom when tragedy strikes. All that stops and the community supports one another through it. We're neighbors first. We lost someone, and we need one another right now."

Sheriff Wise relaxed his stance by a small measure. He scrutinized Granny as if he wasn't sure what to make of her. Finally, deflated, he shook his head. "I didn't come to chase them off," he repeated.

"Maybe. Maybe not," she said, "but you sure stayed until they all went home."

The little orange kittens raced into view and leaped onto my legs, digging their razor-sharp kitten nails into my skin beneath the yoga pants.

"Ah!" I plucked them into my hands and cringed against the new pains in my poor legs. "Lunatics," I whispered, stroking their fuzzy heads. "Were these two any trouble?" I asked. "Did they take their bottles?"

"Yes." Granny reluctantly dragged her gaze away from the sheriff. "I didn't have any kitten food for them to try, so I scrambled up an egg and let them split it. Henrietta lays more than I can use anyway, and the egg was a hit."

I groaned. "I completely forgot to stop."

"It was no trouble," she said.

Sheriff Wise rubbed his forehead. "Can we get back to Mrs. Cooper's secret? Something hidden so completely that only her hiking club knew about it," he drawled.

I waffled. I was glad to have the new tip, but the way he was looking at me, as if whatever I'd uncovered was guaranteed to be silly and irrelevant, made me hesitant to share.

Granny kneaded her hands. "How about I fix us some snacks?" She opened the refrigerator and the sweet scents of fresh fruit salad wafted out.

My stomach groaned in excitement. I took a seat and focused on the sheriff, who chose the seat across from me. "I heard that Mrs. Cooper had a fight with the trail master of her hiking club, so I went to talk to him," I said, attempting to look casual.

"Go on," the sheriff coaxed.

Granny set one plate with a thick slice of her apple cinnamon bread before me and another before him, then centered a butter dish and knife between the plates.

I dug in, gleefully buttering a slice of the bread as I went on carefully with my story. "I didn't know Mrs. Cooper personally, so a hike with her club seemed like a good way to get to learn a little about her." I paused for a bite of the dense buttered bread.

Sheriff Wise sat back in his seat. "I specifically asked you not to do anything like that."

I chewed slower. As long as my mouth was full of bread, I couldn't put my foot in it.

"I know all about your amateur inquisition at the Sip N Sup," he said, obviously displeased. "That was where one of the patrons told you about her hiking club, probably a member of the local card club."

My brows rose.

He nodded. "That's right. I also know you held court with Dorothy Summers and Frederick Kincaid separately, privately. In case you're wondering, I disapprove."

"I wasn't wondering," I said, sitting taller. "Aside from news of her fight with the trail master, I also heard that Mrs. Cooper was seeing a married man in Winchester, but that's yet to be confirmed." I took another bite of bread, letting the moist, sugary morsels dissolve on my tongue and feigning cool when I wanted to grab the loaf and run. "I spoke to the trail master, Oscar, this morning. He said Mrs. Cooper was mad when she arrived, and she took it out on him about nothing at all."

The sheriff stabbed a forkful of his buttered bread with unnecessary roughness. "Go on."

I worked up a smile, reminding myself I hadn't done anything wrong, then filled Granny and the sheriff in on the rest of my morning. I finished my bread in silence and waited for a response.

Granny ferried little bowls of fruit salad to us. "Oh, that's interesting," she said. "Nice work. You went to ask about a fight and wound up confirming a boyfriend. Two birds with one hike."

I beamed. "That's what I thought."

The sheriff's already semi-grouchy expression took a turn for the worse. "You didn't confirm anything," he said. "The trail master could be lying, and even if he wasn't, he had no way of knowing who she was speaking to on the phone that day. It's all pure speculation. There's no way of knowing if any of the information you gathered is good or if you've just been given a complete runaround. Worse, if the trail master did have anything to do with her death, your appearance and interrogation of him today have given him a heads-up that will provide him time to rethink his alibi, cover his tracks, or plot an escape."

"Oscar seemed like an honest guy to me," I said. "I don't think he was lying."

"Oh, you just *know* when people are lying? That's impressive," he said, not sounding at all as if he meant it. "Maybe you can share your insights with me, and I can close all my cases this morning over apple bread and cider."

I frowned. "All I'm trying to say is that you have other, better, suspects than Granny, and every minute you spend looking at her is a minute the truly guilty party has to get away. Heck, a clever man might even realize you're homing in on Granny and plant evidence to help you close your case." The idea had rolled right off my tongue and out of my mouth before I'd had time to think it through. Once it was out, I was terrified it could be true.

"Are you saying that you believe I'll find evidence against Mrs. Smythe here? And when I do, I should disregard it because it was planted by the real killer looking to walk free?" He slid his narrowed eyes toward Granny.

My heart rate rose. "That wasn't what I was saying," I said. Except it really was. Granny hadn't hurt Mrs. Cooper and any evidence that said otherwise was a lie. "Why?" I felt my eyes widen as they locked once more on his steely gaze. "Did you find anything out there?"

He watched me, jaw clenching, unspeaking.

Another thought sprang to mind. "Were you at least able to track the four-wheeler?"

Sheriff Wise shook his head and rubbed his eyes. There were dark crescents beneath them I hadn't noticed before, as if maybe he, too, hadn't slept well last night. "The tracks were lost once they reached the woods."

"But there were tracks," I said. "Granny doesn't own a four-wheeler. That's just more evidence to support the fact I wasn't lying about the intruder or being pushed down the steps last night. It also proves Granny wasn't the killer. Whoever made those tracks was."

"What did you say?" Granny asked, body frozen over the fruit salad she'd been about to offer second helpings of. Her smart brown eyes fixed tight to Sheriff Wise. "Did you accuse Winnie of lying about what happened to her last night? What kind of young woman do you think I raised?"

I popped a grape into my mouth. "Considering he thinks you're a cold-blooded killer, I guess he figures the apple doesn't fall far from the tree."

The sheriff shifted forward, resting his forearms on the table. "My point," he said, "is that I can't go around believing everything I'm told without substantiating it. That's why I'm here. That's what I'm doing. What I believe is irrelevant until I can prove it."

Granny put the lid back on her fruit salad and collected the sheriff's bowl before he could finish.

I forked a berry and smiled. "What about your day?" I asked Granny. "Did you learn anything from your guests before he ran them off?"

"No. We were interrupted before anyone really started talking."

Sheriff Wise grunted. "There was plenty of talking when I arrived. You barely heard me knock."

The look in Granny's eye said she'd heard the knock just fine. "They'd just arrived. We were still on the platitudes and comforts portion."

He laced his fingers together and knitted his brows. "The what?"

"You know," Granny said. "The small talk that happens before things really get going. After a tragedy, the small talk is different. It's made up of comforting words and appropriate expressions of shock and pain. A certain amount of time has to be spent saying how sorry we are that the thing happened and checking to see how everyone is doing in the wake of it before we can go on."

"Grief before gossip," I clarified.

"It's only proper," Granny said. "You have to address the loss before you can speculate on how it happened."

He looked at me.

I shrugged. "It'd be rude to just walk in and start throwing rumors around without

121

saying you felt bad first."

"And we do feel bad," Granny said. "It's awful."

"So, she didn't have a chance to learn anything new from her stitching crew before you interrupted," I said. "How about you, Sheriff? Learn anything good today?"

"I'm learning a few things sitting right here," he said.

I smiled and finished my fruit salad before dropping the bowl into the sink and kissing Granny's cheek. "Maybe I'll run into some of the stitchers at work tonight. I'll apologize again if I do and tell them to reach out for a do-over." Meanwhile, I needed a thirty-minute shower and massive bar of soap. Humility burned my cheeks as I recalled how awful I looked. And smelled.

I grabbed my box and kittens, then headed for the door. I probably needed to clean the spots on my thighs where the little buggers had impaled me before the scrapes got in-fected.

Sheriff Wise stood as I passed. "Now, where are you going?"

"Home," I said, pushing the front door wide enough to fit the box through.

"I'll walk you," he offered, but I was already down the steps and heading across the field toward my place.

"No thanks," I called over my shoulder. "You've got a case to solve."

And I had some brainstorming of my own to do. If the sheriff had intentionally broken up Granny's attempt to gather information, it was safe to assume he'd do the same to me, given a chance, so I had to work fast.

CHAPTER SEVEN

Thanks to a tri-county tractor pull at the fairgrounds and the local FFA banquet, the diner was too busy for me to glean any new gossip. Instead, I spun in circles for nearly four hours, delivering food and refilling drinks for a dozen strangers in logoed trucker hats and a stream of local families, their children boasting giant red, white, or blue ribbons.

I made the most of the situation by including a half-sheet flier for Christmas at the Orchard with each of my customer's checks. I taped a full sheet ad to the side of the cash register and inside every stall in the ladies' room for good measure. I'd made the executive decision before work to amp up my efforts with the holiday event. The couples and handfuls of random shoppers weren't enough, especially after losing a day to the forced closure by Sheriff Wise. We needed to draw in a crowd, and for that I had to think bigger than a few decorations and BOGO coupons. I needed to get folks talking about the orchard in positive ways again, taking pictures and sharing their experiences there, so I enhanced my original plan.

I needed a festival.

Now, Christmas at the Orchard would culminate in a rousing three-day weekend festival! The new fliers promised *Warm Popcorn! Free Sample Ciders! Twenty-Five-Cent Hot Dogs and GAMES!* The refreshments were a complete no-brainer with limited cost on my part, but I'd have to get creative about the games. There was plenty of work to be done, and I blamed Sheriff Wise for pushing me to drastic measures. I had to hustle harder if I wanted to pull in any extra money before the frigid temperatures arrived.

I sent off every flier with a prayer and a smile while skating through a mental list of other ways to get the word out in a hurry. Smythe Orchard's first annual Winterfest would kick off this weekend, and instinct told me that the time had come to sink or swim. The dull pressure in my chest worried there was a good chance I might sink.

I woke the next morning on a surge of

adrenaline, ready to start making preparations for the festival. I'd stayed up late creating lists of everything I'd need for supplies and decor. Sketches of potential displays littered the table and floor beside the couch where I'd fallen asleep. Schematics and logistics plans lay with fliers I'd printed for a mass mailing, and an application for buying ad space in the local paper was still on the printer.

There was so much to be done. My heart kicked into gear at the possibilities. So many things I could accomplish. Such possibilities ahead.

I fed the kittens while I reviewed my notes. *Prizes: Coupons for our products. An item of Granny's baked goods. A sampler of our jams.* It was smart business to hand out samples. Folks would be more likely to try new things and come back for more if they received their first one for free. I turned the list of games around to read it more easily. Each could be made from things already on the property. *Horseshoe toss — paint the shoes and poles to be festive. Guess how many apple seeds in a jar. Pumpkin bowling — paint the pumpkins red and green. Grapevine wreath decorating. Milk bottle ring toss. Tic-Tac-Toe Toss. Face painting. Photo ops.* Photos taken outside the Mail Pouch barn would be great marketing for my future cider shop.

My heart kicked and danced in my chest. If I could get enough interest flowing through town, some of the buzz was sure to get back to Mr. Sherman at the bank. Then maybe he'd come around on his own to see what all the fuss was about, and I would be there to finish the tour we'd started. I might even be able to convince him that loaning me money wasn't a risk. It was an investment.

I snuggled the kittens and looked into their big blue eyes as they worked on the bottles. They stared back in earnest and with full trust until I felt the bonds forming between us. They had an appointment with Doc Austin later, and I was eager to hear they were healthy and thriving. Their little bodies vibrated with happiness as I stroked their fur and rubbed their ears. When the bottles were empty, I set them near their new food bowls and went to dress for the day. If they were still hungry, they'd have to learn to like kibble.

Forty minutes later, I was comfy in my softest pair of blue jeans and a holiday sweater I'd bought online. The soft navy wool had images of snow-topped mountains on it with a log cabin and a decorated pine tree front and center. Crisp white embroidery implored folks to HAVE A GOOD OLD COUNTRY CHRISTMAS. I'd fallen in love with it at first sight.

The kittens and I arrived at Granny's in time to walk to the fruit stand with her. She was in jeans and a red plaid button-down rolled thick at the cuffs. I suspected the shirt had been Grampy's, and I hugged her.

"Are you ready?" I asked.

"Yep." Granny passed me one of two travel mugs in her hands, then grabbed the handle on her collapsible blue canvas garden wagon and dragged it along behind her. The wagon carried boxes of treats she'd made last night and several fresh half-gallons of my specialty ciders from her stock.

"I need to make more ciders soon," I said. "We need to have plenty of options on hand for Christmas at the Orchard."

"Good idea. What do you need?" she asked. "I've got cinnamon sticks and nutmeg in the pantry, but I've been running low on pumpkin spice and a few other things since Thanksgiving."

"I'm not sure." All my tasty flavors were just twists on a traditional base. Some of my recipes worked best with something tart, like Granny Smith cider, while others needed something sweeter like Honeycrisp.

I'd have to see which varieties we had the most of and use those first. "I'll check our inventory and get back to you."

"Text me when you know," Granny said. "I'm going to the market today. I'll pick up everything you need."

My heart swelled with gratitude. "Thanks." I didn't deserve Granny in my life, but I was immeasurably glad she was. Not many people had a best friend, personal cheerleader, and mother figure wrapped in one devoted package.

"I love the idea of a winter festival," she said, not for the first time.

I smiled, watching our words lift into tiny clouds on the morning air. "I'm glad."

"People will love it," she said. "The fall harvest festival is always a hit. I think folks will come back for winter games too."

I slid my arm around hers and squeezed. "We're going to be okay," I said.

"I know." She smiled back, confident and joyful as always. "We've got each other and that puts us both in good hands."

I leaned against her, feeling impossibly lighter. "Cider sampling is on the schedule for today, so I grabbed a few things from home to help entertain children while the adults take their time shopping. I thought I could set up an activity area under the fruit stand."

"Brilliant," Granny said as we arrived at the tent. "How about this table in the corner?"

"Perfect."

She relieved a short display table of its burdens, moving pine cones and fake holly branches to another location before straightening the white tablecloth for me. "There you go. One kiddie table."

I performed a deep bow, then unloaded my messenger bag.

"What is all that?" she asked.

I lined the items along the table where each could easily be reached by little arms. "I printed some holiday-themed coloring sheets last night and added the orchard's logo to them. I found two plastic containers of my old crayons in the craft closet along with a set of holiday stampers and pads. I also have these giant rolls of snowflake stickers."

"You always loved to craft and color," Granny said. "Such a busy and creative mind. You could probably start a preschool with the materials still in my attic."

"Hold that thought, because some of those things might come in handy when I start making the festival games." I thumped a big stack of white paper onto the table's center. "I cut a ream of printer paper into perfect squares for making snowflakes."

Granny patted my shoulder. "Of course you did."

"What do you think about leaving these scissors out?" I presented a basket of my blunt-nose and fancy-edged scrapbook scissors for her inspection. "I thought kids could use them to add a little pizzazz to their snowflakes, and if they want to write their names on them and leave them here, we can hang the finished products inside the tent for added ambience."

"Oh," Granny cooed. "Everyone will love that."

I grabbed an armload of white gourds to weigh down the papers, then turned to survey the scene.

"What's the matter?" Granny asked, instantly picking up on my disappointment.

I rubbed a palm against the wrinkles I felt gathering on my forehead. "I'm thankful for the warm temperatures that keep bringing people out," I said, "but I wish we had a little snow to help sell the whole winter carnival idea. It's hard to be in the Christmas mood when the forecasted temperatures keep being in the sixties."

Granny laughed. "That ends today," she

131

said. "You'll be happy to know the morning weatherman projected falling temperatures throughout the day and snow flurries as soon as tomorrow. Besides, it's December first, and Santa's been ringing his bell outside the bank for weeks. Trust me. Folks know Christmas is coming."

I knew she was right, but I still thought a little snow would help.

Granny unloaded her wagon with a grin. "I thought of you while I was watching my stories yesterday," she said. "Cordelia Addington Wainsworth had a mandatory dinner party for her staff on *The Young and the Pampered,* and she served gourmet cider. Can you believe it? Gourmet cider."

Granny called the trio of soap operas that she'd been watching for the past thirty years "her stories," and I'd believe just about anything happened on one of those. "Cordelia is the really rich lady no one likes, right?" I guessed. "She came back from the dead after that séance at her sister's baby shower?"

"That's the one, but Cordelia was never dead. She faked her death to catch her sister having an affair with her husband. Hence the baby shower," she said.

I shook my head to clear the cuckoo. "And Cordelia served gourmet cider?"

"Yes, and you should too," she said. "The word *gourmet* makes everything sound fancier, then you can charge more."

I preferred, *homemade* or *hand-pressed,* but I liked where she was going with that.

"Why not?" I said. My recipes were more like ongoing experiments, but I doubted anyone would pay money for something labeled that way. "Smythe Orchard now sells gourmet cider."

I raised my hand for a high-five, and Granny slapped her palm to mine.

Aside from the apples themselves, cider had been one of the original products sold at Smythe Orchard. Grampy taught himself the process through research, trial and error. He'd lost a lot of apples at first, trying to get it right, but in the end cider had become part of his legacy.

I'd loved apple cider since my very first taste, and I'd tried different ways to serve it as soon as I was old enough to realize how adding different ingredients changed the flavor. I'd created my first recipe during middle school home economics using Grampy's Honeycrisp cider as the base. I hadn't stopped revising since.

Sometimes, I made cider at home with just a Crock-Pot and whatever apples were on hand, but for the orchard, I used equip-

133

ment inside our press house and followed Grampy's tried and true process. I washed the apples until they shined, then ground them into pulp and pushed the pulp through a press to separate the juice. From there, the juice was strained until only fine bits of apple and sediment remained. The results were heated to destroy pathogens and bacteria and to keep the natural sugars from becoming alcohol. I used the finished products to make my *gourmet* flavors.

"Are you working on anything new right now?" Granny asked.

"No." I'd been sidetracked with plans for the cider shop before we lost Mrs. Cooper. Then, life had begun to unravel from there. Cider making was on the back burner, but it couldn't stay that way, not with a winter festival coming up.

Granny popped open her red camping chair near the register and sank onto the sturdy canvas with a smile. "I predict a crowd today, Winnie," she said, beaming at the orchard gates and tapping her palms against the chair's arms. "We might need to put up ropes and signs that read, LINE FORMS HERE, to control the crowd."

I went to open the gates and returned feeling her enthusiasm in my veins. Maybe this was the day my efforts to spread the word about Christmas at the Orchard finally paid off. Maybe it was the day folks finally caught on and came to see what the campaign was about. I nodded slowly, a broad smile spreading over my face. "I think you're right."

She wasn't.

Two hours later, the only soul we'd seen had politely asked for directions, used the portable potty, then left.

I stayed as busy as my frustrated mind would allow, working steadily through the lists I'd created for Winterfest prep. I arranged horseshoes and pegs on the grass and spray-painted them in festive shades of red and green, made brightly colored signs to stand beside the games I'd planned, and gathered all the necessary materials for general holiday shenanigans. I wasn't sure how Granny had accumulated two dozen sprigs of mistletoe, but I intended to put them all to good use.

I grabbed a sample cup from under the fruit stand tent and tapped the cinnamon cider dispenser. "I don't understand it," I said, swigging the cider and wiping my brow. "Everyone asks how we're doing. Everyone says they support us. So where are they?"

Granny watched the quiet gravel lane.

"They'll come."

"When?" I finished the cider and tossed the cup. Biting wind stung my sweaty face and temples. "What happens if no one comes to the festival?" It was a rhetorical question. We'd lose all the time and money we put into preparations. That was what would happen, and Smythe Orchard couldn't afford that.

Granny reached for my hand. "Don't give up."

I turned my gaze to the empty parking lot. To the sign above the gates bearing the orchard's name. Bearing Granny and Grampy's name. "Okay." I sighed, rolling my shoulders and trying uselessly to dislodge the tension at the base of my neck. "I have to take the kittens to a vet appointment Dot set for them later this afternoon. While I'm in town, I'll mail the fliers I printed last night and take out an ad in the paper." There was still time to turn things around. A lot could happen in a few days. Word could spread. Interest could form. The sheriff might even get his hands on the real killer and clear Granny's name of all the ugly suspicions by then.

Granny patted my hand. "That's my girl."

I gave her fingers a soft squeeze and looked into her tired eyes. "Why do you think no one is coming?" I asked. The answer was probably obvious, but I didn't want it to be. I didn't want to believe people who'd known Granny all their lives were avoiding her or the orchard now. I didn't want them to think bad things about the person and place I loved most in this world.

Granny hooked one ankle over the opposite knee and sighed. "I suppose people think that steering clear of me will put some distance between them and the gossip while they process everything that's happened. No one wants to be seen fraternizing with the local Cider Slayer."

"Well, that stinks," I said.

"Yep."

I freed the cell phone from my pocket and dialed the bank's number. "I need to get Mr. Sherman back out here. If he agrees to the loan, then I can open the cider shop and folks are guaranteed to stop in for a drink." I listened to the prompts and plugged in Mr. Sherman's extension. "My cider shop will be the first like it in the county, maybe even in the state. Curiosity alone will drive people here." I frowned when the call went to voice mail. "No answer."

"He probably has caller ID," she said.

"Probably." It wasn't the first time I'd

called since our gruesome discovery. So far, he hadn't called back.

Granny stretched onto her feet. "I'd better fix the kittens a little lunch. They need lots of nutrition at this age."

"Thanks," I said, gathering the dry horseshoes into my hands. "I'll clean up my mess."

I watched for several moments as she headed back to her place, then I dialed the bank's main line. I couldn't let one man stand between me and my dreams. Mr. Sherman might be avoiding me, but he wasn't the only one I knew at that office.

"Jake Wesson," a familiar tenor answered.

"Hi Jake, this is Winnie Montgomery."

"Winnie!" He cut me off, enthusiasm dripping from the word. Jake was a handsome, kindhearted man who'd worked part time with me at the Sip N Sup during his high school days. He'd landed a job as junior loan agent at the bank after that. "How are you? How's the diner? How's the orchard?" He stopped. "Oh," he caught himself. "I guess I've heard about that. How's your granny holding up?"

"That's actually why I'm calling."

Jake had been the unpopular kid when I'd met him. Too smart and too thoughtful for the teenage girls to notice. Four years later, however, they were lining up for his number, and I found that secretly satisfying. As a woman four years his senior, I could appreciate a man with smarts and kindness. Right now, I was counting on Jake to use both.

I recapped the horrible highlights of my last couple days and explained how important the loan was for the future of our family orchard. "Is there a way you can get the message to Mr. Sherman?" I asked. "He's not answering his office phone or returning my calls. I'm afraid he plans to cut me off without giving me another chance. What happened here wasn't my fault or Granny's."

"Is it affecting business?" Jake asked.

I looked at the silent grounds around me. "Nope. Not at all. In fact, we're celebrating Christmas at the Orchard all week. Maybe longer. And I'm planning a winter festival this weekend."

"I'm really glad to hear that," he said. "I'll put a note on Mr. Sherman's desk. Everyone knows how great your granny's products are. I think I speak for the community when I say that losing Smythe Orchard would be like losing a member of the family."

The notion hit me like a punch to the chest. I'd already lost one member of my family three years ago, and I wasn't willing to lose another. "Jake?" I asked, another important point popping into mind. "Make sure Mr. Sherman knows that Granny didn't do this. She wouldn't hurt Mrs. Cooper or anyone else. And he noticed some discolored leaves on a few trees while he was here," I went on. "They were sabotaged. I don't know why, but the trees aren't diseased. Whatever happened to those few won't spread to the others. I read all about it online, and the symptoms don't match any fungus or infection on record. I think someone deliberately did something to them, and I don't want that to influence his decision on the loan either."

"Who would do that?" Jake asked, sounding sincerely concerned.

"I'm not sure," I admitted, "but I'm going to find out."

"How?"

"Dot might know someone through the Division of Forestry who can help identify the problem." I took a long breath to steady myself. "I just need one more chance to make my pitch for that business loan."

"I'll see what I can do," Jake promised. The compassion in his voice was nearly enough to bring me to tears.

"Thanks." I pulled myself together before

Granny returned with the kittens and set them on the ground.

"Did they eat any kibble this time?" I asked.

"No, but I warmed up a little shredded chicken from my fridge, and they loved it. Cats are carnivores you know."

I shook my head at her. "Keep doing that and they'll never eat kibble. You'll be a short order cook to two ginger dictators for the rest of their lives."

Granny waved her hand at me dismissively. "They're hunters. They're going to like chasing mice and moles and birds soon. They won't need my scrambled eggs and leftover chicken."

I made a face at that imagery. Hopefully they wouldn't bring their catches home to me. The kittens crept into position before me and shrank back on their haunches.

"Oh, no you don't," I said.

They wiggled their little behinds, then pounced, attempting to climb me like a tree.

"No!" I squeaked, pulling a wiggling orange fuzzball from each leg. "No!"

Granny laughed. "They're just having fun," she said. "Come here, Kenny."

I rubbed my palms against stinging thighs. "I hope the vet cuts their nails."

Granny giggled again as the kittens tumbled and rolled together around piles of apples and support posts wrapped in evergreens.

I watched the kittens and puzzled. "When I fill out the paperwork for the vet, should I call them Kenny Rogers and Dolly Smythe?"

"Sure. Or Montgomery," she said, "they are your kittens."

I shook my head. My ridiculous teenage mother had given me my biological father's last name on the birth certificate, successfully setting me apart from everyone the moment I entered the world. She hadn't bothered to take his name when they married, briefly, but I was saddled with it for life. Grampy knew how much my last name and Mom's absence bothered me. He'd even offered to adopt me when I was seven, but my mother refused. She'd come home again from one of her extended absences and claimed she just needed a little money to get her life together so she could take me with her the next time she came. As usual, my grandparents gave her what she asked for. That was the last time I saw her.

I choked down the lifelong knot of emotion tightening in my throat. "Smythe."

Granny nodded, cheeks pink. "Of course." She'd stopped caring about our different last names long ago, but sometimes forgot it was still a needle in my skin.

I cleared my throat a few times, willing myself to get over the things that couldn't be changed and focus on those that could. "I think I'll see what I can do to tidy up the Mail Pouch barn before I go to town. I want things to be in order when I get a second crack at Mr. Sherman."

"Need any help?"

I forced my most assuring smile and shifted my gaze to the driveway. "Nah. Someone has to be here when the crowds arrive."

The Mail Pouch barn was about a hundred yards from the fruit stand, up a gravel road that had been taken over by grass and time. The barn was cavernous and well-cared for, but dirty and currently being used as storage. I had a lot of work to do if I wanted to impress the banker, a man who'd presumably made up his mind about me already.

I propped the doors wide and stifled a sneeze as the dry gritty air puffed out. Inside, dust motes floated before me like a million slips of silver confetti suspended in shafts of sunlight, and I began to drag everything outside that wasn't nailed down. I lined the barn's contents in rows, organizing it now to make disposal and repacking easier later. I stripped away my sweater and knitted beanie cap as I worked, overheating from physical effort. I cleared spiderwebs and old bird nests. Swept the floors and dusted everything in sight. Then, I began to create a visual representation of my future cider shop. I stacked pallets to represent the half wall and counter space where guests would place and pick up orders. I rolled massive wooden spools, left by the local cable company when they'd run service to the orchard many years ago, into formation as makeshift tables. Milk crates served as chairs.

I hauled away trash and brought in holiday décor. I added twinkle lights to the rafters and greenery for centerpieces until the whole thing looked like something straight off of HGTV. I smiled and took a moment to admire my work. It was probably better that Mr. Sherman hadn't seen the space before. It had been a cluttered mess that would have required a creative imagination I doubted the banker possessed. Bankers were about facts and figures.

Maybe that was what I really needed to impress him.

Mr. Sherman had voiced a concern while he was here before. He'd assumed I didn't fully comprehend the financial issues Granny was facing. After all, how could a simple waitress know the first thing about being a business owner. My smile widened as inspiration overtook me. I'd assured him I understood all about what it took to run the farm, but maybe I hadn't made it clear that I also had a creative entrepreneurial mind and very soon, a business degree.

I went to grab my laptop.

Granny appeared in the open doorway a while later. "Knock, knock," she said.

I blinked against the sharp golden sunlight, struggling to pull myself from the work as if I were coming up from underwater. "Hey."

She stepped inside, kittens dancing around her feet. "You missed lunch. I thought I'd bring you something." Her eyes went wide as she set a basket on the giant wooden spool beside my computer. She covered her mouth with one palm as she turned to take in all the changes I'd made. "My goodness. This is fantastic."

I worked through the haze in my mind, barely recalling all the physical changes I'd made to the space before diving deep into the business side of things on my computer. I rubbed my eyes and shook out my hands at the wrists, fingers cramped from typing.

My laptop's battery was in the red. "I improved my business plan," I said. I'd had a vague, blanket-style proposal before, but since pulling up a crate and getting serious today, I'd compiled nearly twenty-two pages of facts, figures, and details. "I still had the templates and notes from a class on entre-preneurship I took a couple of years back. I used them to make an official, professional plan for the cider shop." A prideful smile burst over my lips.

Granny's eyes went misty as she made a slow circle through the tidied space. "That's wonderful." She trailed her fingers over the makeshift tables and countertop. "I had no idea it could look like this in here." She stopped to examine one of the signs I'd printed at home and brought back to post at key locations. The signs had photos to il-lustrate what things would look like once the cider shop was finished. I'd saved the images on my laptop long ago as a project for another business class. I'd opened a virtual cider shop for a grade back then, explaining in essay after essay how cider making was a blend of nature and science, and for me, a lifetime of memories. I'd originally collected images of cafés and tea shops from around the world to use as inspiration for the assignment. I'd printed them today for impact and hung them throughout the barn.

I powered down my computer, then went to wrap an arm around Granny's shoulders. "We can do this," I said. "I ran the numbers, and we can really do this. Once it's up and running, the orchard will make more money than it ever has, which means you can save for retirement and give more to the community at the same time. We'll rent the space for showers and private parties. Sell tickets for special tasting nights, and I can finally serve all the ciders I want, in any flavor I want, any time I want. We just have to get this business plan to Mr. Sherman."

She nodded, speechless, as a fat tear rolled over her round cheek.

I moved to face her and took her hands in mine. "Granny. We can really do this."

She pulled me against her and wrapped me in a hug. "Thank you," she whispered, and I felt the sobs begin to come.

CHAPTER EIGHT

I had to shower and change before taking the kittens to the vet or facing anyone in public. Dust and cobwebs from cleaning the Mail Pouch barn had attached to my skin, hair, and outfit like a second layer of clothing, and that was no way to approach the banker. So, I traded my jeans and sweater for a nice-fitting pair of black chinos and a cream-colored blouse. Then, I blew out my hair and applied a little Maybelline magic to my lips and eyes. Looking my best seemed like a good idea once I'd resolved to see Mr. Sherman in person.

The kittens thoroughly hated the car ride. They mewed and climbed and panicked all the way into town. I made a mental note to buy a pet carrier for them to travel in. The box just didn't do the job anymore, and I'd spent a significant portion of the drive afraid that they might get on the floorboard beneath my feet.

I stopped at the general store for the pet carrier and wound up with one hundred dollars' worth of kitten supplies. I wasn't sure quite how. I'd left Kenny and Dolly in the car, window cracked and hoping they wouldn't use their needle-sharp claws on Sally's leather upholstery, then wiped out the pet aisle before throwing my credit card at the cashier and jetting back to Sally. The kittens hadn't missed me. They were lazing in the sun on the dashboard until I tucked them safely into the carrier and got back on the road.

At the bank, I lowered the windows to half-mast and locked Sally's doors before heading inside. I didn't have an appointment. Just a little hope, lots of determination, and what I thought was a brilliant business plan. As for the kitties in the car, a cool breeze, secured carrier, and seasonal temperature would keep them comfortable until I returned.

I stood tall, chin up, and walked as confidently as possible in three-inch heels. I was a gum boots and sneakers girl, but businesswomen wore heels.

The air inside the bank was scented with cinnamon, and a quiet but upbeat Christmas tune was dancing through speakers.

"Winnie?" Jake's voice broke the bank's

museum-like silence, and I turned with a smile. He stood in the doorway of a small windowed office with his name on the glass. "What are you doing here?" he asked, heading my way with a broad smile. "I get a phone call and a visit? Must be my lucky day."

I kissed his cheek and grinned. "You inspired me earlier, so I drew up a proper business plan." I handed him the manila folder in my semi-sweaty grip. "It's the first time I've done it outside of class, but I think I got everything covered. I had a good start the first time Mr. Sherman came out, but I realized I needed a lot more." I rubbed my palms against the thighs of my pants in case he wanted to shake hands for any reason.

"Mind if I take a look?" Jake asked. "I'm a business proposal junkie."

"Would you?" I hadn't expected the offer, but I loved it. "I was just here hoping to get it onto Mr. Sherman's desk, but I'd love feedback if you're willing."

"Sure." Jake tipped his head toward his office door. "Come on in. Can I get you something to drink while I go over things? Coffee, tea, water?"

"No." My mind ran to the kittens locked in my car. "I can't stay." I sighed. "Dot talked me into taking a pair of kittens she found in the national park, and they have an appointment with Doc Austin in about ten minutes. This was only meant to be a quick pit stop."

"I completely understand," Jake said, attention fixed on the open folder in his hands. "I'll look it over, then get it to Mr. Sherman as soon as he comes back."

I looked toward the wall of larger offices. Mr. Sherman's light was off.

"He's out on a visit now, but I expect him any minute," Jake volunteered.

"Thank you," I said, sincerely. "I really do appreciate this."

"Anytime."

Back in the car, the kittens cried for an escape. They'd pressed themselves against the little gate at the front of their carrier and stretched skinny orange paws through the holes toward me. I stroked the soft fur of their arms and promised they'd soon be free, then headed the rest of the way over to the town's beloved veterinarian's office.

Doc Austin had been a large animal vet for thirty years, mostly dealing with local livestock and horses until his retirement. Then, like most men his age in Blossom Valley, he'd gotten restless and gone back to work a year later. Now, he leased clinic space on Forrest and Vine, but he also made house calls. He said he went wherever the work took him. He boarded pets at his home while owners took vacations, and he even provided daycare at the clinic for elderly and very young pets while their humans were at work. Basically, he was the previous generation's version of Dot, and I loved him. It didn't hurt that he had been a lifelong friend of Grampy's.

I parked in the animal clinic's lot and unfastened the seatbelt from the kittens' carrier.

Mildred, the receptionist met us at the door. "Come on in," she said, ushering us inside. "I was so glad when Dot called to say you were taking these little sweeties. What happened to them was tragic, and you've got all that space out there on the orchard without a single pet. You're in for a real treat now. These guys will make everything more fun."

I handed her a jug of my cider with a bow around the center. "This is for the office, from the orchard."

She hugged it to her chest. "Thank you."

"Of course. And you're right about the kittens. They've been an unexpected joy." Kenny and Dolly had only been in our lives for a couple of days, but I already couldn't imagine life without them.

"Good." Mildred's bottom lip jutted forward. "Lord knows your granny could use a little comfort right now. It's hard to be on the business end of the rumor mill. I know."

My muscles tensed. "Do you think folks really believe Granny hurt Mrs. Cooper?" I asked. "No one came out to see us today."

She frowned. "Didn't the sheriff shut you down?"

"Yesterday," I said. "Not today, and he was just looking for any evidence that might have been left behind by the killer, who isn't Granny," I added for good measure.

"I thought your Granny closed up shop after Thanksgiving," she said, sounding puzzled. "What's she doing open today?"

"Christmas at the Orchard," I said. "We're going to start staying open all year, weather permitting, and I have a big winter festival planned this weekend." I dug a flier from my purse and passed it to her. "You should come. Tell folks about it. It's going to be a lot of fun."

She looked at me as if I'd grown a new head. "The trees are dormant all winter."

"Yes, but our products are still available. We make cider, pies, jams, and jellies regardless of the season. We've always sold them to the general store and local restaurants.

Now, we want to sell direct from the orchard. Winterfest is my way of helping folks see they can visit Smythe Orchard for our goodies any time of year."

She still looked confused. "You plan to keep the fruit stand going?"

"Only seasonally. I'm going to open a cider shop in our Mail Pouch barn where people can come and spend some time with friends and family over hot apple cider and a slice of granny's pie anytime."

She nodded and headed for her desk. "That sounds lovely. Make yourself at home, and I'll get your new patient forms together. The doc is finishing up with another appointment, then he'll be right with you."

As if on cue, Doc Austin appeared in the hallway. "I won't be a minute, Winnie," he said, lifting a finger and vanishing through another open door.

The receptionist waved a stack of papers from beside her desk. "I'm going to put you in exam room three."

I grabbed the carrier and froze as motion caught my eye outside the window. It took only seconds for me to recognize Oscar and his grubby old fishing hat. I watched curiously as he moved quickly along the sidewalk and across the busy street. Where had he been coming from? Aside from the vet clinic, there was only an orthopedic shoe store, pediatrician's office, and a beauty shop. Could he have followed me? Goosebumps rose on my skin as I considered the reason why he might. Could he be Nadine's killer? Keeping tabs on me in case I'd seen through his lies and planned to tell someone? *Like the sheriff.*

"Winnie?" Mildred asked.

"Coming." I followed her to a closet-sized room at the back of the building, thankful I could no longer be seen from the window. Mildred handed me a clipboard, pile of blank forms, and a pen before making herself scarce.

I started by scratching out the words *Kenny Rogers* on the second form then printing Dolly's name in its place.

Doc Austin arrived a few minutes later, his puffy white hair as thick and wild as Albert Einstein's. He wore Wrangler jeans and a West Virginia Mountaineer's T-shirt beneath his lab coat. "Sorry to keep you waiting," he said, a welcoming smile across his lips. He opened the gate on the pet carrier immediately and with enthusiasm. "I heard all about these little guys from the rehabilitation specialist in the national park. You and Dot saved their lives."

155

"It was all Dot," I said. "I'm just feeding and housing them. Dot was the one who did the rescuing."

"You always were a humble one. You still driving your Grampy's cars?"

"Yes, sir," I said. "I drove Sally here today."

He chuckled. "That's cause she's your favorite. Always has been. Personally, I like the eighty-four SVO. I was with him when he found her, you know?"

"I believe I have heard that story." I smiled. "Took the two of you three years to find all the parts she needed."

He folded his arms and grinned. "Those were good times. Your grampy was a great man."

"Yes, sir."

He slid his glasses onto the bridge of his nose and shot me a mischievous look. "If you're ever looking to unload her, I know a guy who'd pay her full worth and treat her like a queen."

"I'll be sure to keep that in mind," I said, enjoying the warm moment with a man who'd loved Grampy once too.

"Well." He cleared his throat. "Let's meet these little survivors." He pulled the kittens into his arms and turned them over with practiced skill. "Boy," he said, then looked into Kenny's eyes, ears, mouth, and nose. "He's healthy. Clean. No ear mites or fleas that I can see." He did the same for Dolly. "Girl," he announced, then weighed them both with a little effort. Neither wanted to hold still long enough to get a reading, but the doc managed. "One pound six ounces and one pound nine ounces. What are you feeding them?"

"Some formula Dot left me, plus some kibble, but they prefer Granny's scrambled eggs and shredded chicken."

He belted out a hearty roar of laughter. "Well, that sounds about right," he said. "There's no need for special treatment. These two are big enough for kibble, so feel free to move away from the bottles, and tell your granny they will be just fine without a personal chef."

"I'll tell her, but I don't think it will stop her."

He chuckled again. "Probably not. Now it's time for the ouchy part. Shots." He set the kittens carefully on the floor where a trio of feathery toys awaited, then opened a cabinet at eye level and swung his head back to avoid putting his eye out in the confined space. "This is why I need to expand," he said. "Closets don't make sufficient exam rooms."

I grinned. "You could always stop being so likable and good at your job," I suggested. "At least a few folks would go elsewhere. Then you could have your closets back."

He got out a pair of vials and read the labels. "I guess you're right. Everything's a matter of perspective. It's easy to forget the little annoyances are sometimes blessings. It's like fussing over where to store all the extra food after a party."

"Did you say you're expanding?"

"As long as the banker will allow it, that's the plan." He scooped up the first cat and administered the shot, then rubbed the spot carefully to soothe Kenny.

Dolly charged him, jumping onto the doc's left pant leg and scurrying up by her nails before being pulled off and set onto the table. "Yeow!"

"Sorry," I said. "They do that."

He sprayed a little mound of what looked like orange Play-Doh out of a can and onto the paper table cover. "How about some cheese?" Both kittens dug in, and Doc Austin administered Dolly's shots while she ate. She didn't seem to notice.

Ten minutes later, I'd written a check for two kitten exams and was on my way back to the car.

I slowed at the sight of a paper wedged beneath my windshield. I buckled the carrier inside, then grabbed the page and turned it over in my hands.

Three little words were scratched across the page:

LEAVE IT ALONE

My heart rate spiked, and my mouth went instantly dry. I struggled to breathe through the panic.

I scanned the street, but no one in sight paid me any attention. Couples moseyed hand in hand along the sidewalk a few blocks away. Distant shoppers ducked in and out of storefronts. Nothing unusual. No signs of someone sinister. I turned back to the words etched beneath my fingertips and felt a distinct pang of unease.

Oscar had been outside the vet clinic earlier, and he'd been moving away at top speed when I spotted him.

I locked myself inside the car and dialed the sheriff's department. The woman who answered the call instructed me to stay put and wait. I did as I was told while examining every male passerby in search of Oscar and wondering if he might be the lunatic trying to scare me to death.

Sheriff Wise's cruiser pulled into the space beside mine a few minutes later. He came to stand beside my door with genuine concern on his unreasonably handsome face. "You okay?"

I cranked Sally's window down an inch and stuck the note outside. "Do you believe me now?" I asked. "Who else would harass me like this and tell me to leave things alone besides the true killer? Who obviously isn't my granny."

Sheriff Wise snapped a pair of blue latex gloves over his big hands, then took the note. He sealed it inside the equivalent of a gallon freezer bag before reading it. His brows lifted, and he turned his attention back to me. "This note says nothing about your granny, Nadine Cooper, or her death."

"It's another threat," I croaked. "It's clearly from the killer, and this time he walked right up to my car in broad daylight. You can't ignore that." I bit my tongue against the urge to announce Oscar as my new number one suspect. The sheriff had already made his feelings about my opinions crystal clear. Plus, the last time I'd given him an opinion, I'd told him I thought Oscar was a nice guy.

"I also can't assume this note is from the killer," Sheriff Wise continued. "How do I know you haven't aggravated a whole slew of people lately? Anyone could have written this message about any number of things."

My jaw sank open. "You know exactly what this note is about, Colton Wise," I snapped, angling my mouth toward the inch of open window up top.

One corner of his mouth inched up. "What did you say?" he asked.

My heart stopped. "What?"

"Did you call me Colton?"

Had I? I raced mentally backward over the exchange, and heat rushed over my face. *I had!* Nosily reading all his family's Facebook posts had left me feeling as if I knew him far better than I actually did. "So?" It *was* his name.

He rocked back on his heels, looking victorious for no reason. "I don't believe I've ever introduced myself to you that way. Which means you've been asking around about me."

"No, I haven't." I responded too quickly and his smile grew.

I really hadn't asked anyone about him, but I'd spent hours digging up information online, and I suddenly wondered if he knew.

"You sure about that?"

I bit the insides of my cheeks and pulled my chin back. "Yes. I have to go."

"Anything in particular you wanted to know?"

"Please find my stalker," I said, starting Sally's engine and shifting into reverse. "Goodbye."

He stepped back, eyes twinkling. "You can call me Colton," he said. "If you want."

"No, thank you." I checked my mirrors four times before backing up. I was thoroughly rattled for no good reason, and I didn't want to take out an innocent bystander in my haste.

"That's fine," he said. "Some people are into that. Men in uniforms. Positions of authority. You can keep addressing me as Sheriff if that's your thing."

"No." I nearly poked my eye out trying to get sunglasses onto my face. "Not me." I cleared the parking spots and pulled the shifter into drive.

"Well, you have to call me something," he said with a grin.

I could think of a few options, but I kept them to myself and stared straight ahead as I motored past him.

"Colton it is, then," he called, his reflection rocking with laughter in my rearview mirror.

The Sip N Sup was its normal kind of busy when I clocked in for my shift the next night. It would have been a great time to ask questions and gather information, but I couldn't seem to get the note from my windshield out of my mind. It wasn't that the message had been especially scary when I really thought about it. It was more about the fact I lived in such a small town that whoever was threatening me must always know exactly where I was. I didn't like this new feeling that nowhere was safe and I couldn't hide. I found myself scrutinizing male faces in search of Oscar or someone who looked as if he might be the one trying to scare me. I surveyed their heights and builds seeking a match for the man who'd knocked me down the press building's steps.

"Winnie?" Birdie Wilks waved a hand before my eyes. She and her card club were on their fourth carafe of coffee, and I was beginning to think one of them was spiking the pot with all the hooting and hollering going on.

"Yes, ma'am," I answered, moving in her direction with a smile. "Y'all sound like you're having a terrific time over here. Maybe I ought to join a card club."

"You should," Birdie said, and a number of the women burst into another round of laughter. "We're already having great fun thanks to you," Birdie continued.

"Me?" I smiled, a little unsure where this

conversation was going and if I wanted to hear it. I cast a look around the room to count the number of folks who might be about to hear something I didn't want them to.

"Yes. We were just discussing how you marched right over to that hiking group of Nadine's and asked the trail master what on earth he was arguing with her for."

Another round of laughter ripped through them.

I blushed. "You said they argued." And they had. Oscar admitted it.

"We know what we said. It's just that gossip doesn't normally go that way. Normally," she drawled, "someone hears a juicy tale, and they pass it on. Then the next person does the same until everyone knows, and the person they're all talking about doesn't have a clue that their little secret has been hung out to dry like underpants on a clothesline."

"It's funny because I let Oscar know people were talking about him?" I guessed.

"The way we hear it, you did more than let him know," Birdie said. "I heard he was so worked up when he got home, he didn't know if he should scratch or wind his watch."

"I didn't mean to upset him. He seemed

fine when I left," I said, suddenly realizing that if Birdie's card club was telling me this, a whole lot of other people had heard about it too. Like Sheriff Wise. I rubbed my temples. He hated when I asked questions about Mrs. Cooper. And *he thought I'd been asking around about* him, I reminded myself, blushing furiously again. "I'll apologize to Oscar the next time I see him."

By closing time, I had a mental list of things I wanted to do when I got home, starting with looking more closely at the trail master. Was he truly flustered by my questions or was he upset because he'd lied to me? What had he been doing near the vet today before the threatening letter had appeared on my windshield?

I also had a lot more to do in preparation for the Winterfest. I'd mailed the fliers and placed the ad in the paper yesterday, so people would soon learn about the event on a mass scale, and Mildred was sure to tell people about my future cider shop. I'd seen the intrigue in her eyes, even if she'd pretended to blow me off. Which reminded me. I had to make a few more gallons of my specialty ciders soon.

What I needed more than anything was for Sheriff Wise to announce Granny's innocence publicly or at least make it clear that she was no longer a suspect. From what I'd read online, he was a good detective, and there was no way even a bad detective could truly believe Granny was behind any of the bad things happening in Blossom Valley.

I grabbed my coat and clocked out with images of Mrs. Cooper in my mind. She must've confided in someone about her boyfriends, but who? Did she have a best friend I didn't know about? A sister or a beloved hairdresser? If I knew who she'd talked to about her love life, I could contact the men in question, and surely one of them would be able to shed some light on her last few days for me.

I waited for Freddie to walk me out at closing. He was vigilant about keeping watch on anyone leaving alone after dark, and I appreciated that more than ever as he peeked under my car and into my back seat before I climbed inside. Something about the darkened lot had given me goosebumps and kept me from setting foot outside without a chaperone. Thankfully, Freddie didn't mind being anyone's white knight, and as a bonus, there wasn't another note under my wiper. I waved goodbye as I pulled onto the road, feeling infinitely safer strapped into Sally's cockpit.

I took the main road back through town, then turned onto the county route that led to the orchard. Streetlamps were fewer and farther between as I headed deeper into the countryside. The inky path before me twisted and curved like a black satin ribbon wound tightly through the mountains.

Sally hugged the asphalt, unaffected by the things that had me clutching her wheel. Electricity and intuition had the hairs on my neck standing firmly at attention, despite the distance I'd put between myself and the dark Sip N Sup parking lot. *I'm safe,* I reminded myself. *I'm safe and almost home.*

The earlier threat clung to my thoughts like static on flannel. *Leave it alone.* I'd provoked someone dangerous, and I needed to do exactly as the note instructed. I needed to trust the sheriff to get things done right.

Except I couldn't.

I had to save Granny's reputation and her orchard. I had to identify my stalker before he got his hands on me instead of a piece of paper and a marker.

I slowed instinctively for the next downhill curve then blinked as a set of headlights flashed on in my rearview mirror. The growl of an engine broke the still of the night. The vehicle lurched forward, closing the distance between us at unsafe speeds. I nudged Sally's pedal lower, hoping to navigate the upcoming curve safely, then look for a place to pull off and let the speed demon pass. The deep ravine on my right would keep me in place until then.

BEEP! The driver suddenly blared his horn. A moment later he began to flash his lights as well.

As I slowed from shock, the truck knocked into my bumper. The impact sent me left of center, tires squealing all over the road. I jerked Sally back into my lane as an oncoming car sped past in the opposite direction. Behind me, the psychopath tailgated closer, until his headlights and grill were no longer visible in my mirror. I stomped the gas and charged downhill at a reckless pace, taking my chances on the winding road before me, unwilling to allow my assailant to catch me and spin me over the cliff.

I tightened my aching grip on the wheel, struggling and desperate to keep Sally between the lines as we flew down the mountain. A log truck blinded me with its bright lights as I rocketed around the next curve, and I whimpered with fear as Sally rocked in the wind from its passing.

I jerked the wheel toward the first available inch of berm at the base of the hill and braced myself as the offending pickup barreled past at double the posted speed, headlights flashing, horn screaming, engine roaring.

I pried my trembling fingers off the wheel and cried as the truck vanished into the night.

CHAPTER NINE

I called the sheriff's department after I calmed down. I reported the crazy driver and told police dispatch everything I could remember about the incident. The report would be filed for me, and I'd get an emailed copy to use at the body shop where I'd have Sally's bumper looked at.

I forced myself back onto the road and drove home in fear the crazy truck might reappear around every turn. When I finally arrived, I collapsed onto my couch, still in my uniform and too exhausted to bother with pajamas or any other portion of my usual bedtime routine.

I dragged the pink patchwork quilt off the back of my couch and over my body, my mind racing, pulse settling. I had a feeling the truck that had attempted to run me off the road was connected to the note I'd found on my windshield and that the sheriff would be looking for me in the morning, but there wasn't much I could tell him. I didn't get a license plate number, a look at the driver, or the make and model of the truck. Even as it roared past me, it was little more than a dark blur to my tear-filled eyes.

I fell asleep determined to make tomorrow a better day. Tomorrow, I'd be a woman of action instead of a sitting duck waiting to see what awful thing would happen to her next.

I woke at dawn, then hurried to help Granny with the kittens who'd slept at her house because of my late shift. I didn't tell her about the incident with the truck. Partially because I wasn't ready to talk about it, but also because I wasn't hurt and didn't want to worry her about something that was already over and couldn't be changed. When we parted ways, I took the kittens home and prepared to make a few specialty ciders with the ingredients Granny had picked up for me. She was certain she could handle the orchard customers on her own, assuming anyone showed up, and if business somehow got busy, she had a clutch of her girlfriends on standby. Though, neither of us thought it would come to that.

I had the day off from the diner, and a growing list of things to do before the festival, starting with the ciders. I lined stockpots on the four burners of my stove and poured a jug of plain cider into each. As the contents heated, I measured ingredients from bags and boxes into cups and bowls, then clustered them together beside the pots where they were headed. I chopped fresh apples, peeled oranges and lemons, then began to stir the fresh flavors into the waiting ciders. Orange juice and lemon zest in one pot. Cinnamon and sugar in another. A chai tea bag here. Caramel and vanilla extract there. Soon, the ciders were simmering, and the delectable scents of all my favorite things floated heavily in the air.

I repeated the processes several times before checking the clock and switching gears. I bottled and labeled the final products, then stowed them in my fridge. It was almost time to go to town.

I had plans to price materials for the cider shop and meet contractors about potential renovations. Afterward, I'd stop by the bank and corner Mr. Sherman about my business proposal, then lure him back to the orchard with promises of free cider and sweets. I'd finally realized that Mr. Sherman was the key to my ideal cider shop scenario, but he wasn't the only way to make the dream come alive. After feeling like a victim in my personal life the last few days, I'd resolved not to make the same mistakes when it came to business.

And I made a backup plan.

As backup plans went, mine wasn't very good, but that was why it wasn't Plan A. In the backup scenario, I would drain my savings account and open the cider shop without Mr. Sherman's help. I'd be a dead broke entrepreneur praying her business wasn't one of the thousands that failed every year, but I'd have a cider shop. If the shop succeeded, I could pay myself back with the revenue instead of paying the bank. If the business failed, I'd lose everything. My dream. My business and my life savings, not to mention all hope of helping Granny save her orchard. The terrible backup plan also depended on me having enough money to open the shop at all, and the only way I could know that for sure was to start getting quotes for everything. Since the barn had never been anything except a barn, the renovations needed were extensive and daunting. Heating and cooling, duct work and plumbing, electrical updates, and a septic system for starters. I needed a contractor to divide the space, put up walls, install floors and ceilings, a kitchen and bathrooms, plus a dining area. After all that,

I'd still need décor, tableware, and appliances. I had no idea what any of it would cost, but I was going to find out. Today.

A honking horn drew my attention, and I grabbed my jacket with a smile. Dot had the day off, too, and she'd volunteered to keep me company. She'd even said she'd drive. So my day was off to a fantastic start.

Dot waved from behind the wheel. She wore torn blue jeans, knee-high brown boots, and a tan sweater with narrow layers of lace along the bottom. Total country chic. Her signature look, outside of the park ranger uniform. I'd chosen soft, dark washed skinny jeans for the day and paired them with my favorite cowgirl boots and a pale gray V-neck sweater. I brought my black motorcycle jacket, knit scarf, and hat in preparation for the predicted temperature drop this afternoon.

I tossed my purse on the floorboards, then buckled up beside her. "Good morning!"

"Hey!" she said, adjusting the volume on her favorite country station. "How are the kittens? And Granny? And you?" She gave me a bright smile and shifted into drive.

"The kittens are fine," I said. "Healthy. Growing. A bit rambunctious, but the internet says that's to be expected. Granny's a trooper. She's trying to gather information from the gossip mill by plying folks with cider samples. She hasn't gotten anywhere so far, but she's trying. I'm at my wit's end with absolutely all of this."

"Today will be better," she said. "Where should we go first?"

"Higbee Plumbing on Market. From there I made appointments with another plumber, three electricians, and two general contractors. They'll all want to see the barn eventually, but right now I'm only looking for ballpark figures. I took a ton of photos to help them get a feel for the space."

"Good thinking ahead," she said, turning onto the county road at the end of Granny's drive.

"Thanks." A bandage on her forearm caught my eye. "Hey, what happened to you?" I asked, pointing to the injury.

She rolled her eyes. "I was bitten. I don't want to talk about it."

I smiled. Dot would tell anybody anything, unless the story threatened to embarrass her, and those were my favorite kinds of stories. "Please?"

"No."

"Come on. I could use the pick-me-up."

She slid her eyes my way. "You assume the tale of my injury will make you happy."

I nodded fervently.

"Fine, but you can't repeat it. Not to anyone."

I mimed locking my lips and tucking the key into my pocket.

"I had to lead a workshop on animal safety for a bunch of preschoolers at the nature center yesterday. They were on a field trip, and I was explaining the dangers of approaching wild animals."

"And something bit you?" I gasped. "While you were teaching kids about safety? That's awful." Dot had led similar preschool sessions before, and they normally ended in something for me to laugh about because unlike animals, children never liked her. "So far this isn't one of my favorite stories."

She groaned and let her head tip over her shoulder. "I haven't told you what bit me."

I grinned.

"When I corrected a kid for tapping on the snake tank, he spun on me. The kid, not the snake."

My mouth fell open. "The kid bit you?"

"Yep. I had to update my tetanus shot after being bitten by a preschooler during a presentation on how to stay safe around wild animals."

A loud and inconsiderate bout of laugher bubbled out of me. "That was a much better story than I'd expected. I especially

176

enjoyed the twist ending."

"I was due for the shot anyway."

I gave her my widest, goofiest grin.

She turned onto the main drag through town and shot me a curious look. "Have you run into Hank yet?"

I felt the smile slide off my face. "Thankfully, no. I have enough problems already."

"Well, good. Rumor has it he's still complaining about the way things ended between the two of you. He says it was all a misunderstanding and you should've let him explain."

"I don't even want to know where you heard all that," I said. I had enough problems without opening that can of worms again. "Leave it to Hank to break my heart one Christmas, then come back a year later to stir up trouble again."

Hank had lied to me for months, visiting and interviewing with a big oil company in Ohio while pretending things were fine with us and even alluding to a Christmas proposal. Instead, he'd landed a huge money-making opportunity with the out-of-state company and made the announcement over Thanksgiving turkey at his mama's house. He was moving after the new year. Somehow he managed to be shocked when I didn't celebrate his good news. Worse, he'd expected me to drop my entire life and move with him. We weren't even engaged. Why would I do that? What would happen if we'd broken up and I was isolated in Ohio? I finished his mama's lovely holiday dinner with smoke curling out of my ears, and I cut him loose after pumpkin pie and ice cream. I hadn't looked back since.

Okay, I looked back a lot, but he didn't need to know it.

"Well, he's looking for you," she said. "It took him all of two minutes to hear about the mess with Mrs. Cooper and your granny, and he's hoping to lend his shoulder should your weary head need a place to rest."

I pretended to gag. "I have pillows." Pillows were great. They didn't make life-changing plans behind my back.

The friendly reminder that news traveled fast brought something else to mind. "Have you heard anything about me confronting Oscar, the trail master?"

"Yep." She nodded. "Everyone has. Folks think it's great that you're going after answers like you are. Protecting family is one of Blossom Valley's most cherished virtues."

That was true. Depending on the situation, protecting family occasionally trumped all else, including basic laws, manners, and a bevy of other things. Too bad all those supportive people weren't coming out to the orchard to buy a bushel and support Granny. "Birdie Wilks said I upset Oscar. I didn't mean to, and I wish I hadn't, but I can't help wondering why he was upset. He made it sound as if there was barely an argument between him and Mrs. Cooper. More like she was just in a bad mood and took it out on him over trail mix and the fact he gets regular spray tans at Sunny Buns."

Dot wrinkled her nose. "Well, there's a visual I could've lived without." She slowed to the reduced speed limit through town. "He probably knew it looked bad. Them fighting right before someone killed her. I'm sure he didn't want any fingers pointed his way."

"Could be," I said. "I saw him outside Doc Austin's office a few minutes before I received that awful note under my wiper."

Dot slid wide blue eyes my way. "What?"

"I didn't see him leave it, but I have been wondering. Is he innocent or just a really good liar?"

"You think he could've killed Mrs. Cooper?" Dot asked.

"He was quick to offer up a pair of nameless boyfriends." Had he only wanted to shift my attention away from him?

"The whole town's got a hold of that bone," Dot said. "It's been a long while since something this bad happened here. Now, gossips are having the time of their lives fielding and relaying all sorts of information, and the conspiracy theorists are speculating Mrs. Cooper was a rogue agent from a federal bureau of some sort or possibly a member of witness protection."

"That all sounds very exciting, but I'm willing to bet the reason behind her death is simple, whatever it is. As far as I can tell, she had a small humdrum life like the rest of us and a crotchety attitude unlike most. She probably made someone mad or hurt their feelings and they lashed out. It was probably an accident. Heat of the moment. You know?"

"Makes more sense than thinking she was a rogue operative in hot pink heels and pedal pushers," Dot said. "Hey, have you been able to remember anything else about the truck that ran you off the road last night?" I'd called Dot the moment I'd arrived safely at home. She'd stayed on the line with me until all the tears had passed and offered repeatedly to come over despite the hour.

"No. Why?"

"No reason. I just thought I could help keep an eye out for similar vehicles and take note of the drivers."

"The truck was black, I think, or maybe dark blue." I pictured the flashing headlights and my heart raced all over again. "It wasn't a small truck, but it wasn't a giant one either." I groaned. "I'm a terrible eye witness. I made a statement over the phone, but I had so little information the deputy I spoke with wasn't sure anything could be done with it."

Dot released the steering wheel with one hand to pat my shoulder. "You were scared to death. I'm not sure I'd have had the presence of mind to know it wasn't an elephant chasing me."

I squeezed her hand on my shoulder. I didn't know what I'd do without Dot in my life, but I was sure I'd cry a lot more. "Turns out Sally's fine," I said, finding the silver lining. "There was a little paint left on her trunk from when the truck pushed me, but I think it'll buff out. No need to file an insurance claim and raise my rates."

She offered me a fist, and I bumped it.

Several hours later, we'd survived all of my scheduled appointments with potential contractors for the cider shop and an avalanche of information on costs, products, warranties, and availability. My head spun, but Dot helped me organize all the paperwork between meetings so I could keep it straight later when I had to make the tough decisions. The heartbreaking truth was that I simply couldn't afford to do what I wanted without a small loan or a big miracle.

We headed toward the ice cream parlor on foot after the final meeting. I needed a chocolate malt to drown my sorrows and possibly a few french fries to drag through it.

I zipped my coat against the biting wind. Temperatures had plummeted as promised and a flurry of snow floated in the air, melting quickly as it hit the ground. Holiday décor seemed to have popped up on street lamps and in shop windows overnight. SEASON'S GREETINGS banners hung from light posts and wreaths hung on shop doors. Strings of chasing lights wrapped leafless trees and squatty shrubs along storefronts. Despite the bonus weeks of lovely weather, winter was on its way.

There was no one else in line for ice cream, so we were on our way back to Dot's ride in no time. She pumped the straw in and out of the thick creamy malt as we leaned into the frigid wind. "What if you get another kind of loan?" she asked.

"Maybe it doesn't have to be all or nothing. You could use your own money for as much as you feel comfortable with, then get a personal loan for the rest if Mr. Sherman won't approve a business loan for the whole amount."

"Maybe," I said. "I just wish Mr. Sherman would take a chance on me. Forget the trouble the orchard's in. I want him to trust that I will be good for the money, and I will successfully reach my goals."

"He'd be crazy if he doesn't," she said. "And I don't think he's crazy. Cheers to nothing but good news ahead."

We tapped our takeout cups in a toast and straightened our postures as the wind relented its wrath. Winter was coming, but the day was beautiful. The sun was bright against the majestic autumn-colored mountains. I had a big chocolate malt and my best friend at my side. Anything seemed possible. Maybe Dot was right. If Mr. Sherman didn't budge on the business loan, there was always another way to get where I wanted. There was only one way to find out.

"I left a significantly improved business plan with Jake a couple days ago," I said. "He promised to pass it on to Mr. Sherman for me. It might mean more coming from a junior loan officer than from the person wanting the loan," I said. For all I knew, Mr. Sherman loved the revised plan and was drawing up paperwork for my loan as I spoke. Maybe another impromptu drop in at the bank was in order.

A tall, dark-haired man in sunglasses rounded the corner ahead of us and I nearly swallowed my tongue. It took me a minute to realize it wasn't Hank. Though it would have been just my luck to want so desperately to avoid him, then literally walk right into him.

"Has he called yet?" Dot asked.

"Hank?" I squeaked.

"No." She slid me a sly grin. "Mr. Sherman."

"Oh." I sighed. "No. I haven't heard back, but I was just thinking the bank isn't too far from here. If Mr. Sherman's not in, Jake might be."

"Someone was just talking about Jake," Dot said. "I can't remember how he came up, but I said I remembered him from when he worked with you at Sip N Sup, and the other person said he's as sweet as ever, but all grown up and handsome now." She wiggled her malt cup and watched me, waiting for confirmation.

"He's definitely grown into his height and filled out nicely, but I've always thought he was handsome. He was just a little more awkward about it five years ago. He seemed just as kind and ready to help as ever when I met with him. He's one of those rare good guys, I think."

"I don't think good guys are rare," Dot said. "I just think the one guy you caught turned out to be a toad. We should go say hi." Dot pointed her cup at the bank as it came into view across the street.

"Perfect," I said. "I'll invite Mr. Sherman back to the orchard if he's in."

Dot hit the button at the crosswalk. "Excellent."

I steeled my nerves and felt my stomach rock as I prepared to face the man who held the fate of my dreams in his hands.

"Hey, what did you decide to name the kittens?" Dot asked as we hurried across the street. "I've been thinking about them, and I kind of like Harry and Sally or Apples and Cider. Pumpkin and Spice. Something like that."

"I went with Kenny and Dolly."

Dot's eyes went wide and she bounced on her toes as we landed outside the bank. "Love it."

"I thought you might." I pulled the glass door open and motioned her ahead.

The bank was quiet as usual, still scented

like cinnamon and playing soft but upbeat holiday tunes. I smiled at the six-foot Christmas tree that had sprung up in the front window, boxes of trimmings and twinkle lights at its feet, then led the way to Jake's office and leaned through the open doorway. "Knock, knock," I said.

Jake's fingers froze on the keyboard and a broad smile split his face. He pushed away from the desk and greeted me with a hug. "Twice in a week? When did I get so lucky?" He released me and his gaze landed on Dot. "You're both here to see me? Clearly, I'm doing something right."

"I stopped in to see what you thought of my business proposal. Dot just wanted to say hello."

She lifted her hand in a hip-high wave. "Hello."

He hugged her. "It's great to see you again. It's been years. I think everyone in town comes through here except you."

"Direct deposit," she said, "and cash machines. I spend most of my banking hours in the national park."

"Still." He rocked back on his heels. "Couldn't hurt to stop in and see me some-time."

Dot blushed. "I guess not."

Mr. Sherman's voice caught my attention,

and I slipped away from my friends. He opened his office door and ushered another man in a suit to the front door. When he turned back, I was there.

"Hello," I said brightly. "How are you? You look well." Actually, he looked startled and a little confused. "We don't have an appointment," I said. "I just wanted to stop in and personally invite you to come back to the orchard and finish that tour we started. I'm sure you have my business plan by now, and I'd love the opportunity to finally show you the space where my cider shop will be one day. I think once you've seen the location, you'll understand the value my shop will bring to the orchard and our community."

His shoulders and chin fell an inch. "Let's step into my office."

I followed on his heels, performing a silent fist pump for Dot and Jake, but they were engrossed in a private conversation, oblivious to my wild excitement.

Mr. Sherman unbuttoned his jacket and took a seat behind the desk, then motioned for me to take the seat across from his. The office was simply decorated, well-organized, and speckled with photographs of Mr. Sherman and other middle-aged men sailing and fly-fishing. "Miss Montgomery," he began, pulling a folder I recognized as my own off a stack at the corner of his desk, "it's very nice of you to stop in again, and I appreciate the amount of work you've done on the business plan Jake delivered to me on your behalf. It shows great initiative."

"Thank you," I said quickly, feeling an imminent *but* coming on. "If you have any questions or concerns, I'd be happy to answer or address them." I folded my hands over my knees to keep them from bobbing. I was twenty-eight years old, so why did it feel as if I'd been called into the principal's office? "Granny's got a great lineup for this week's cider tasting," I rambled, leaving him no room to ask his questions. "It's all part of my Christmas at the Orchard program. Folks are loving it, and I have a winter festival planned as well. I hope to make it an annual tradition."

He watched me, arms resting in parallel on his desk, framing my folder. Confliction flickered over his brow. "Miss Montgomery —" he began again.

"Look," I said, inching forward on my seat. "Smythe Orchard is a risk, yes, I know that. Granny clued me in on the financial problems a few weeks ago, but the problems aren't with the product or the orchard. She took a lot of time off to grieve after losing

Grampy, then she didn't know how or where to start when she was ready to re-open. Some shady out-of-town contractors took advantage of her when she called around looking for farmhands to gather the harvest, and it was a downhill snowball from there. Every obstacle was bigger than the last, each delay led to more debt, and eventually the orchard wasn't able to regain its footing. It's sad and unfortunate, but the financial state of the orchard doesn't reflect its potential. It only reflects the impact of Granny's grief on the business, and the results of a marriage made at a time when husbands handled everything and women maintained the house." It pained me to say it because Granny was a strong independent woman and my role model, but until Grampy passed, she'd never even pumped her own gas. The day I'd learned that was the day I learned that strength comes in many forms and with many definitions. "Don't invest in the orchard," I said, feeling guilty but knowing all the banker saw was numbers, and our numbers were bad. Plus, the current owner was loosely suspected of murder. "Invest in me instead."

His gaze flipped up to meet mine. "You?"

"Yes. My credit is perfect. My savings are substantial. I've never been in any kind of trouble and my current GPA is 4.0. I'm one hundred percent responsible in all aspects of my life, and I would never be reckless with money. Mine or anyone else's."

He sank back in his seat and tapped his finger against the edge of his desk.

I held my breath and mentally berated myself for the outburst.

"All right."

"All right?"

He nodded. "You wrote one heck of a business plan, and you have a point. The family orchard could go out of business tomorrow, and it wouldn't necessarily stop your cider shop from succeeding, especially considering the sizable revenue you've projected for renting the space for events. Maybe your Granny will turn things around with your help and the Smythe Orchard will last another generation or more in this community, or maybe it will only produce enough apples to satisfy your cider shop's needs. Either way, the two are separate concerns for me." He rubbed his forehead. "It's hard to gauge the sound versus faulty investments sometimes, but I'm willing to come back out and take another look at your future business site."

"Thank you," I said. "I'm sound and so is my plan. With it, I can get the orchard stable again too."

He shoved onto his feet with a chuckle and extended a hand to shake. "I miss the optimism that comes with youth."

I accepted his hand, then let him corral me toward the door. "Thank you. You won't regret this."

"It's just a visit, Miss Montgomery. I'll do my best to keep an open mind." He lifted his arm to check the time, then dropped it back to his side. The distinct tan line on his wrist sent a flood of nostalgia through my heart.

Images from a thousand fishing trips with Grampy crashed over me like tidal waves. I'd learned grief was like that, arriving in sudden and unbidden attacks, summoned by things as silly as a stranger's tan line. Still, in that moment, I could hear his laugh and smell his aftershave. Granny wore Grampy's wristwatch now, but I'd never forget how much his father's gift had meant to him, or how much Grampy still meant to me.

I waved goodbye with an ache in my chest, then hurried in Dot and Jake's direction.

Dot was the first to notice my approach. She halted their conversation mid-sentence. "Well?"

"He agreed to come again and see the barn!"

She grabbed both my hands and we pretended to scream silently for a few seconds, then separated like normal people. I tossed hair off my shoulders. She adjusted the hem of her sweater. "Time to go?" she asked.

"I think so." I hugged Jake goodbye, then waited while Dot dug in her purse for something.

"Jake?" Another bank worker approached on shiny patent leather heels. She smiled sweetly at me, then paused while Dot handed Jake a receipt from her purse.

He pocketed the paper and smiled, then turned to the waiting employee. "Yes?"

The woman's voice was soft but audible. "Mr. Bentley is on line one. He'd like to talk to you about Mrs. Cooper's property."

"Great," he said. "Put him through."

Dot grabbed my elbow and hauled me toward the door, then pushed me outside. "I just gave Jake my phone number," she said. "Is that insane? And all I had to write it on was an old receipt. I hope it wasn't for deodorant or razors. I don't want him thinking I'm sweaty or stinky. Or hairy." She made a horrified face, then looked longingly over her shoulder at the bank behind us, as if she might return and ask for a look at the receipt. "I thought about asking him for his phone so I could type my contact information in, but I didn't want to be presumptuous. I am a few years older. He might think I'm gross or something."

I laughed. "It's a four-year difference, not forty. He'd be crazy not to call," I said, replaying her sentiment when I'd been worried Mr. Sherman wouldn't call.

She smiled.

I kept an eye on the bank as we climbed into Dot's Jeep. "Did you hear that lady tell Jake that Farmer Bentley wants to talk about Mrs. Cooper's property?"

Dot reversed out of her parking spot and eased onto the road. "What? No. I was trying to get out of there before Jake unfolded that receipt with my number on it. As soon as I gave it to him I felt like a complete moron."

"He'll call," I said again. "One of the tellers told Freddie's wife that Farmer Bentley has been buying up properties for months. Do you think he could want Mrs. Cooper's land too? Do you think it seems a little soon to be asking about Mrs. Cooper's stuff?"

Dot shrugged. "I don't know how any of that works, but I am a little surprised he'd want more land at his age. He already has one of the largest farms in the county, and he's at least your granny's age."

Those had been my thoughts exactly. I hated to wonder if a nice old man could be a killer, but if I was right about his intentions, moving in so fast on a property that wasn't even for sale yet struck me as significant. "Did you know Mrs. Cooper had a son in Tennessee?" I asked, recalling his Facebook update.

"No. Since when?"

"About forty years, I guess. His Facebook profile says he's a real estate developer in Nashville. I wonder if he gets her property now that she's gone?"

"Probably," Dot said. "Why?"

I wasn't sure, but I suddenly couldn't help wondering if Mrs. Cooper's death had more to do with her land than her surly disposition. "I think I should talk to Farmer Bentley," I said. I wanted to know why he was in such a hurry to get ahold of that property. And if he'd been in touch with her son before he called the bank to ask about it.

What if he'd offered to buy the land before her death, and she'd said no?

CHAPTER TEN

Mr. Sherman didn't call that afternoon. So I spent the night obsessing over whether or not he'd call at all, and I woke exhausted for my early shift at Sip N Sup. I left the kittens with Granny before racing out the door, still wiping sleep from my eyes, a travel mug of black coffee in one hand and a slice of toast caught between my teeth.

The temperature had plummeted overnight, leaving the air crisp and the grass coated with the sparkling evidence of an overnight frost. Very good news for my upcoming winter festival. I finished the toast with enthusiasm, watching each puff of breath become a little cloud of ice crystals and float away as I headed for the car. I hauled the zipper on my coat to my chin before sliding behind Sally's wheel and adjusting the vents to circulate her heat.

I'd finished all the games and displays for the festival while I'd fretted over Mr. Sherman into the wee hours, and Granny had spent her evening stringing lights and greenery along the entire perimeter fence, giving the orchard an inviting and magical glow. She'd even painted and erected multiple large wooden signs announcing Winterfest and Christmas at the Orchard. The results were fantastic, festive, and fun. Anyone who could drive by without stopping now was either a grinch or a scrooge, and I didn't want them here anyway.

Granny had also arranged another lunch with the stitching crew. It was a secret meeting this time, so hopefully they'd make it to the gossip without being interrupted. As an added bonus, I suspected that she might learn even more today than she would have before because time had passed and everyone had had more opportunities to hear something useful they could share.

I took my time getting to work. It was the first time Sally and I had been back on the road together since the crazed truck had tried to kill us. The drive was lovely, but the view from just outside the Sip N Sup was not.

Hank's familiar silhouette was parked at the counter, clearly visible through the large windows. I gripped the wheel a little tighter and felt my stomach flop. It had been a year since our ugly breakup, but I wasn't ready to face him. I let my head drop against the seat back and considered calling in sick. I'd never done that before, but with everything that was going on, I was sure Mr. Kress would forgive me.

I scanned the lot for signs of his overpriced foreign car so I could park as far from it as possible and not be tempted to kick the tires on my way inside. I didn't see it, but my gaze caught on the sheriff's cruiser, and I groaned.

I took another look inside the diner, and Sheriff Wise lifted his cup in my direction, letting me know I'd been spotted.

Now, I couldn't leave or the sheriff would assume I was avoiding him and come looking for answers I didn't want to give. New plan. I'd go to work, act completely natural, and avoid both men.

I pulled Sally into an open space around back and counted to ten before getting out.

I didn't work a lot of morning shifts, so I couldn't help wondering if the sheriff normally had breakfast at my place of employment, or if he was there on business. Asking about me and Granny. Listening to the local gossip flow from a dozen sexagenarians all hopped up on caffeine, carbohydrates, and syrup.

I yanked the strings on my apron corset-tight as I crossed the lot to the back door and slipped inside. I would not let the sheriff or Hank ruin my day. *Let the sheriff ask about me,* I thought. It was fine by me because there was nothing nefarious to be found. Maybe that fact would finally get him pointed in the right direction — away from me.

I clocked in four minutes before my shift started and gave Mr. Kress a grouchy thumbs up. I should've had more coffee before leaving Granny's, but I'd been in a hurry. Losing sleep was making my lifelong aversion to mornings worse by the day.

I strode into the dining area on sheer determination and the sounds of clanking silverware. I spotted Hank immediately. He was seated at the end of the counter, looking like a young Patrick Dempsey. His crisp white button-down and designer wool coat made my ridiculous heart skip a beat. I'd always been a sucker for a clean-shaven, nicely dressed man.

"Miss?" he said, lifting his mug from the counter and stunning me with his confident smile.

I grabbed the pot and told myself not to pour it in his lap. The sheriff was watching. "Hello," I said politely refilling his mug.

"Can I get you anything else? Maybe just the check?"

He chuckled. "Thanks, but I just ordered. It's been too long since I've had my Sip N Sup usual."

"Enjoy." I turned on my toes and reconsidered the steamy pot in my hands. His usual consisted of two eggs, two sausage links, hash browns, and pancakes with a bottomless cup of coffee. Hank wasn't going anywhere for a while. I never understood how his lean, athletic frame seemed to magically absorb the calories without impact. If I added creamer to my coffee, my pants wouldn't zip.

"Winnie." The sound of my name on his tongue turned me back around, and I hated myself for the way I still responded to him. Even after the lies and secrets and deceit. I hated him for not being honest with me and for not including me in his major life decisions when we were supposed to be getting engaged. Sadly, parts of me would always love him for the lifetime of shared dreams and tender memories that had come before the bad.

I returned to him silently, a determined smile in place. "Yes?"

Hank rolled his cool blue eyes up at me, peering through the thick black lashes his mama gave him and looking like someone who belonged on a billboard instead of inside a small-town diner. "I think we should talk," he said, his voice low and pleading.

My tongue stuck to the roof of my mouth and my breaths quickened. I felt the heat of two dozen sets of eyes on me.

"I can't. I'm . . ." My mind scrambled. What was I? Too mad? Too hurt? Plain unwilling? "Working."

He nodded and slid one hand over mine when I rested it on the counter between us. "Another time, then. Why don't I come over and pick you up tonight? We can go for a ride or walk through the orchard for old times' sake. Sort things out."

I closed my eyes against the rush of powerful memories. When I reopened them, I found Sheriff Wise watching from his stool across the way. There was inexplicable interest in his eyes, maybe even a little misplaced heat.

Hank lifted my hand in his and gave my fingers a squeeze. "What do you say?"

I jerked back to reality and yanked my hand away. "Stop."

He recoiled as if I'd slapped him. "What? Why?"

"You know why," I hissed.

He froze, hurt and anger plain on his face. "Winnie, it's been a year," he said. "It's time we talk."

My head began to shake before he'd finished speaking. Too many emotions squirmed and twisted in my heart and mind. It wasn't his fault that my father had never bothered to contact me after my mother dumped me off with her folks and ran away, but Hank's decisions to sneak off and plan a different life had cut me to the bone, and I couldn't relive it. Not for him or anyone else. "There is no more *we*," I whispered. Then, before I said anything more or a renegade tear fell, I took my coffee pot and ran away.

Sheriff Wise stared past me in Hank's direction, his expression fathomless as I bolted for the ladies room. He'd clearly heard the exchange and judging by the sympathetic expressions all around the room, so had everyone else. It wouldn't be long before the entire town heard about it too.

Freddie hit the order bell, and I changed directions, glad for the distraction. I set the pot back on the burner and blew out a long steadying breath. In keeping with my continuously horrific luck, Hank's meal sat on the shiny service area between myself and the kitchen. I tipped my head back and let my eyes fall shut. A moment later, I pulled myself together and gathered the plates. Hank was right about one thing. It had been a year since our breakup, and I hadn't gotten the closure I'd wanted back then, but I'd had enough time to let it go. I couldn't allow what Hank had done in the past to keep interfering with my life in the present.

It was time to move on and deliver his giant breakfast.

"Got it," I called into the busy kitchen before heading back to the counter with a slightly more genuine smile in place. My feet stopped short of Hank's now empty seat. A crisp green twenty sat beside his still steaming mug of coffee. Behind me, the little bell over the front door jingled, and Hank strode along the sidewalk outside the windows disappearing into the crowded parking lot.

Granny and the kittens were at the fruit stand when I returned home. Christmas music piped through the CD player near the register, and Granny's red nose was brighter than Rudolph's. The temperature had plummeted by at least twenty degrees since yesterday, and winter was undeniably upon us. Thankfully, Granny wasn't alone.

A small group of folks with stiff Northern accents chatted animatedly about their luck finding Smythe Orchard. They'd come to enjoy a day in the national park and over-heard a few locals discussing the cider.

"We love cider," the tall brunette said. "I buy the grocery store out of stock every time they bring it in."

"I do the same thing," her friend said, lift-ing another half-gallon into her arms. "But I've never had so many delicious gourmet choices."

Granny smiled when she saw me. "Here she is now," she announced. "The woman behind the best apple cider in town. My granddaughter, Winnie."

"The best cider in town?" the taller woman cooed, "I think you mean in the state or maybe on the East Coast." She and her friend moved in my direction, a pair of men in their wake. "Truthfully, this might be the best cider I've ever had."

The unexpected compliment lifted my spirits and sent a rush of heat across my cheeks. "Thank you."

"How do you do it?" she asked.

"I start with the very best apples," I said, tipping my head toward the orchard. "Then, I play with the recipes, tweaking and fine-tuning until I get the results we sell here.

The flavors have evolved over time. It's an ongoing quest for perfection."

"She's been making cider and using it in recipes all her life," Granny added. "She was raised here, and I guess the whole thing is just second nature to her. She's something to behold in the kitchen."

I leaned against her side and wrapped my arm around her back. "I get the dedication honestly. Granny cooks and bakes. Makes pies, jams, breads, anything you can think of from her homegrown fruits. She turns these apples alone into far more and better things than I could ever dream."

The taller woman watched us, appraising. "You know what?" she said, passing her items to the man behind her, "I write for a travel magazine called *Beautiful America,* and I'm always looking for places like this to feature in our "America's Best Kept Secrets" section. If you're interested, I'd love to talk to you more about your orchard. Maybe take a tour. See how the magic happens." She dug a business card from her purse and handed it to me.

Granny slapped her palms together. "We're interested," she said, "and everything you've got there is on the house. You can write about that in your blog too."

I laughed. *And that,* I thought, *is one small*

reason the orchard is in deep financial trouble. Granny hated taking money for anything. Not the strongest business model. But she was right this time. *Beautiful America* was a wide-reaching magazine for travelers that featured destinations no one heard of until their products showed up on the pages of the magazine. *Beautiful America* was online, but it was also in stores across the United States and several other countries, making this clandestine opportunity priceless. If this woman really followed through with a story on Smythe Orchard and my cider, it would boost our sales and increase our customer base instantly. "I'll bring the tractor around," I said.

While Granny worked her magic, retelling the tale of how she and Grampy had come across the failing orchard and simply knew they wanted to build a life on it, I looked the woman up on my phone. I used her business card as a guide and found she had enough followers on any social media platform to populate a small town. Photos of the orchard began appearing before my eyes with tags like #hiddengem and #sneakpeek. Better still, people were responding. "She called us hidden gems," I told Kenny and Dolly as they rolled end over end in the grass, growling like a pair of wild lions.

"Easy," I said. "Be nice to your sibling." I took a step in their direction and they sprung apart. "Thank you."

They darted forward, and I yipped as they jumped onto my pant legs and climbed furiously up my thighs. "Ah!" I jumped as their needle-sharp claws nicked the skin beneath my jeans. Doc Austin's trimming of their nails had done little to diminish their ability to climb. "No, kitty." I peeled Kenny off first and Dolly followed suit. Back together on land, they tore out of sight. I rubbed my stinging thighs. "Goofs."

Granny returned an hour later with the blogger and her friends. I said a heartfelt thanks and goodbye to the woman who'd turned my day around.

"Can you believe that?" Granny asked as their rented SUV bounced back down the long gravel lane. "What a nice lady and a needed stroke of luck."

"She liked my cider," I said, feeling a fresh surge of pride and enthusiasm.

"No. She *loved* your cider," Granny corrected. "She took four different kinds with her."

I beamed. "Which four?"

"Honeycrisp original, cinnamon, caramel . . ." She ticked the flavors off on her fingers and looked to the sky for help when she got stuck, "and the tart one made with the Granny Smiths."

I pointed at Granny. "I think those should be the ones we set out for Mr. Sherman when he comes back to visit," I said. "Being recognized in that magazine will have to impress him." I mentally backtracked over the flavors Granny had listed. "I should probably think of a name for that last one before the cider shop opens. I can't list it as 'the one with Granny Smiths' on the menu."

Granny scooped Kenny off the ground and rubbed behind his ears. "You're going to need a name for the cider shop too."

I fought the urge to bounce a palm off my forehead.

She heaved a sigh, her gaze drifting to the horizon. "It's hard to enjoy the moment when I can't get Nadine off my mind."

I rubbed Granny's arm. "I know what you mean."

"I should've been nicer to her."

I smiled, remembering Mrs. Cooper's commanding presence. "She didn't make it easy," I said, "and you couldn't have known something would happen to her."

Granny leaned against me. "Maybe, but being kind is always the right thing to do, and I let her get under my skin every time. Have you given anymore thought to what might've happened to her?"

"Continually."

"Me too," she said. "Any new leads?"

"No, you?"

"No."

I let my head drop back, posture deflating. "What about your lunch with the ladies?"

"They all had plenty to say, but none of it was new. And a few of them were downright disappointed the sheriff didn't come back this time." She snorted. "Apparently he's 'dreamy' and 'a real catch,' " she said using air quotes. "I'm not clear on which one of them thought they were going to catch him, but it's probably for his own good that he didn't show up."

I laughed. "There must be something in the water. Dot gave her number to Jake at the bank yesterday. She's regretting it now because she's four years older than him, but what's done is done."

Granny shot me a droll look. "The age difference didn't seem to bother my stitching crew. Some of them have new hips older than the sheriff."

I laughed. "Did you have a nice visit otherwise?"

"It's always nice to be with friends," she said softly. "Oh, I almost forgot. The crew got a whole pack of new orders today and an invitation to the state Knitwits convention. The Knitwits are a group of knitters, but they're adding needlework to this year's lineup and invited us to attend. Expenses paid."

"That's great!" I said. "You should definitely go. Your group does amazing work."

She rolled her eyes. "They want to showcase our rude patterns."

I laughed. "Oh."

"And we need a group name and photo."

I sighed. "More names. Maybe we can brainstorm together later."

"Deal," she agreed. "Maybe you can add some hard ciders to your lineup."

The afternoon turned frigid and rainy as we chatted and planned for the future. For Mr. Sherman's visit. For a cider shop on the property and for ways to bring more people out to celebrate Christmas at the Orchard.

When twilight demanded it was closing time, I joined Granny in her kitchen for hot cider and sandwiches. "It's too bad you didn't learn anything new from your girlfriends today," I said, still stuck on the fact they thought Sheriff Wise was dreamy and not sure how to bring it up again. Sure, he had kind eyes when he wasn't glaring at me, looked impressive in a uniform, and his jaw-line was square enough to make sculptors weep, but he was a real pain in my backside.

"The stitchers mostly wanted to talk about what you've been up to," she said. "They wondered how I felt about you confronting Oscar and challenging the sheriff at every turn."

"I'm not doing that," I said. "I mean, I confronted Oscar, but I was polite about it, and I'm not challenging the sheriff."

"Maybe not intentionally," she said, "but I can see how some folks might view it that way. No judgment," she hurried on, "and for the record I'm proud. Grampy and I raised you to have a backbone and to do the right thing anytime you can. Obviously I didn't hurt Nadine, and you're doing your best to make sure everyone knows it. I think that's nice."

"*Trying* is the key word there." I paddled an orange slice around my mug of cider with a cinnamon stick. *Failing* was more accurate.

"Once the ladies left, I had the police station receptionist over for pie."

"Oh yeah?" I asked, using the cinnamon to dunk a bobbing cranberry. "You didn't tell me that."

"I was processing."

I didn't like the sound of that. "What did she tell you?"

"Nothing about Nadine's murder. She said that was all under wraps while the investigation was open, and the sheriff specifically asked her not to talk to me about it. She had an interesting question for me, though."

I stilled my cinnamon.

"She wondered how you were doing after being run off the road by a crazed lunatic in a big black truck."

"I'm actually not sure how big the truck was," I said, offering an apologetic smile. I winced under her intense look of dis-approval. "I didn't tell you because I wasn't hurt and I didn't want to worry you. There's enough tough stuff going on in your life already without me serving up another tale of disaster."

Granny shook her head slowly, heartbreak evident in her eyes. "We have to be able to tell each other anything. You know that, and we don't get to decide for one another what they can or can't handle."

"I know."

"Good." She peeled the foil off an apple cake, then grabbed a knife to cut it. "Do you think the truck that chased you could have been driven by the same man who was

211

in the press building the other night?"

The same one who'd left me the threatening note.

"Probably," I admitted.

"Could that man have been Oscar?"

I tried yet again to visualize the trail master and compare him with the memory of the man who'd bowled me over leaving the press house. "I'm not sure." I accepted a slice of apple cake and lifted it with my fingers, unwilling to wait on a fork. "All I know is that I'm desperate to figure out who's doing these things and get him arrested before the threats go any further. I'm doing my best, but all I've gotten so far is discouraged."

"Just don't let it stop you," Granny said. "You never know when you're just one move away from getting what you want. That's why I scheduled another lunch date for tomorrow. Even when our first few tries don't pan out, we have to buckle down and keep going."

I sucked a drop of cinnamon icing off my thumb. "Who's coming over this time?"

"Pastor Gerber," Granny said. "I figure, if there's a soul in this town who hears everything, it's him, and as a bonus, he can't lie about it."

"You're hitting up the pastor for information," I deadpanned. "Have you thought of the eternal consequences?"

She rolled her eyes. "It's just lunch. It's not like I'm asking him to commit a felony."

My phone vibrated on the table between us, and I turned it toward Granny with a smile. "It's Mr. Sherman."

CHAPTER ELEVEN

"He's coming!" I tossed the phone onto the table like a hot potato. "Oh my goodness. He's really coming!"

Granny pressed her hands to her chest. "When?"

"Tonight," I said. "Now."

"Oh, dear." Granny turned in a small circle, then burst into action. "How much time do we have?" she asked, snapping pink rubber gloves over her hands.

"I'm not sure," I admitted. "He said he was finishing up at the bank and heading here on his way home." According to my phone, it was approaching five o'clock, and thanks to daylight savings time, it was already dark. Luckily, Mr. Sherman and I had already decided the potential small business loan was for my cider shop, not the orchard, and he'd seen the orchard before anyway. Also, the Mail Pouch barn had electricity. Sure, it was only a light bulb on a swinging chain, but at least it wouldn't matter that night had fallen, and all the taste testing could be done at Granny's place.

We buzzed around the kitchen together, cleaning and organizing everything in sight while brainstorming the pastry selections we should offer with my cider. Twenty minutes later, Granny's kitchen looked amazing, but there was no sign of Mr. Sherman.

"How does it look?" I asked, feeling a rush of nerves heat my cheeks and flip my stomach. I'd filled three of Granny's glass tea dispensers with cold cider recipes, then lined them on a quilted table runner made by my great-grandmother. Beside those, I added two thermal dispensers with hot cider. Orange slices, cinnamon sticks, cranberries, and mint leaves floated visibly behind the glass of the cold dispensers. The contents of the final two dispensers, however, were a visual mystery, but hopefully a treat for the taste buds.

"Perfect," Granny said. She set fresh glasses and mugs out for tasting, then lined the back side of her table with a mini-buffet of treats made from the orchard's fresh ingredients.

I placed a stack of small plates, forks, and

napkins beside the buffet. "What else?" I asked.

Granny examined the spread. "Music?"

"Yes!" I brought up a holiday station on her radio and set it to play softly. "Perfect. What else?"

"I think that's it," she said. Her gaze flipped to the black cat clock above her sink, its eyes and tail swinging in time. "Five-thirty-five. He should be here any minute."

I blew out a long thin breath. She was right. The bank closed at five, and the commute was less than ten minutes. "He's probably finishing paperwork or reviewing applications." I doubted the bank staff stood at the time clock like diner employees, waiting to punch out. "He might even be approving my loan request." Probably not, but a lady could hope.

Granny lit a pair of candles on her baker's rack, adding cinnamon and vanilla scents to the already mouthwatering aromas filling her home. "There," she said. "I think that's it."

I agreed. The room was perfect. Inviting. Enticing. Everything I could want for atmosphere on such an important night. Even the aged stone fireplace along the back wall had a little fire going and two orange kittens dreaming happily on the hearth. *If they woke and climbed Mr. Sherman's legs, I would die on the spot.* "Maybe I should move the kittens into one of the bedrooms while he's here."

A sharp rap on the door canceled my thought.

"He's here!" Granny stage-whispered loudly enough to be heard outside.

She took a long audible breath, then went to answer the door.

I shoved a bite of apple torte into my mouth to stabilize my nerves.

"Mr. Sherman," Granny said, "Welcome. Come in. We're so glad you were able to make the time for a second visit. How are the roads?"

"Slick," he said, shaking rain from his hat. "It took a little longer than I expected. I didn't mean to keep you waiting. Hello, Miss Montgomery."

"Hello." I swallowed hard, feeling the pressure of the moment in full force. This was it. This was my chance. "I'm so glad you're here."

Granny stepped closer to the overflowing kitchen table and made a face at me.

"Oh." I rubbed sweat-slicked palms against the thighs of my pants. "Well, you've been at work all day, and you probably want to get home, so I won't keep you long. We've set a display of samples here for you to taste test. It's a small selection of the gourmet items I plan to sell in the cider shop."

Granny splashed a few ounces of the first cold cider sample into a glass and passed it his way. "These are all Winnie's recipes," she said. "I think you'll find it hard to choose a favorite."

He accepted the drink with a small smile. "Thank you."

I filled a plate with bite-sized bread and pastry samples, then passed that to him as well. "I make the ciders, Granny bakes the treats," I said. "Everything you'll sample tonight is proprietary." Meaning the recipes belonged only to us. They could be used by us, sold by us, put into cookbooks by us, anything we wanted.

"Good." He nodded as he chewed.

I wasn't sure if the word was meant to be a comment on what I'd just told him or a compliment on the fritter he'd pushed between his lips. I didn't care.

"Would you like to sit?" I asked, offering him a seat at the end of the table where a bit of room remained.

"No, thank you." Instead he circled the table, working his way through the cider selections and sugary offerings. Each time his cup neared empty, Granny traded him for a new one and told him about the recipe. I did the same for his plate.

Twenty minutes later, based on Mr. Sherman's satisfied expression and the fact our buffet had been nearly wiped out, I guessed things were going well. "Can I answer any questions for you about our products or processes?" I asked.

He looked up from his mug of hot cider as if he'd forgotten we were there. "What are the production costs for these items?"

"Production costs?" I looked at Granny.

"I have all the ingredients on hand," she answered promptly. "They don't cost me a thing."

Mr. Sherman's expression soured. Wrong answer. Everything cost something and he wanted to know the total when every spoonful of sugar and pinch of salt had been figured in.

"I can get those numbers to you," I said, "for the breads and pastries as well as the ciders."

He nodded. "What will you sell them for?"

I hadn't decided.

"What will your margins be?" He asked before I could think of an answer to his first question. He wiped the corner of his mouth with a napkin and turned his full attention on me.

"Individually?" My voice cracked. I'd only considered the big picture costs like renovations and monthly/annual overhead associated with daily operation of the cider shop. I'd based my projected sales on current cider and product numbers. I hadn't broken it all down per product. "I'll get those figures to you first thing tomorrow."

Obviously unimpressed, he looked at the clock.

I was losing him.

"How about a walk?" I suggested. "Some mountain air to go with the sweets." I smiled.

He didn't.

Granny passed me my coat, then threaded her arms into a wool number of her own. "I'll come along so you won't have to walk back alone."

My heart swelled. "Thanks."

Outside, the wind whirled fallen leaves into soggy cyclones at our feet.

I hurried along beside Mr. Sherman and Granny, struggling for the right thing to say. "I'm confident our Mail Pouch barn is the perfect location for this kind of shop," I said. "There's nothing more perfectly West Virginian than sipping cider on an orchard nestled in the Blue Ridge Mountains, except doing it inside an iconic location like this one."

Mr. Sherman slowed slightly. "I don't disagree, Miss Montgomery, but it's my job to be thorough and prudent. I know we've said that the cider shop is separate from the orchard, and that investing in your new business is different than investing in Mrs. Smythe's older one, but how can that ever be one hundred percent true? Your proposed location is on her property, a location that's receiving a lot of bad press right now." He stopped to face me under the moon and stars, cold wind battering our hands and cheeks. "I'm not saying it's fair. I'm just voicing facts that I believe will inevitably impact your new business. Folks are already cautious where the orchard is concerned. How can I know that the pattern won't continue or even worsen after I've approved your loan? In that scenario, granting the money doesn't help you at all, instead I will have done you a great disservice by putting you in a position of debt you can't repay."

I pulled my hands inside my coat sleeves to curl my fingers against the cold and frustration. "It's true that the orchard isn't getting as much business as it did before, but how do we know that folks are pulling away from the farm intentionally and not merely acting out of routine? Granny's never had the farm open this late into the season before. Maybe people aren't coming because they normally don't. Maybe they still think of the orchard as closed after Thanksgiving. Most of the guests we met today told us they'd stopped in after receiving my flier or driving past and seeing the signs up."

"And what about your wildly successful Christmas at the Orchard campaign?" he asked.

I pursed my lips. I'd definitely oversold that the last time I talked to him. "It's bringing in new customers as well," I hedged, "and people will continue to come as they realize we're open. The winter festival I have planned will go a long way toward that end. I'm in the process of contacting all the tour companies we've worked with in the past, and I've taken out an ad in the county's *Gazette.* Right now, the change is new, and change takes time."

Mr. Sherman offered a pitying smile.

I could practically hear his inner voice asking, *How much time do you think the orchard still has, Miss Montgomery?* And, *How long do you believe your new cider shop can succeed with dismal sales and a lack of customers?*

Sadly, I didn't know.

"Mr. Sherman," Granny said, "I can understand your concerns about my business impacting Winnie's. I've thought about that, too, and I'm willing to get a surveyor out here who can divide the property. I can make the acre or two around the barn and down to the road separate from the rest, then put that in Winnie's name."

"Granny!" I gasped. The cold knife of separation sliced through my core. "I don't want that," I whispered, working to control my tone through the shock. "We're a team. The orchard and cider shop need to support one another, not pull apart." My insides twisted at the thought of being cut off from her. "No."

She stepped closer and gave me her usual loving smile. "It's only a formality. Divided on paper alone. In case you haven't thought about it, or guessed, the whole shebang is yours when I go anyway."

I felt the squeeze inside me tighten. "No."

She sighed, then turned her smile on Mr. Sherman. "It's an option we can pursue if it comes to that. Meanwhile, there's an access road behind the barn that could be properly graveled and used as an access point for cider shop patrons if we need to disassociate this place from mine."

Mr. Sherman peered into the night beyond the barn, probably trying to discern the overgrown path the cable and electric companies had used to run services to the property. "I'm not sure this barn can ever be disassociated from your family's legacy, Mrs. Smythe, but I certainly appreciate the thought you've given this."

He dipped his chin and began to move again. "To be honest, I'm still bothered by the condition of your trees. I'm no farmer, but I do enough gardening and have spent enough time in nature to know what I saw the other day wasn't a sign of good health. Something was clearly wrong with them."

Granny shot me a look.

I shook my head infinitesimally. I'd have to bring her up to speed on that later.

"Maybe if you had something for collateral," he suggested.

Granny's gasp cut through his words, and I turned, half-sick with the knowledge Granny and I had nothing aside from the farm, which was more baggage at the moment than buoy.

Her eyes were wide. Her stare fixed to the Mail Pouch barn. Still several yards away, doors parted. The distinct flicker of flames glowed against the walls inside.

"No!" I burst into a sprint, terror clawing

at my chest.

This couldn't be happening. I couldn't lose the barn. Grampy loved the barn. *I* loved the barn. I'd pinned all my hopes to it, and I couldn't watch it go up in flames.

I swung the doors wide, and a cloud of acrid smoke rushed out. The space was trashed, crates broken, signs ripped down, but the fire was contained inside an old metal barrel I'd posed as a hostess stand. Someone had stuffed the barrel with chunks of broken crates and my holiday décor, then used it all as kindling.

"Oh, Winnie!" Granny wailed, her voice and footfalls arriving several moments behind me. Her hands cupped my shoulders, and she turned me to her for a hug. "I'm so sorry."

I pulled away, determined to look as grown-up as possible while on the verge of tears. Mr. Sherman had just said there could be a problem with opening my shop here, and now he was present for the proof. He was witness to the second crime on Granny's property this week. "Mr. Sherman," I began softly, turning to see if he'd left again, the way he had before.

This time his gaze clung to the floorboards beyond the fire. His long shadow stretched and wobbled over a line of letters carved

into the historic wooden floorboards.
STRIKE TWO.

CHAPTER TWELVE

The sheriff interviewed Granny, Mr. Sherman, and me while one of his deputies examined the grounds outside the barn and another picked through the mess around us. Floodlights had been erected to assist in the efforts when my light bulb on a chain had left too much to be desired. The process was still slow going. Darkness and intermittent rain made outside searches doubly awful, but the deputies worked diligently and without complaint. Hopefully this time one of them would find a clue about who'd trashed the place and started the fire. I knew in my bones that person was also Mrs. Cooper's killer and needed to be stopped.

I waited as patiently as possible through the search process happening inside the barn. My hands itched to clean up the mess and erase the crazed lunatic's mark from my future cider shop, but I couldn't risk damaging potential evidence. Instead, I wound and unwound a loose thread from the hem of my sweater around one fingertip and listened to the sheriff's interviews. Granny and Mr. Sherman gave identical statements to mine. We'd found the mess together. There were no signs of the vandal. No one fled the scene this time or escaped on a hidden four-wheeler. The night had been perfectly still as we'd made our way from Granny's house.

When the inspecting deputy finally took his leave of the space, I got busy righting toppled crates and tossing splintered ones into the burn barrel. *Who would do something like this?* My furious mind played the question on repeat, but that was exactly the problem. Wasn't it? No one knew who would do this. In a town so small I'd probably served eight-five percent of them coffee or a burger at one time, no one seemed to have a clue who'd killed my neighbor, broke into our press house, left a note on my car, tried to run me off the road, or vandalized my future cider shop.

"Winnie?" Sheriff Wise approached me, his hat clutched to his chest. "How are you holding up?"

I nodded, not trusting my tongue to hold its angry thoughts.

"My men are walking Mr. Sherman to his

car and your granny back to her house. I told her I'd see you home. When you're ready," he added

I scanned the room for Granny. She stood between the open barn doors with a deputy, her gaze on me, brows raised in question.

"I'm okay," I told her with surprising calm. "I'll call you when I get to my place."

"All right." She returned a small smile, then took the elbow offered by the deputy, and began the cold, dark walk home.

Sheriff Wise leaned against one of the giant wooden spools I'd positioned as tables throughout the space. He braced his palms on either side of his hips. "Cool barn."

Something had changed in his demeanor tonight. He wasn't as brooding, taunting, or hostile as he'd been at the other unfortunate run-ins. I bristled, illogically irked that he had the nerve to change himself on me and without notice or apparent prompt.

"I know you and I got off on the wrong foot," he began, "but I want you to know I'm sorry this is happening to you and your granny."

Was this some kind of new tactic to gain my trust and lure a confession from me? Or had he possibly wised up and realized Granny and I were innocent?

"I'm also sorry I was harsh with you the

other times we've spoken. I can be fast to assume the worst, I guess." He lifted one shoulder with an impish grin. "Hazard of the job."

The unexpected speech put a damper on my temper. I realized I was angry about the vandalism and had planned to point my wrath at him. A convenient target. Now, he'd ruined that.

He shook his head and released a low chuckle. "Apparently I've become so accustomed to criminals professing their innocence that I've picked up the bad habit of assuming the worst in everyone. It wasn't fair of me to do that to you or your granny."

"What brought on this confession?"

He shifted his gaze away. "A compilation of things, I suppose. For one, I've been asking around about you and your granny for days. No one's had a bad word to say about either of you, and everyone I've met had some kind of beef with Mrs. Cooper. Furthermore, it seems less and less likely that these peripheral events are unrelated to the murder since I can't find a soul who doesn't think you're a saint. Which leads me back to believing crimes like this," he motioned to the barn, "are likely the work of the killer who is, in fact, trying to stop your ill-conceived investigation."

I chewed my lip and considered him. "So you believe Granny didn't hurt Mrs. Cooper?" I asked for clarity. "And you know I'm not running around trying to cover anything up or redirect your suspicions, or whatever it is you've accused me of?"

"I think all those things are highly unlikely," he said carefully, shifting his weight against the giant wooden spool. "Besides the fact it would be unthinkably dumb for your granny to have murdered her known nemesis and left the body to be found on her own property while scheduled tours were in progress, I also believe Mrs. Cooper's death was an act of passion. I've spoken to your granny several times this week, and she's no dummy. Also, I've seen her become passionate about many things. Farming. Her late husband. Her community. You. When we spoke about Mrs. Cooper, her mood consistently fell somewhere between nostalgic appreciation and exhaustion. I'm not sure the woman even has a temper."

I smiled. "I've never seen it."

The sheriff smiled back, and it reached his eyes for the first time in my presence.

I paused to enjoy the dimple that appeared on his left cheek and the kindness in his eyes. He really, finally, believed me.

"Well," he said, breaking the sudden and inexplicably tense silence, "why don't I help you finish up in here?"

He wanted to help me finish what? Cleaning?

Before I could ask for clarification again, Sheriff Wise grabbed the broom I'd leaned against a far wall and began to sweep the ash and splintered wood toward the open doors. "Got any music?"

"Sure." I started a playlist on my phone, then busied myself in the work, unsure what to make of the strange new camaraderie brewing between us. I tossed crumpled signs and broken crates into the barrel of melted holiday décor and tried not to stare at the handsome sheriff sweeping my floor.

"You really should call me Colton," he said, hoisting a toppled pallet off one of my printed café photos, "if we're going to be friends."

Is that what was happening? We were becoming friends?

"I'll try." My heart warmed senselessly at the thought. Though I couldn't imagine why he'd want to be my friend, especially after the front row seat he'd had to my unforgivable behavior toward Hank this morning. I'd replayed the exchange a thousand times in my head after he left, and I died a little more each time. I must've looked impossibly moody and juvenile to Colton and anyone else who didn't understand my history with Hank. Regardless, I'd been unfair. Hank hadn't done anything to provoke me, and I owed him an apology.

I forced my thoughts back to the crisis at hand. "What do you suppose was the point of all this?" I asked. "I get the point of the message left behind, but why would anyone want to trash this place? If the fire had gotten out of control and burned this down, the entire country would be short a piece of its history."

The sheriff leaned on his broom, just inches from the set of jagged letters carved into the floor. "Honestly, I think all of this constitutes a threat." He cast a conflicted gaze around the room before fixing it on me.

"Go on," I urged. Clearly there was something more he wanted to say. "I need to know."

"I think the manner in which this message was delivered is a distinct escalation from a paper tucked under a windshield wiper. This threat is permanent and was made using something that could probably kill you. The potential of fire damage was likely by design, meant to show you he's in control. I think he wants you to see that he knows you and he knows what you care about. Also, that he's willing to take it away if necessary."

I took a step back, eyes wide, mouth dry. "What?" My mind jumped to the one thing left on earth that I truly cared for above all else, my life included. *Granny.* Did the man who did this know that too? Would he go after her next?

"I think it's more important than ever that you make it clear you've taken the warnings to heart and are leaving my investigation alone. Someone clearly has an eye on you."

My knees buckled and my stomach pitched. I took a seat where I stood, then leaned forward and told myself to breathe.

"Hey." Heavy footfalls rattled the boards beneath me. A moment later, Colton crouched into view. "I'm not trying to scare you. I'm trying to help you see the danger. You can trust me to get to the bottom of this without your help. I know I'm relatively new around here, and you don't know me very well, but I'm excellent at this job."

I lifted my gaze to meet his. Everything I'd read online had confirmed his last statement. "I was only trying to help clear Granny."

"I know," he said. "For the record, that choice was misguided and dumb."

I narrowed my eyes and bit back a scathing retort. He sighed, lowering himself onto his backside before me. "If I put myself in your position, I suppose I can see how you thought you were helping."

We stared at one another for a long quiet beat. The figurative wall that collapsed between us resulted in a floodgate of zigzagging energy. My pulse leaped, and my cheeks heated.

"I got a flier for your winter festival in the mail today," he said. "I'm thinking about coming."

"Oh, yeah?"

He bobbed his head. "I thought I might even come around early and help you set up. It seems like a two-woman show out here most days, and you're probably going to have a couple hundred people that night."

A couple *hundred*? Hope soared in my heart. "You think?"

"Yeah. That's my best guess based on how much these people seem to love you guys and this place. Plus the fliers were pretty good."

I smiled. "I guess I could use some help, then."

Colton's gaze fell away momentarily, and it came back to me a little shyer, less sheriff-like. He stretched onto his feet and offered me a hand. "Then it's a date."

My mind latched on to the word *date*. I stared into his inviting blue eyes, trying and failing to will his intentions out of him.

He cocked his head at my hesitation and let his hand fall back an inch. "Or not."

My cheeks flooded with heat again, and I hiked up my smile before sliding my palm over his. "It's a date." I was on my feet with an easy tug from his hand. Electricity ran up my arm and into my chest. I pulled in a sharp breath.

Considering all my other peculiar responses to Colton Wise lately, I should have been prepared for the shock of his touch, but I wasn't. I could only imagine the expression on my face as I tried to form it into something casual and friendly.

Colton held on to me a beat longer than absolutely necessary. Had he felt it too?

I stepped back, freeing his hand and shoving my electrified palm into my pocket.

He kept his eyes on me, a peculiar expression etched over his features. "That man you spoke with at the diner this morning —" he began.

"Hank." I cut him off. I knew where that was going. "I was out of line."

"The two of you were a couple once?"

I stifled an eye roll. As if he hadn't heard

all the gory details of my abandonment by now. "We broke up last Thanksgiving. Why? What are people saying?"

"Nothing," he said, looking a bit mystified. "Of all the people I asked about you, no one ever mentioned a boyfriend. I just assumed you didn't date."

"Why wouldn't I date?" I asked, feeling a bit slighted by the comment. "I mean, I don't date now because the last attempt turned out to be a huge mistake, but why would you assume I didn't date at all?" I crossed my arms over a suddenly hollow center. Did he think there was something wrong with me?

"It's just that most folks said you keep to yourself. You work. Go to school. Help your granny. I figured it didn't leave much time for dating, and people you went to high school with actually said the words, 'Winnie didn't date.' Kids who recognized your name from college said you didn't go out with them or hang out at the party scene. I guess I can't understand why no one bothered to mention Hank."

I was suddenly profoundly thankful for a community who'd protected my privacy when faced with a prime opportunity to dish some excellent gossip. "I didn't date in high school because my mom did. She got

237

too serious with someone, which is how I came to exist." I shook my head, willing myself to shut up. He hadn't asked for an ugly backstory. "I don't hang out with my classmates in college because they're all under twenty-three, and I passed that birthday five years ago. I'm officially an old maid in comparison."

He smiled cautiously. "And Hank?"

That was a good question. "I've known Hank all my life. He's a decent guy, though a little too driven by money, appearances, and prestige in my opinion. We had things in common once and started dating a few years back. It ended poorly, but before that he'd been the only man who'd kept my interest or given me that little zip of excitement when he came near."

Until now.

I pushed the pointless observation aside.

He pulled the buzzing phone from his pocket. The words *Detective Hanson* were centered on the screen. Colton rejected the call.

He returned to his broom without comment, suddenly detached from the moment, the conversation, me.

"You okay?" I asked. "Was that call about Mrs. Cooper?"

His gaze snapped back to mine. "No. That

was nothing."

"Doesn't seem like nothing."

His Adam's apple moved slowly as he swallowed, apparently regrouping. "I'm thirty-three," he said finally.

"What?"

"You're five years older than your classmates, so you feel like an old maid. I'm wondering what that makes me in your eyes. Being five years older than you."

I didn't answer. We both knew that wasn't what he'd been thinking about.

"I never asked about the truck that came after you the other night," Colton said a few seconds later. "I was out on another call or I would've come to see you."

"It's fine," I said absently. "A little paint on Sally's bumper from the nudge, but it'll buff out."

A flash of interest lit his eyes. "There's paint?"

"Not much. No damage."

"You're going to have to show me that when I walk you home. If there's enough paint there to get a sample, I'll be able to name the make and model of the truck that hit you."

"Sounds good," I said, still distracted by the fact he'd avoided a call from a detective then seemed temporarily out of sorts over it.

I pumped up the volume on my favorite country Christmas songs and got back to work. I used the time to mentally review the conversations I'd had with Mr. Sherman before we'd arrived at the barn. Had he made up his mind about my loan? If he said no now, how would I know if it was because of me or the creep who kept committing crimes on Granny's property? How could I get him back out here for one proper uninterrupted visit? Wait until the killer was caught? Would Mr. Sherman consider it then or was my fate already sealed with him?

A few songs later, the barn was clean, and the lazy patter of rain had stopped.

Colton hefted the final pallet onto a stack against the wall as something scratched at the back of my mind. "What's up?" He tugged off the work gloves he'd donned for the heavy lifting and gave me a curious stare.

"I've been thinking about the business loan I applied for. One of Mr. Sherman's concerns about the orchard is the condition of our trees. He found some unhealthy-looking leaves on his first visit and assumed the trees were sick, but I know they aren't. Not with any kind of disease that will spread and hurt our yield anyway. I've seen diseased trees. That's not what this is, but what if the tree problem is related to our case?"

Colton wiped a sleeve across his brow and headed in my direction. "My case, and what do you mean?"

"I think the trees were sabotaged, and I can't help wondering if whoever poisoned them is the one behind everything else." I hadn't thought the tree situation could be connected to the murder at first, but what if it was? "What if hurting the trees was the first crime in this crazy spree? What if Mrs. Cooper had been headed home from our place, caught the person in the act, then threatened to tell on him. He might've killed her to shut her up."

Sheriff Wise set his hands on his hips. "I meant what happened to your trees?"

In the wake of every other crime happening this week, I'd completely forgotten to tell him. "Bring a flashlight. I'll show you."

I was back at the Mail Pouch barn first thing the next morning with some wood stain, putty, and a sanding block, prepared to erase the simple two-word threat from my barn and my life. Colton had collected soil samples from the trees on his way out the night before, and I was certain he'd find the culprit once he figured out what had been used to hurt the trees. He also managed to get a little paint off Sally's bumper, but he wasn't convinced it would be enough to identify the truck that hit me. Still, he'd promised to try.

My breaths were visible in the cold air as I huffed and puffed over the carved wood, using all the elbow grease I could muster against the threat on the floorboards. My sanding block lost its grit before making much of a dent in the jagged gashes, and putting my weight into it wasn't doing much either. "I was afraid you'd give me a hard time," I muttered to the angry letters staring up at me, "but I came prepared." I worked the wood putty from my pocket and applied it liberally to the deep groove of the first letter, then used a small plastic putty knife to smooth it out. Once that dried, I'd sand again, repeat the process as needed, then stain. I gave the rustic floor a long exam. I might have to stain the entire surface a much darker color than I'd planned, but it beat the alternative of opening a homey cider shop with a threat carved into the floor.

My phone rang, and Dot's face graced the screen. I wedged the device between my ear and shoulder as I finished filling in the rest of the letters. "Hey, you!" I answered, thrilled by the distraction. "I thought you had to work this morning."

"I do. I stopped for coffee at the Sip N Sup on my way over to the park," she said softly.

"Why are you whispering?" I whispered back, ducking my head and raising my shoulders to my ears, as if whatever affected her might come across the line to me as well.

"Farmer Bentley just walked in," she said. "I remembered you saying you wanted to talk to him, so I thought I'd tell you he was here. Then, you won't get any ideas about going to his home where he could kill you if he's a murderer."

"Jeez. I wasn't going to go knock on his door." Farmer Bentley was at least seventy, but I wasn't dumb enough to initiate a chat with any potential killer alone.

"Well, now you don't have to," she whispered. "Get over here."

I hesitated, my gaze drifting back to the recently puttied floorboards. Did I really want to talk to a murder suspect at all?

"Are you on your way?" Dot prompted.

"I told Colton I'd let him handle the investigation from here," I said. "Someone vandalized the Mail Pouch barn and he stayed to help clean up. He was really nice and helpful, and he said he thinks Granny's innocent, but I'm in serious danger, so I promised to leave this alone."

"Colton? You mean, Sheriff Wise?"

"Yeah." I rubbed my forehead. That was going to be a long conversation once she got me alone again.

"And you told him you'd leave this alone, so you're leaving this alone?"

"Yeah," I sighed. "I think I have to."

Dot made a soft raspberry sound. "Get down here!"

"I can't!" I yelped. "I just told you —"

"Do you remember that time in sixth grade when you thought our homeroom teacher was a dancer at that gentlemen's club off Route 20?" she asked, interrupting my complaint.

"I don't see how that's relevant."

"No?" she asked, her voice hitching an octave.

I flopped back on the floor and crossed my legs. "It was an honest mistake. I saw a bunch of skimpy clothing on her passenger seat when I was crossing the lot before school."

"Uh-huh," Dot said. "And you asked her why she had them, even though it was none of your twelve-year-old business."

"Hey, we had a right to know who we were locked in a school with all day," I protested, "and those clothes were utterly inappropriate for public view."

"And you got a detention by sneaking in at recess to go through her desk in search of proof she worked at the gentleman's club," Dot continued.

"I found the truth, didn't I?"

Mrs. Crosby and half the female faculty met on Wednesday nights at the old Skate-A-Way rink for roller derby. I'd had no idea there was such a sport or that women enjoyed doing it in outfits that were highly inappropriate for school.

"Uh-huh. Give your regrets to Colton. I'll make sure Farmer Bentley doesn't leave before you get here." Dot disconnected.

I hauled myself off the floor and dusted my backside with both palms. Dot thought she knew me so well. As if a lifetime of friendship had somehow given her a key to my brain.

Ridiculous.

I shifted foot to foot, admiring my work on the barn floor and trying desperately not to wonder why Farmer Bentley had been allegedly buying properties all over town and using them for nothing. His behavior didn't make any sense, but neither did most of what had happened this week. Could he have wanted Mrs. Cooper's property too?

Had she told him no? Would he poison our trees to try to convince Granny to sell the orchard once the trees began to die?

I tapped my toe.

I paced.

The wood putty needed time to dry before I could do anymore with the floor, and I had to make a trip into town for more holiday décor anyway. If I left now, I could visit with my best friend before she went to work . . .

Sally and I made good time getting to Sip N Sup, probably because the roads were clear and I was excited to see Dot.

She waved when I walked in.

"Good morning," I said, scanning the room to see who was there.

Dot tipped her head to indicate the corner booth where Farmer Bentley sat alone. "I didn't have to do a thing to keep him there. I thought I'd have to strike up a conversation about my mama and hope he knew her, but he's on his third cup of coffee going through those files. Hasn't looked up once."

I leaned inconspicuously back for a look around her shoulder at the thin, gray-haired man in saggy Wranglers and a flannel button-down shirt. He seemed content. I definitely didn't want to bother him.

"Go ahead, ask," Dot said, smiling like a know-it-all.

"What?"

"You want to know what's in the files."

I dragged my gaze back to her. "Do you know what's in the files?"

Dot waved at Reese, and the perky blonde waitress headed our way.

Reese smiled at everyone she passed, corkscrew ponytail bobbing behind her.

"How is that she can make crossing the diner look like fun?" I asked.

"I can't be sure," Dot mused, "but I'm leaning toward youth and beauty."

"We're not old," I told her.

Dot rolled her eyes.

"Hey, y'all," Reese said, leaning her hip against the counter beside me. "What's up?"

Dot shot Farmer Bentley a look. "He's your table, right?"

"Sure. Why?"

"Can you get a look at what's in those folders he's looking at? Don't let him know you're looking. Try to peek and report back to us?"

Reese laughed, straightened her apron, and sashayed away.

I looked to Dot for interpretation. "Was that a yes?"

"Reese never says no to anything."

Reese grabbed a coffee pot and went to check on Farmer Bentley. He covered his cup with one hand. No more coffee. Reese struck a hands-on-hips pose and said something that drew the man's attention to me. As he looked my way, she repositioned herself closer to his shoulder and craned her neck for a look at his open folder.

I waved when he held my gaze, a definite question in his eyes.

Beside me, Dot lifted a coffee mug to her lips. "Do you think he knows what we're up to?"

"I don't know."

Farmer Bentley's eyes suddenly widened and he spun on Reese. Her lips moved quickly though I couldn't hear what she said as he slapped the file shut.

Dot jerked around on her seat to pretend she hadn't been watching.

Anxiety pricked and snapped at my skin.

Reese sauntered back with the coffee pot a moment later, looking gravely disappointed. "I didn't get a very good look. Official papers, maybe legal documents, and some aerial maps. He caught me peeking before I made heads or tails of it."

"Thanks for trying," Dot said. "You did great."

Reese didn't look satisfied. "It wasn't my

best work. He's quick for an old guy."

I couldn't help wondering if he was quicker than Mrs. Cooper. My tummy sank with the ugly thought.

The service bell rang and Reese smiled. "That's me," she said, lifting a hand to Freddie in recognition of the order. He nodded from the kitchen.

"Wait," I blurted before she could dart away. "Why was Farmer Bentley looking at me?"

"Oh." She wrinkled her nose. "I improvised and told him you were picking up his tab. You can add my extreme willingness to help you to the tip." She filled a mug with coffee and slid it my way. "This one's on the house."

"Gee, thanks."

Reese dropped me a wink and flitted away. I really needed to learn to walk like that.

Dot climbed off her stool. "I'll let you take it from here. I've got to get to work."

"Okay." I climbed down beside her. "I guess I'm going to see a man about a folder." I practically had to now. If I was paying for the man's meal, I should at least get to ask him a couple questions. I knew I was being nosy and I'd promised Colton I wouldn't, but I really wanted to know what Farmer Bentley was studying over there.

And why.

I crossed the diner self-consciously after watching Reese float around, then paused at the tableside. "Hi, Farmer Bentley."

He folded his arms over the closed file. "You bought my meal."

I forced a smile. "Seems so."

He worked his jaw side to side, appraising, before asking, "Why?"

"It's part of my pay it forward campaign," I improvised, unsure where the lie had come from without notice, and a little disappointed by the fact that it had.

"What's that?"

"It's when someone does one nice thing for three people, then those three people do nice things for three more people each, and kindness spreads through a community. Sometimes farther."

He pinched one of his big gray caterpillar eyebrows between his thumb and first finger, probably trying to decide if I was full of manure. A small, wry smile tugged his lips. "I could get behind something like that."

Guilt twisted in my core for lying to the old man. Now, I really needed to do three nice things to make up for it. I took a deep breath and slid onto the bench seat across from him. "Can I ask you something?"

His caterpillars crowded together. "Depends."

"When I was at the bank yesterday, I overheard someone say you were interested in Mrs. Cooper's property. Is that true?"

He turned his attention to the stack of files under his protection and began to cram the wad of unruly pages into line. Corners and headers of legal documents and letters poked free in every direction. He'd been hasty snapping the files shut in front of Reese and hadn't taken the time to straighten them up. A rush of color bled across his cheeks and over the top of his balding head.

I hoped he wasn't the one who'd been telling me to *leave it alone,* because if that was the case I'd just completely outed myself as Meddlesome Montgomery. I glanced outside, debating making a run for Sally. I didn't need to keep talking. I could pay his bill and leave. Or I could stay and ask the questions burning holes in my heart and mind.

The diner door opened before I found my tongue, and Oscar stepped inside. He held my gaze as he strode forward, choosing a booth across the way and sliding onto the bench that faced me.

Fear lifted the fine hairs along the back of

my neck and curled my toes inside my boots.

Was it a coincidence that Oscar had turned up here? Now? Or was I right to fear he'd been following me? Blossom Valley was small and the diner was popular, I reasoned, turning my gaze back to Farmer Bentley.

I dug deep for a few drops of bravery, then pressed on. I needed answers before paranoia ruined my small-town life. "I've also heard that you recently purchased some other properties around town."

His brows raised slightly but he maintained a steady frown.

"Are you planning on expanding your business?" I asked congenially.

He slid out of the booth, buttoned his jacket to his chin, then pulled the mess of files against his chest. "I think I'll pay my own bill, thank you."

"Farmer Bentley," I called after him. "Wait."

He shot me a warning look, then marched woodenly to the register.

I slumped against the padded vinyl seat back and watched as he paid, then climbed into his old tan and cream Ford pickup and trundled away.

"Well?" Reese asked, manifesting pleasantly at my side. "Was I right? Were those legal papers in his folder?"

"I don't know. He never opened them in front of me."

"Bummer," she said. "You want some more coffee?"

"No, thanks." I hadn't touched the first cup. Good thing it was on the house.

I pushed onto my feet, and left Reese an unreasonably large tip. My first of three acts of kindness. Then, I scurried out the door avoiding any more direct eye contact with Oscar in case he was a killer.

Sally's engine purred to life as I twisted her little silver key and stared, forlorn, at my reflection in the mirror attached to my visor. The meeting with Farmer Bentley hadn't gone very well, but I'd been close enough to spot a familiar logo on several of the papers trying to escape his secret files. The thick blue and gold initials, E.M., stood for Extra Mobil, a major US oil company. What I didn't know was why a small-town farmer would have so many papers with their initials. Sadly, I had an idea of who might be able to guess.

Hank.

CHAPTER THIRTEEN

Six hours later, against my better judgment, I'd swallowed my pride and offered to drive Granny to Hank's sister's birthday party at the local park pavilion and party hall. The pavilion was fine in better weather or when the sun didn't set before dinner, but it wasn't great for fall or winter events. Tonight, the building was alight with activity. Sounds of music and laughter spilled from the windows and door. The pavilion, on the other hand, was loosely occupied by displaced party-going smokers huddled around a glowing firepit.

"Ready?" Granny asked, bundling up before stepping into the cold.

Not even close.

I scanned the lot for signs of Hank's beloved sedan, but didn't see it. Maybe he'd ridden with his folks, or if I was lucky, he'd left town.

We walked arm in arm along the stone

path toward the packed party hall. I shuddered at the sight of the fire. It would take some time before the sight of open flames reminded me of s'mores and hot dogs again instead of threats and menacing murderers.

We slid into the party as a couple with a sleeping toddler hurried out.

"I hope there's tater salad," Granny said. "Someone always brings a killer tater salad to these things. I've tried recreating it at home, but I can't touch the flavor. There must be a secret ingredient."

"I'll check out the buffet when I drop the gifts off," I said. And while I was over there, I'd be sure to look for Hank's mama's dump cake. Nothing I'd ever eaten compared to that hunk of heaven. It involved crushed pineapple, canned cherries, and a vanilla cake mix that made regular appearances in my dreams.

Granny unfurled her scarf and gave the room a sour look. "It's a shame this is the best hall we have in Blossom Valley. It hasn't been updated since my prom."

I would have laughed, but it was true. The place was old, with yellowed walls and a water-stained ceiling. Gina and her family had done a good job of camouflaging the worst eyesores with signs and streamers, but no matter how they dressed it up, it was still an old stone building at the local park.

Some folks used our local church halls for parties, which were affordable but had restrictions. No alcohol, for example, even locally made wine. When the pastors had tried allowing that, a few troublemakers ruined it by bringing in moonshine. They argued the moonshine was also locally made, but the church didn't think it was the same. So, the alcohol ban was back in place. Plus, some popular music selections were frowned upon for their content and the church insisted all parties ended by 9:00 p.m. House parties were hard to end at all and always left a mess for the owners. That whittled the choices down to the park hall and Dante's Italian, the only restaurant in town with a private room. Dante's party room only held thirty people, which didn't make for much of a party.

This town needed my cider shop.

Granny handed me the presents, then went to mingle. I recognized most of the faces as I made my way through the crowd. Some of the partygoers were locals; others were members of Gina's family whom I'd met during my time spent with Hank. The gift table was piled high with cards, packages, and well-wishes. I made a little space for our gifts beside the basket meant for

cards. Granny had gotten Gina a gift certificate for the beauty parlor, and I'd found a
photo book of the nation's remaining Mail
Pouch barns. Gina was a talented photogra-
pher with a little in-home studio everyone
loved to visit, and I'd known she'd appreciate the book as soon as I saw it. Gina had
taken dozens of pictures of our barn over
the years, and I hoped she'd be willing to
sign a few of her framed shots for my cider
shop's décor.

By the time I returned to where I'd
started, a hug line had formed in front of
Granny. She smiled and laughed and
hugged each person, as if she didn't have a
care in the world. At the moment, she probably didn't. I envied her ability to compart-
mentalize like that. I hadn't been gifted with
that particular talent. My mind never
stopped working, and I carried my every
worry everywhere I went.

I smiled and stood supportively at her side
while folks shared their condolences for the
mess she'd been in all week. I cringed when
an elderly man asked her pointedly about
how she was getting by. She responded with
stories of our kittens' hijinks and how they'd
been spared from becoming orphans when
Dot had brought them to me.

She didn't mention last night's intrusion,

the threat, or fire.

She also didn't mention Mrs. Cooper's untimely demise or the sheriff's brief and misguided notion that she might have caused it.

Just hugs, humor, and hospitality as she invited everyone, personally, for a visit to the orchard. She even sold the suddenly frigid temperatures as "perfect for our new campaign, Christmas at the Orchard, and the upcoming first annual Winterfest."

The crowd listened with rapt attention and went along behaving as if everything was fine, at least where Granny was concerned. Me, on the other hand, folks eyed warily. My presence had no doubt reminded them of my ugly breakup with Hank last Thanksgiving. I shifted my gaze away from a pair of staring ladies I only vaguely recognized, and I fought the urge to go home. Talking to Hank tonight was a terrible idea, especially after I'd blown him off publicly at the diner. What was I thinking? I should've invited him over privately to apologize and ask my questions instead of showing up unexpectedly at his large family gathering.

Gina breezed into view, sliding between two older gentlemen and scanning the crowd for something. She spotted me a moment later. "Winnie! You came!" She ran to me on four-inch heels and wrapped me in her arms. "I didn't think you'd come." Gina was every bit as attractive and athletic as her brother, but with less drive to make a name for herself somewhere. Gina was happy where she was and with *who* she was. I appreciated that in a human.

"You look amazing," I told her. "Twenty-four looks good on you."

"Thanks." She blushed and the rush of color reached all the way to the tips of her ears, emphasizing delicate pearl earrings. Her platinum blonde hair had been teased within an inch of its life and piled into a bouffant Dolly Parton or Marie Antoinette would be proud of. "I keep telling my folks I'm too old for these big parties, but they won't let them go. Someday, when I meet the right guy, I'm going to deplete their party fund permanently on the best darn country wedding anyone's ever seen. That ought to put an end to the crepe paper and balloons for a while. At least until they rebuild the nest egg." She laughed.

I hoped my cider shop would be up and running before she got married. Gina would want to have the ceremony and reception in Blossom Valley, and she deserved a nice indoor option in case of weather that didn't involve water-spotted ceilings.

She stepped back and looked me over. "Do you realize we haven't run into one another since last Christmas? You look fantastic." Gina made a slow circle around me. "It looks like you've lost a few pounds, not that you've ever needed to, and your hair's longer. I like it. It's great." She came back to face me, a bright smile on her lips. "Honey, you look hot."

I snorted. "Did you say someone spiked the punch?"

Gina crossed her arms still smiling. "It's not just the physical stuff. You're happy. I can see it in the glow of your skin and twinkle of your eye." Her jaw dropped. "You're seeing someone."

"No." I shook my head, smiling back. "I'm overwhelmed, stressed out, and frequently terrified these day. Does that count?" I guessed it made sense that she would assume I looked this way while in a relationship. She'd only known me while I was dating her brother, and if she swapped *terrified* for *infuriated,* then my current emotions matched up pretty closely with where I was at the end with Hank.

Her smile drooped slightly, and she inched closer. "I heard about Mrs. Cooper. It's just awful."

I nodded.

"How's your granny doing?" Sincerity colored her words as she cast a careful look in Granny's direction. The only thing bigger than Gina's hair was her heart.

"She's resilient," I said. "Determined. She'll be okay."

"Good." She stepped back and resumed her cheerful smile. "Speaking of determined, I hear you're about fit to hang out a private eye shingle. Chasing leads. Searching for justice. You're causing quite the stir with all your sleuthing."

"It was stupid of me," I admitted, "but Sheriff Wise was looking at Granny as a possible suspect, and I wanted to protect her so I thought I could look into things too."

She pursed her shiny pink lips into a little cat-that-ate-the-canary smile.

I squirmed, unsure what the look might mean. "He's new here, and I'm not, so I figured I could help."

"And?"

I laughed. "Turns out he did *not* want my help."

Gina rolled her eyes. "City," she said with a grin. Being the opposite of country, which we all wore proudly and valued highly, *city* could either be a straight-up insult or an excuse for doing things wrong. Sometimes both. "I heard he came here from the FBI in Clarksburg."

I chuckled, imagining Colton in a black suit and shades. Maybe I was thinking of the secret service. "Actually, he worked homicide with the Clarksburg police, and he partnered with an FBI task force, but he never worked for the bureau."

"Look at you," she cooed, "knowing all about the good sheriff."

"I read up on Colton when he first looked at Granny as a suspect."

"I guess you two have gotten close. Spending time together on this investigation."

"No." I pursed my lips. "Nothing like that."

"But you call him Colton," she prodded.

I plucked the fabric of my shirt away from my chest. Too many people in one room. It was beginning to get a little warm.

"Wait a minute." Gina narrowed her eyes and took a small step closer to me. She angled her torso forward, as if we were about to share a great secret. "Is he the one you're seeing?"

Hank arrived at his sister's side, a cup of punch in each hand. "Sorry this took me so long. I got hung up with Aunt Betty at the cake." He passed her a cup, then turned to scowl at me. "I'm a little surprised to see

262

you here. I thought you were planning to steer clear of me until I went home."

Home. What did he know about home? *This* was his home. Ohio was somewhere he'd moved less than twelve months ago.

No wonder I left him.

Gina paled. "Oh, no, no." She shot him a disbelieving look. "You two are not going to fight at my birthday party. Mama will kill you."

"Who's fighting?" he said smartly. "Winnie isn't even speaking to me. She made that abundantly clear at the diner yesterday morning. In front of everyone."

The apology I'd planned was suddenly heavy as lead on my tongue and unwilling to move.

Gina fisted a handful of his fitted V-neck sweater and pushed him toward the exit. "Outside," she snarled under her breath. "Don't you dare let a single soul see you with anything other than a smile on your face tonight. You might get to go home in a few days, but I live here, and I don't want to spend another few months avoiding gossip about some big mess my brother made before he skipped town."

"That wasn't my fault," he said over his shoulder as she forced him past me. "I wanted to surprise her with a proposal and a house. *She* dumped *me.* You know that."

"Out."

Hank snaked a long arm out and grabbed my wrist, towing me in their wake. His fingers pressed against my pulse point, and I hated that my heart rate skyrocketed in response. I loathed the fact he now knew it.

Forced through the front door and into the cold, Hank and I stared at one another.

I wiggled free of his grip, then gave Gina my best forced smile. "Happy birthday."

"Thank you for coming," she said pleasantly. "Don't forget to eat something and have a slice of cake after y'all sort this out." She shot her brother a pointed look, then turned on her heels and went back inside.

Hank blew out a long shaky breath, then extended his hand toward the pavilion. "Can I interest you in a seat by the fire?"

I eyeballed the collection of smokers rocking with laughter, red plastic cups in their opposite hands, and caught the tail end of a fishing story. "Sure." I scanned the pavilion for a table upwind of the smoke and far enough away from the other occupants that we might have a little privacy in case things went poorly. "How about here?"

I took a seat on the picnic table's top and planted both feet on the seat. "I'm sorry about the way I behaved at the diner. I was rude and I shouldn't have been. It was juvenile and uncalled for. You were just being nice."

Hank took a seat beside me, leaving at least a foot of space between us. He dropped his folded hands between his knees and tilted forward at the waist, his expression caught somewhere between confusion and disbelief. "I overheard you and Gina in there. You're seeing someone."

"No," I said and laughed. "I'm actually a giant mess right now, but she thought I looked happy and assumed I was dating. I'm not."

"Are you happy?" he asked.

I thought about the week I'd had. About my life and all the moving parts. "Yeah," I sighed. "I am."

Hank pressed his lips tight. "Did I ever make you happy, Winnie?"

My heart broke a little for him. For me. For what we'd lost and would never recover. I swiveled on the cold wooden tabletop for a better look into his eyes. A familiar pang of regret twisted inside me. "Listen," I said softly. "I'm obviously still hurt about how things ended between us, which is ridiculous. I know, and I'm working on it. It wasn't fair of me to put all the blame on you."

Hank stilled. "I never meant to hurt you. I know you think I lied to you."

"Not lied." I shook my head, cutting him off, hoping to make him understand before I lost my nerve. "You didn't tell me what you were up to, and I know you said it was meant to be a surprise, but it felt like betrayal. If I had really been the right girl for you, I would've seen what you did as romantic or exciting. But I hate surprises. I like to know things. I want to be included on major decisions like leaving my hometown, and I would never move out of state with someone who wasn't my husband. Maybe not even then. I don't know, but I hated that you didn't know any of that. We'd been together for years." My throat tightened, and my eyes stung. *Why hadn't he known those things?*

I wiped my coat sleeve under my eyes. "Obviously we were in trouble long before things ended between us. People who aren't talking drift apart. I guess that was what we did. By the end, I didn't know you anymore, and you didn't know me." I cleared the lump of emotion caught in my throat. "In the name of honesty and communication, I want to tell you why I'm really here apologizing to you tonight instead of hiding out

266

at the orchard waiting for you to leave town again."

Hank watched me silently, his pale eyes searching. "Okay," he said gently. "You can tell me anything, Winnie. I should have told you everything when I had the chance." He scrubbed a heavy hand through his thick dark hair, then left it gripping the back of his neck. "Why are you really here?"

"I want to ask you about Extra Mobil."

He frowned. "I work for their competitor. You know that. Don't you?"

"It's a general question." I waited, giving him a chance to change his mind.

He didn't.

"There's a local farmer buying up properties around town but not doing anything with them. I thought it was a little strange because this man is old enough to retire, and there hasn't been any news of his farm expanding. Then, I saw him at the diner with a folder stuffed full of papers, and a lot of pages had the Extra Mobil logo on them. I wondered if you have any idea what that could mean?"

"How can I even guess? You haven't given me any information." He turned toward me, bumping his knees against mine. "What's this about?"

I considered being coy, but I didn't have

the energy. "I'm trying to find out if this farmer might've had something to do with Mrs. Cooper's murder," I said. "I promised Colt— Sheriff Wise — I'd stop asking so many questions because whoever killed her knows I'm trying to find him and he's threatened me multiple times already."

Hank's fair skin paled. "What?"

"I know I need to listen to the warnings, but I can't seem to let it go. And honestly," I ranted, "who's to say the killer will leave me alone anyway? It's not as if the threats say, *Stop what you're doing and I'll leave you alone.* Even if they did say that, why would I believe a killer?" I kneaded my frozen hands on my lap, wishing we were closer to the fire and at the same time wanting desperately to move farther away. What if someone overheard us? "I think the best thing I can do right now is just figure out who's threatening me and get them into police custody. Don't you? Then I won't have to worry anymore." I turned pleading eyes on Hank. "Right?"

Hank looked as if he'd sucked a lemon. "Who are you?"

I snorted a humorless laugh. "Winnie Mae Montgomery," I said, offering him my hand.

Hank accepted the gesture. "Well, it's nice to meet you Winnie Mae Montgomery," he said. "Let me think about this." He rubbed his palms together, then cupped them around his mouth and puffed warm breath against his skin.

I burrowed deeper into my coat. "Who would have guessed that Mrs. Cooper's sudden death would turn my life upside down?" I whispered.

"I suppose," he began, "based on what little you've told me, that this farmer could be working with the oil company toward some end goal. Maybe he's being paid to pick up the properties for some reason? Maybe the oil company wants control of the parcels but doesn't want them to be in the company's name. I can't guess why. I'd have to think a little longer on that theory. Maybe this guy knows the oil company is coming this way in search of acreage to drill on, and he's capitalizing on that by buying up land so he can lease mineral rights to them later. That could make a nice supplemental or retirement income." He frowned. "It's hard to say with so little to go on. Can you tell me who the farmer is?"

I considered that a moment, but I didn't want to put Hank in danger by sharing too much. If Farmer Bentley was the killer or involved with the murderer somehow, he'd want to get rid of everyone who knew about

269

him. On the flip side, if Farmer Bentley had nothing to do with any of the bad things happening to me, I didn't want to be the one unfairly spreading rumors and gossip about him.

"Winnie?"

"I'm thinking." If I didn't tell Hank, and he really wanted to know who was buying up the land, he might ask someone else. Then, people would know we'd been discussing this, which was bad for both of us. "It's Farmer Bentley," I said as quietly as possible, hoping the snap and crackle of the fire covered my words.

Hank nodded. "Are the properties adjoining? Do they butt up to his land or to one another? Is he possibly trying to accumulate one large portion of land?"

"I'm not sure," I admitted. "I don't even know where all the properties are, only that he's buying land and not using it. And he called the bank to ask about Mrs. Cooper's land while I was there. I overheard it myself."

"I guess it wouldn't matter if the acres are all connected if he's only planning to lease the mineral rights to Extra Mobil."

I rolled the new theories and ideas around in my crowded mind. "Buying land has to be expensive," I said. "Is there enough money in what you're talking about to justify the initial costs? How soon would he see a return on the investment?"

"I don't know how much he's paying for the properties, but given the right circumstances, mineral leasing can be lucrative."

I smiled. "Thanks, Hank."

"Don't mention it." He slid off the picnic table and offered me his hand. "I'm hungry and it's freezing out here. How about we go inside and get some tater salad and dump cake?"

I took his hand and laughed. "I love tater salad and dump cake."

"I know," he said, giving my fingers a quick squeeze. "I did pay a little attention sometimes."

I spent the rest of the evening at ease, mixing and mingling with neighbors and friends. Gina made me line dance, which I pretended to hate but didn't, and I ate my weight in dump cake while Granny showed off photos of the kittens as if they were her grandchildren.

I let the warm moments settle into my soul, and I savored the carefree night.

Tomorrow I'd have to find out where Farmer Bentley's new properties were located and if they were connected. More importantly, I needed to know if Granny's land was next on his list.

CHAPTER FOURTEEN

The kittens were sound asleep when I got out of the shower that night. I crept around, trying not to wake them. It was official — they owned me. I tiptoed to the kitchen for a hot cup of peppermint tea, then carried it softly back to my couch, where I'd booted up my laptop for a little light research. I started with a look at the county auditor site, where property owners were listed alongside details on the parcel numbers and purchase prices. Hank had asked me where Farmer Bentley's new properties were located, and the auditor seemed like the right place to find out.

I sat back several minutes later, frustrated. The database only showed one property in Farmer Bentley's name, and that was his current residence. One he'd owned for thirty-one years. I sipped my tea and considered the facts. For starters, I'd heard the woman at the bank tell Jake that Farmer

Bentley wanted to talk to him about Mrs. Cooper's property, but what if that was a coincidence? What if the man on the phone was a different Mr. Bentley? What if Farmer Bentley had made the purchases, but I couldn't find them because he'd made the purchases under another name?

I scanned the website and discovered it could take up to ninety days for new sales to be recorded and reflected online. I could make a trip to the auditor's office and ask a clerk in the morning, but that seemed like a quick way to irritate my stalker. Maybe I could just call.

I pulled my feet onto the couch and tucked them beneath me, letting the smooth peppermint tea grease the wheels in my brain. If I couldn't learn anything about Farmer Bentley's alleged new shopping habit, which I assumed had a connection to Extra Mobil, then maybe I could learn more about Extra Mobil.

I typed the company's name into my browser and started with their official website. It didn't take long for me to learn Extra Mobil had made a massive land grab in a neighboring county several years back and was already up and running to the tune of $700 million in revenues. Now, they were looking to expand. It was the sort of news reported all the time in West Virginia over the last few years. So often that I'd stopped paying attention as long as Blossom Valley wasn't involved.

I read several more articles on the nearby plant including a particularly interesting interview with Charles Crowder, the company's CEO. Crowder used the opportunity to boast about his company's positive financial impact on the county, reducing local unemployment numbers and raising the average household income. I had to admit the company's annual revenue was impressive. There were a whole lot of zeros behind that second number. Maybe Hank was right about the farmer trying to work ahead of the game and call dibs on land to be drilled on, should Extra Mobil turn their eyes on our town.

My stomach rolled. The idea of having a mega corporation like Extra Mobil set up shop in Blossom Valley with its loud, destructive, and invasive drilling equipment made me uncomfortable. We weren't that kind of community. We were a cozy, country town with a national park and river. We catered to outdoor enthusiasts and fall foliage seekers. We weren't industrial and we didn't want to be. We didn't have the space or constitution for it.

I rubbed my eyes and finished my tea before it went cold. I needed a new subject.

I brought up Nadine Cooper's Facebook page. It had been updated again. Funeral arrangements were set and the extended family had begun posting their favorite memories of Mrs. Cooper along with prayers and well-wishes for her son.

I followed the link to his page then breathed a little easier as I read. Apparently Timothy Cooper Jr. bought rundown buildings on the outskirts of Nashville then turned them into high-rent apartments and condos. I wondered again what Farmer Bentley planned to do with the properties he'd purchased and whether or not Timothy Cooper Jr. had wanted his mother's land for himself. Blossom Valley was no Nashville, but it was gorgeous and normally peaceful in the extreme, the perfect setting for one of those celebrity spas or rehabs. Though I didn't want either right next door.

My mind wandered back to Colton as I scrolled through Mrs. Cooper's Facebook photo albums. Why had he left a rapidly growing and successful career in Clarksburg to protect and serve a tiny town in the hills?

"Wow." I stopped on a string of Mrs. Cooper's photos that appeared to be from a professional photo shoot. She wore a blue one-piece bathing suit with a plunging neckline and sheer white wrap. Although modestly done, the repetitive collection seemed completely frivolous and a bit risqué for someone with a forty-year-old son. These shots and all the others sharing the album had the same three-word hashtag: #MillionDollarMama. I laughed. Granny still used a VCR and landline while her arch nemesis had multiple social media accounts and shared photo sessions with hashtags. Maybe some of the crazy rumors were true. Maybe Mrs. Cooper really did have a secret double life.

I rubbed my eyes as fatigue latched onto my bones and begged me to sleep for as long as possible. "One more search," I said through a hearty yawn. This time I searched for the hashtag Mrs. Cooper seemed to favor. What the heck was #MillionDollar Mama supposed to mean? Was it just something she'd made up to make herself feel good, or was it part of something much bigger like #RoyalWedding?

The search results came back in bulk. Mrs. Cooper wasn't alone. Million Dollar Mama was more than a hashtag on her endless photos and selfies. Million Dollar Mama was an identifier for patients of Dr. Manny Davis, a plastic surgeon in Winchester, Virginia.

Mrs. Cooper had been seeing someone in Winchester all right, and she'd been representing him for years in online ads and new client recruitment pieces. No wonder her hiker friends thought she looked half her age. She was sneaking off to get plastic surgery, then telling them the results were from communing with nature!

I tipped my head back and puffed an ugly laugh. Faker. That explained the bulging buttons I'd noticed on her blouse too. Granny's nemesis had probably had a boob job!

My phone rang, and all humor drained away as I stared at the unknown number. I imagined the killer somehow knew what I'd been doing online and had called to threaten me verbally. "Hello?" I squeaked.

"Hey." A warm and slightly familiar male voice greeted me.

"Hey." I waited, unsure, and frowned against the little screen. The voice sounded a lot like . . .

"This is Colton," he said. "Sorry to call so late."

"Colton," I parroted, wholly confused. "What's wrong? Has something happened?"

"No. Nothing like that. I just had an update to share, and I wanted to touch base with you after last night and see if you're feeling any better."

"I'm fine," I said, feeling a strange flutter of nerves. "I worked on the damaged barn floor a little. I think it's going to be okay."

"That's good news." He sounded genuinely relieved. "How'd you do it? Sanding?"

"I tried. That wasn't getting me anywhere so I used a little wood putty. Tomorrow I'll sand some more. Probably stain the whole floor."

"You might try lacquer," he suggested.

"Maybe. You said you have an update for me?"

"Yeah." He paused. "I got a call from the lab. That soil sample I took came back positive for high levels of herbicides."

I was right. "Someone really did sabotage our trees."

"Yep," he said. "I'll figure out the who and why."

"Okay," I agreed. "Any luck with the paint from Sally's bumper?"

"Still waiting on that." He was quiet another moment. "How are you doing on your promise to leave my investigation alone?"

I stared at the guilty glow of laptop light on my skin. "I'm doing great," I said, quickly closing the lid and tossing the evidence of my lie onto the cushion beside me. "Very well. Thank you." I dragged a decorative pillow over the laptop for good measure. "Why?"

I held my breath through the long pause that followed.

"I know firsthand how tough it can be to stop a curious mind," he said. "It's easy to make yourself crazy wanting answers to questions you shouldn't have, but you can't always ask them." He chuckled softly, as if the words were part of an inside joke. "You don't want to seem presumptuous. Don't want to be that overconfident, clearly misled moron."

"What?"

Colton cleared his throat. "How about this? If you get any strong urges to investigate, call me instead."

"Call you?"

"Use this number. It's my personal cell phone."

I rolled the unexpected offer around in my cluttered head. "Are you sure?"

"I'm positive. I don't want you drawing any more unwanted attention from your stalker, so let me help. If you feel like falling off the wagon, I'll be your sponsor."

I laughed. "So. I'm an addict now?"

"Aren't you?" Bass rumbled in his tone.

I shivered as my gaze traveled to the partially hidden laptop beneath my throw pillow. I needed to tell him what I'd learned about Mrs. Cooper and my suspicions about Farmer Bentley.

"Well, it's getting late and I don't want to keep you," he said. "I just thought I'd check in."

"Okay. Thank you," I added, a bit breathlessly.

"Have a nice night."

"You too." I disconnected the strange call. I'd have to tell him what I'd learned the next time we spoke. Right now, I needed to make more specialty cider for the festival.

I shuffled into the kitchen, replaying the short conversation in my mind.

The trees were sabotaged. Exactly as I'd suspected, but what did it mean?

I couldn't promise not to wonder who would do such a thing, but I could let Colton figure it out without me. I hadn't realized how thoroughly shaken this week had left me until I saw the unknown number on my phone screen. For a moment, I was certain the killer had been watching me somehow, through the windows or maybe from behind the couch. My skin crawled at the thought. As much as I wanted answers, I would definitely take Colton up on his offer. I'd call him to talk out my questions and voice my concerns. He was the perfect man for the job. He was on the same case I was, had access to much more information than me, and he had an outstanding record of bringing in the bad guys. As a surprise bonus, he was also easy to talk to and a pretty good listener.

I set a pair of clean stockpots onto the stove, then filled them with traditional cider and flipped the burners to medium. Adding generous doses of turmeric, ginger, and cinnamon would give the pretty amber liquid a delicious and healthful boost, not to mention fill my home with multiple mouthwatering aromas. I stirred the warming cider with pride and inhaled the enchanted steam as it lifted into the air.

Several minutes later, I turned the burners off and covered the pots to let the new cider flavors cool slowly. I let my mind wander over Colton's strange phone call. Maybe I'd call him back tomorrow and tell him about Mrs. Cooper's selfie addiction and her connection to the plastic surgeon in Winchester. While I had him on the line, I'd see what he knew about Farmer Bentley and the new Extra Mobil plant. Maybe Colton knew which properties Farmer Bentley had purchased. Maybe he also thought the local land purchases and oil refinery plant were connected.

I went to brush my teeth while I waited for the ciders to cool. I loaded my toothbrush with paste, feeling satisfied with myself and my plan. Then I went to work erasing the impact of too much soda and dump cake on my teeth.

A low drone outside the window caught my attention and pricked my ears as I rinsed and spat. A distant vehicle? My gut clenched. An ATV? My imagination?

I wiped the corners of my mouth, then hustled into the front room, senses on alert, listening hard for the sound to grow louder.

And it did.

The kittens stirred. They heard it too. I stroked their little heads and shushed them, praying the rider outside tonight wasn't the same man who'd flattened me on the steps outside the press house, then escaped on a four-wheeler. I held my breath as the growling engine drew nearer, becoming more distinct.

I pressed myself against the front wall and used one finger to peel back the corner of my curtain. Outside, a four-wheeler rolled to a stop and revved its engine. The rider was dressed head to toe in black, exactly like the last man who'd showed up uninvited and on a four-wheeler.

"Oh no," I whispered, thinking of my night's research and the conversations I'd had with Farmer Bentley and Hank. I hadn't listened to my stalker's warnings, and my bullheadedness had brought the killer to my doorstep.

I swiped my phone to life and pressed redial on my most recent call.

The ATV jerked forward and raced away, turning at the corner of my house and charging along the side only to sweep around the back and reappear at the front window. His headlight sliced a circle through the night, flashing outside each pane of glass as he passed.

"Winnie?" Colton asked, his voice on alert.

"There's a man outside my house on a four-wheeler," I said in lieu of hello. "He's racing around in big loud circles, and I don't know what to do."

"Lock the door," he said. "Try to keep your eye on him without alerting him to your presence, and don't hang up the phone. I'm on my way."

I shifted my gaze across the wide expanse of grass outside my window to the little white farmhouse where Granny lived. I didn't want to stay on the line. I wanted to make a run for her house, to be with her in case this thing, whatever it was, went pear shaped. But I couldn't do that. This nut was here for me, and I needed to keep her away from him.

"Winnie?" Colton said, the distinct slam of a car door carrying through the phone. "Breathe."

"Okay." I watched in horror as the rider pulled a bottle from his pocket and turned it upside down. Piloting the vehicle with one hand, he poured the contents of the container over the grass as he rode.

"Can you still see him?" Colton asked.

"Yeah." I could see him, I just didn't understand what he was doing "He's pouring something on the ground."

"What?"

My heart clenched painfully as a dozen unthinkable possibilities jockeyed for position in my head. "I don't know." And I absolutely didn't want to find out. "Hurry."

CHAPTER FIFTEEN

The four-wheeler took off, making big circles again. This time the rider extended one arm at his side, the white bottle gripped in his gloved fist. I ran from room to room, watching from the windows in fear of what might come next.

"He stopped," I said softly to Colton, voice quavering as I peered through the back door's ruffled curtain.

The rider tossed the bottle onto the ground and dug into his pocket.

I squinted and stared through the window, begging my eyes to see better in the dark. "I think that was a lighter fluid bottle!"

Sounds of a roaring engine echoed across the phone line. "I'm almost there," Colton said. "Four minutes out. I'll radio dispatch to add a fire truck."

"He's moving again!" I spun away from the door and bolted through my home, sliding haphazardly over laminate flooring on fuzzy-sock-covered feet.

A tinny voice rose in the background on Colton's side of the line. A radio? Dispatch, perhaps? A few familiar words and phrases cut through my rattled brain as I raced to keep my eyes on the man outside my home. *Trespasser, fire, Smythe Orchard.*

The rider stopped several feet from my front porch and revved his engine. Taunting. His dark silhouette was nearly invisible against the backdrop of night. Only the plume of exhaust in the chilly night air and low rumble of his engine assured me he was real.

"What's happening now?" Colton asked.

"He's just staring at the front of my house." I leaned back a few inches and heaved a shuddered breath. "I don't understand what he's doing," I said, but the minute the words escaped my mouth, I knew. He was punishing me.

The rider lifted one arm over his head. I watched with bated breath. What did it mean? Was it a signal to others waiting in the shadows? A flame sprung into existence from his fisted hand.

"Lighter!" I screamed.

The man's head jerked in the direction of my voice.

I clamped trembling fingers over my

mouth. "There was lighter fluid in the bottle, and he's going to set it on fire."

"Three minutes," Colton said, his voice icy and hard. "Cavalry's on the way."

Panic rocked painfully in my chest. Adrenaline beat in my veins. "What do I do?"

"Keep your eye on him. Don't go outside."

I nearly laughed. "There's no way I'm going outside." *Unless he lights my house on fire.* The invisible vice around my heart tightened further. "Do you think he'll do it?" I asked, my words coming in pants. Until that moment I'd naively hoped the theatrics were only meant to frighten me.

But what if he was done warning?

"Two minutes," Colton ground the words out sounding as dangerous and determined as I was fearful and weak.

A gunshot rang out, and I yelped.

"Was that a shotgun?" Colton demanded.

My heart hammered in my throat as I lifted the corner of my curtain for a better look at what was happening in the dark. The lighter's flame was out. The rider's profile was visible. His head was turned away.

"What's happening?" Colton snapped.

I couldn't speak. Couldn't move. Couldn't breathe.

"Winnie!" he yelled. "Does the rider have a gun?"

288

"No." My stinging eyes filled with tears as I followed his gaze to the small figure holding his attention across the field. "It's Granny," I whispered.

She stood defiantly before him, outside her home in nothing but her night coat despite the freezing temperatures. Her beloved shotgun, Bessy, in hand. Was she going to shoot him? I bit my lip against the urge to say the words aloud. I shouldn't have even thought them, but there she was, facing off with a man threatening to burn her land, and I wasn't convinced she wouldn't do it.

"Have her hold him there," Colton said, sounding strangely relieved. "Give me ninety seconds. I can see the orchard's lane from here."

"She can't see me," I said, reaching for the door's knob. "Should I go out and tell her?"

"No." He hesitated. "You'd better stay put. I'm almost there."

I gripped the knob, wanting to go to her, but not wanting to become a distraction to her. The standoff was bone-chilling. I reminded myself to breathe when my lungs began to burn from a lack of oxygen.

The man flicked his lighter back to life in one hand, gunning his engine with the other.

Granny shot a second round into the air.

"Now what happened?" Colton barked.

A set of fast-approaching headlights bounced in the distance, making their way up the lane in our direction. He was almost here.

Granny turned toward the headlights.

The rider dropped the lighter and grabbed his handlebars, launching the four-wheeler in Granny's direction.

"No!" I tore open the front door and flew outside as a patch of flames erupted in the grass.

Granny's scream barely registered before it was silenced by the impact that threw her small frame onto the ground.

"Granny!" I leaped from my porch, catching air and landing hard before scrambling upright once more. I darted through the small patch of flames, already fizzling in the frosted grass.

The ATV spun hard, kicking a line of loose earth and stones behind it as it changed trajectory, rocketing away from Granny and the large truck tearing up our driveway.

I slid onto my knees at her side, arms extended, prepared to help her up and check her wounds. To tell her it was going to be all right. Colton was here and an ambulance was on its way.

Her eyes were closed.

"Granny?" I stroked hair off her pale face and patted her cheeks, but she didn't move. "Granny!" I pressed my head to her chest, hugging her where she lay. Her heart beat faintly beneath my ear. Her chest rose and fell in small shallow puffs. Bessy lay at her side a few feet away.

I did this to her. The truth was a punch to my gut. I'd brought her attacker here with my incessant questions and determination to learn his identity. She hadn't done anything wrong.

Colton's truck thundered to my side and rocked to a hard stop. "Winnie!" He jumped from the cab, feet in motion as they hit the ground.

I sat up, peeling myself away from Granny.

Relief washed over his features as he took me in. Then he caught sight of Granny. "Tell me what happened." He knelt beside me, immediately examining Granny with steady, practiced hands.

A blast of light washed over us as a bleating fire truck and wailing ambulance bounded up the gravel lane in our direction, illuminating the night.

I turned my eyes to track the four-wheeler humming invisibly in the distance, too far gone to catch now. Little more than a small white dot of a headlight against the horizon.

"I think she hit her head when she fell," Colton said. "There's a good-sized flat stone in the grass back here and some blood behind her ear. "Are you hurt?"

"No." Anger laced the word. I wasn't hurt, but I should be. Me. Not her. I dragged my tear-blurred gaze back to Colton as he stripped out of his jacket and placed it over Granny's torso. "Why didn't you chase the ATV?" I demanded. Why was he here and not out there making an arrest? Making that guy pay? "We could have had him. Now he's gone."

Colton leveled me with a fathomless stare. The muscle along his jaw clenched and released.

"Why?" I croaked, shooting a pointed look at the dark, silent mountain where the psycho had escaped.

I spun back on Colton when he didn't answer, feeling the fires of guilt and revenge burn hot in my belly. "Why did you stop?" I repeated. "Didn't you see him?"

Colton shook his head once in the negative, arresting blue eyes fixed on mine. "All I saw was you."

Emergency vehicles filled the space around us. A pair of deputies included.

Colton stood to wave them in our direction.

I pushed onto shaky legs beside him, wiping frantically at falling tears.

He took notice. "It's not your fault," he said quietly before the uniformed men and women arrived. "None of this. You got that?" He was wrong, but I didn't have it in me to argue.

"Why'd she come out here?" I whined, wrapping trembling arms around my middle to keep from falling apart. "Why didn't she stay in the house? What was she thinking?"

Colton lifted a palm to slow the approaching responders, then curled me against him with the opposite arm. The act unleashed the worst ugly cry I'd had in years, but he spoke confidently to the newcomers over my sobs, filling them in on what had happened, directing them on what to do and where to go. I hid my face until the crowd had fully dispersed.

Colton stepped back, his shirt soaked, when I finished. "She called dispatch before she went outside," he whispered. "They knew what was going on when I called it in. First responders and my deputies were already en route when she came outside to protect you."

I processed the possibilities of that. "You

got here first."

Colton gave one sharp dip of his chin.

"Sheriff?" A pair of EMTs arrived beside us with Granny on a gurney.

"How is she?" I asked.

"We're going to take her in," the older paramedic said. "She's going to be all right. There's an ugly goose egg at the back of her head that's going to need stitches, and she's got plenty of mild lacerations and contusions, but nothing broken. We'll take good care of her."

I looked at each of their faces, searching for the thing they weren't saying. "Why won't she wake up?"

Their gazes swept to Colton.

The older paramedic kept his face neutral when he swung his attention back to me, but I could see it wasn't easy for him. "We'll run some tests at the hospital. We'll know more soon."

They didn't know what was wrong with her. Which meant they'd lied to me. How could they be sure Granny would be okay if they didn't even know why she wouldn't open her eyes?

I followed them to the ambulance in a dreamlike state because this couldn't be my reality. I was numb, and I couldn't take my eyes off Granny's slack face or motionless body. My ears began to ring, and my vision blurred around the edges as the EMT pressed an IV needle into her arm.

"Does she have any allergies to medications that you're aware of?" a low warbling voice asked.

"No."

"Would you like to ride with her?"

I nodded, unable to find my tongue again.

Colton put a hand on my shoulder. I didn't have to look to know it was him. "I'll go with her," he said, then more quietly, he added. "You don't have to go alone." He helped me into the ambulance bay when I didn't respond, and I took a seat on the bench beside the gurney.

Colton sat stoically at my side. Somewhere in my addled mind I realized that between teasing me and accusing me of crimes, Colton Wise had become my friend.

I clutched Granny's hands in mine as the doors thumped shut. "Find the person who did this," I whispered.

"That's a promise."

When Dot brought me home from the hospital the next morning, an inch of snow had already blanketed the ground. She'd stayed up with me through the night, drinking gallons of terrible cafeteria coffee and begging for Granny to wake up.

She didn't.

I hugged Dot goodbye and dragged myself inside to feed the kittens.

Funny how everything looked the same, but I felt completely different. There were no signs of the fear I'd felt just hours before, no indication a lunatic had terrorized me, threatened the orchard with fire, or put Granny in the hospital. My stomach tightened with the awful visceral memories, but my living room was bright with sunshine. Two orange kittens snoozed peacefully on the couch. The paradox of my internal and external realities was unsettling. It reminded me of the days following Grampy's funeral when the world just snapped back into motion as if our lives hadn't been tossed completely upside down.

Granny will be okay, I reminded myself. The scans didn't show any irreparable damage. She just had to open her eyes, which the doctors were confident she would do when she was ready. So, why wasn't she ready? Didn't she know I was scared and alone out here? Didn't she know how worried I was that the doctors were wrong, and I'd lose her too?

I cringed at the selfishness and anger in my thoughts. Granny had taught me to be a silver-lining seeker, and I needed to apply that lesson now more than ever. I also needed sleep. I needed to clear my head and start again when I was up to it.

I curled onto the couch with the kittens, scooting them close to my chest where I could feel their purrs reverberating in my heart. What had happened to my small ordinary life? I didn't want to run from monsters or solve crimes or live in fear. I wanted everything to go back to the way it had been a week ago when Mrs. Cooper was alive, fighting over nonsense with Granny, and I was happily planning my cider shop.

Had it really only been a week?

I closed my eyes and nuzzled against the kittens' fur, then sent up a fervent prayer for Granny. Whatever else happened, I needed her to come home.

I woke seven hours later feeling stiff but rested.

The kittens were asleep on the windowsill, their water was overturned, and their dry food was gone. They'd clearly had a party and I'd slept right through it. I stretched my aching muscles and headed for the shower.

Late-afternoon sunlight streamed over me as I made an appointment with Mrs. Cooper's plastic surgeon in Virginia and polished off the end of a turkey and swiss sandwich while leaning over my kitchen sink. I swept crumbs down the drain to avoid dirtying a dish. Whatever defeat I'd felt as I'd fallen asleep had worn off with rest or been washed away in the shower. My mind and muscles were alert, ready, and filled with resolve.

I called off work when the sandwich was gone, then I checked with the nurse working the phones on Granny's floor to see about an update. There weren't any changes in her condition, so I didn't need to hurry back to visit. I had time to make a quick trip across the river.

I grabbed my coat and keys, then brought up the business address for Dr. Manny Davis on my phone. I was eternally thankful for the last-minute cancellation that had made my appointment possible. I wouldn't be able to concentrate on anything until I knew who hurt my granny, and to do that, I needed to know who killed Mrs. Cooper. Maybe her plastic surgeon in Winchester could shed some light on the subject, especially since she might have recently dumped him.

I bypassed Sally and grabbed the key to the little red SVO this time. With luck, I'd fly under the radar of anyone looking for me in my usual white Mustang. Just to be safe, I donned large black sunglasses and pulled my coat's hood over my knit cap before turning out of Granny's driveway, then I hunkered down inside my coat and tried to be less noticeable.

I crossed the river without a tail and enjoyed the beautiful drive to Winchester. It was too cold to put the windows down, but the Mustang floated around the gently winding strip of highway forged between two ancient mountains. I didn't need the brake until I hit the Winchester exit. After that, I barely needed the gas.

I'd never been to Winchester before, but I was surprised to find it was a lot like Blossom Valley. Small, country, filled with pickup trucks and folks who looked like my neighbors passing outside the windows. The posted speed limit waffled between twenty-five and thirty-five, so I was passed by folks on bicycles, tractors, and foot while I waited at every light through town. Usually twice.

Eventually, I took the last open spot in a small lot when my GPS insisted I'd arrived. The building was much newer than the others around it and the style too modern to fit in. A mini-billboard at the edge of the crowded lot had the hashtag #MillionDollar

Mama printed beneath a larger-than-life photo of five women with slinky sequined dresses and perfect figures.

I climbed out feeling more than a little self-conscious about my figure, and absolutely certain I had the right place. Most of the women in the ad were twice my age and looked vastly better than me. I brushed nervous fingers through my bangs, fanning the long, side-swept strands over a few budding age lines. Then, I fixed my posture and hurried inside.

The smattering of patients in the lobby looked up as I entered. I hustled to the desk and scribbled my name on the line as illegibly as possible in case anyone tried to confirm I'd been there. Still putting my nose where it didn't belong.

The room was spa-grade fancy with slightly dimmed lights and a bubbling water feature. The color palette was endless shades of beige on beige, from seating and carpet, to walls and artwork. The whole thing felt oddly unsettling. I concentrated on the classical music drifting softly from hidden speakers and helped myself to a cup of tea from a stand in the corner. A little beige sign encouraged guests to "Enjoy a cuppa."

"Miss Jones?" the receptionist called. "Miss Jones?"

No one moved.

I gave the room a long look before I realized she was talking to me. "Oh! Here!" I abandoned the tea and rushed in her direction, eager to get out of the waiting room and into a private space where I was less likely to be recognized by anyone who might want to hurt me.

The nurse gave me a wavering smile. "I just have a few papers for you to fill out while you wait."

I took the clipboard and grinned.

"Right this way." She led me down a long beige hallway to a small exam room with startlingly white walls and multiple photos of people before and after various surgeries. Smaller noses, fewer wrinkles, bigger breasts, tighter thighs. "Consultations are painless. You can even take off your hat and sunglasses if you'd like."

I pried my gaze off the results photo of a very successful tummy tuck. "Thank you." *But no thanks.*

Alone, I wondered if Dr. Davis would ever use his trained surgeon's hands for harm. I'd come in search of information on Mrs. Cooper, her life, known enemies, and general state of mind before her death, but what if I'd been so worried about being seen by the killer while I was leaving town that I'd unintentionally come to visit him?

I shivered as I filled out the pile of forms on the clipboard, then froze at the sound of a familiar voice outside the exam room door. "Thank you for agreeing to reschedule on such short notice, Doctor."

"Of course," a second man said. "It's no problem at all, Sheriff Wise. Nadine Cooper was important to me."

I abandoned the paperwork I'd been falsifying and went to peek into the hallway. How was it possible that Colton was *here*? *Now?* The door moaned as I turned the handle and pulled it open an inch.

Colton stood outside my room, sheriff's hat in hand, beside a man in a lab coat who couldn't have been ten years my senior. That was Dr. Davis? Somehow I'd expected a baby boomer on a misogynistic power trip, not a sweet-faced thirty-something in a Mr. Rogers cardigan and Harry Potter glasses. Maybe he'd gotten a little work done himself.

Colton twisted at his waist, scanning the narrow hallway. His gaze hung on my slightly opened door for a long beat. "Is there somewhere we can talk privately?" he asked.

"Certainly." Dr. Davis walked through the open door across from mine and into a small beige office.

Colton followed, dragging the door closed behind him until it touched the jamb without latching.

I crept across the hall to listen. If I could get the answers I needed to satiate my curiosity without ever coming face-to-face with the potentially deadly doctor, all the better.

"Of course not," Dr. Davis answered. His voice rose sharply in response to a question I hadn't heard.

"You're sure?" Colton asked.

I set my hands on the wall and leaned in close, hovering my ear outside the nearly closed door.

"I would never have a relationship, like the one you're describing, with any of my patients."

I blushed on his behalf. At least he was polite enough not to mention the fact Mrs. Cooper was old enough to be his mother.

Sheriff Wise went through the usual questions from there. I'd heard them asked a thousand times on my favorite television shows. *Did Mrs. Cooper have any enemies? Did the doctor have any idea who might've wanted to hurt her? Did she seem upset or distressed the last time they spoke?*

I stiffened in anticipation of that response.

Oscar, the trail master, had overheard Mrs. Cooper breaking up with someone on the phone the last time he'd seen her, and I believed that man was Dr. Davis. Furthermore, Oscar said Mrs. Cooper told the man on the phone she was seeing someone else. *Another plastic surgeon!* Considering she'd been one of Dr. Davis's spokesmodels for the last few years, there had to be a good reason she'd left, and he had to hate it. Maybe Dr. Davis did have reason to lash out at her.

"Not at all," he answered smoothly. "Mrs. Cooper seemed fine the last time we spoke."

"Pfft." The dismissive sound was out of my mouth before I'd thought better of it.

Colton shifted in his chair, eyes fixed on the door.

I sprang upright.

"Miss Jones?" the nurse's voice sprouted in the silence behind me. "Can I help you with something?"

Torn between the urge to provide a plausible excuse for my blatant eavesdropping and an absolute unwillingness to speak at all, I covered my mouth and ran.

"What's going on out here?" the doctor asked as I rounded the corner at the end of the hall and darted through the monochromatic waiting room.

"I found your next appointment, Miss Jones, listening at the door," the nurse tattled.

"Miss Jones?" Colton's voice echoed.

I bolted into the parking lot, doubly thankful I'd had the forethought to drive a different Mustang for this adventure. *He didn't see me,* I thought to myself, gunning the engine to life. *No one knows it was me. I'm fine. It's fine.* I hooted in relief as I pulled the shifter into reverse and slid out of the parking space, keeping one eye on the office door behind me.

Miraculously, no one followed.

I eased into traffic feeling slick as a whistle and supremely victorious.

Two traffic lights later, the flashers of Colton's patrol car lit up my rearview mirror.

CHAPTER SIXTEEN

I pulled into the next parking lot and got out my license and registration. I highly doubted Colton was pulling me over for a traffic violation, and I was positive his authority ended at the river, but what else could I do?

He rolled his cruiser into the empty spot beside me and took his time getting out. Eventually, he knocked on my window.

I forced myself to roll it down.

"Fancy seeing you here," he said with a tight smile.

"I guess it truly is a small world." I handed him my papers. "Hope you don't mind me asking, but what seems to be the problem, Sheriff?"

He kept his hands at his sides, knees slightly bent for a look in my open window. "I'm not trying to give you a ticket," he said. "I was just trying to get your attention before you hurried off again."

I lowered my dark shades to the end of my nose. "Well, I'd say you've succeeded. Seems like a phone call would've worked too."

"Where's the fun in that?"

I dropped my sunglasses into my purse, then pulled the hood on my coat down, slightly irritated because he still hadn't come out and told me what he wanted. I could only assume he intended to scold me for meddling again. I caught his amused gaze as I peeled off my knitted hat and fluffed my fully mashed hair.

The wind changed and the mouthwatering, buttery scents of melted cheese and fresh-baked breads wafted over my face. My stomach rumbled in response.

Colton braced his hands on his hips, drawing my attention back to the sheriff's uniform, coat, and badge. "You tore out of Dr. Davis's office mighty fast. Why was that?"

Answering felt like a trap, so I kept my mouth shut.

"I don't know if you're in the market for advice," he said lightly, "but I feel your disguise was lacking, and the alias probably wasn't your best work either, Miss Jones."

I tapped my thumbs against the steering wheel, unwilling to bite.

"Were you thinking of having some work

done and change your mind?"

I grimaced. What was that supposed to mean? "You think I need some work done?"

"No judgment," he said, "everyone has something about themselves they wish they could improve."

"And what would you like to improve?" I asked, daring him to point out a flaw.

He squinted down at me against the biting wind and afternoon sun. "My ability to keep you out of this murder investigation could use some work," he said.

"Funny," I said flatly.

Colton shifted his weight, losing his good humor. "Not really. It's becoming nearly impossible to keep tabs on you, let alone keep you safe and catch a killer at the same time."

"Maybe you should just follow me around," I suggested. "Whoever is behind all this seems to be back there already. The two of you would be bound to run into one another."

Emotion flashed over his features, there and gone before I could label it, and his serious sheriff stare was fixed back in place.

I glanced away, unsure what to make of the fleeting expression I'd seen. "Did you pull me over to yell at me?" I asked. "I know I broke our deal, and I deserve it."

Colton rocked back on his heels, relaxing his stance. "Nah," he said smoothly, yanking my shocked gaze back to his face. "I pulled you over to see if you'd want to split some fries and maybe grab a milkshake with me."

My eyes flicked to the delicious-smelling burger joint in front of us, and my traitorous stomach agreed before my mouth could.

Colton grinned. "We can talk about what you were doing at Dr. Davis's office while we eat."

"Great." I climbed out and accepted his offered arm, then let him lead me inside an adorable fifties-themed soda shop.

The intoxicating scents were doubly potent inside the building, and a walk past the ice cream display case to the hostess stand added fresh-baked waffle cones and homemade fudge to the air.

A woman in a retro uniform and white apron greeted us. "Two?"

"Yes, ma'am," Colton answered kindly, removing his big sheriff's hat and clutching it to his chest.

"I'm Ginny," she said. "It'll be my pleasure to take care of you today, Deputy."

"Sheriff," Colton corrected, with an easy smile.

"Sheriff," she agreed. Her attention drifted

briefly to me. "You picked a great spot for a date."

I fidgeted under her, albeit quick, appraisal. She was blonde and beautiful, at least five years younger than me, and clearly interested in Colton. It didn't take her long to return her attention to him, apparently satisfied that I wasn't much to worry about. I couldn't blame her. Unlike Ginny, with her adorable outfit and face, I was bundled in a puffy winter coat and plagued by sweaty hat hair. I probably even had little red marks on both sides of my nose from wearing sunglasses all day.

"It's not a date," I said.

Colton's gaze jumped to mine.

"Is that right?" Ginny's smile grew.

"Yep," I assured. "We're just a couple of friends who ran into one another by utter coincidence and decided to get some food."

Ginny smoothed her palms down the sides of her uniform, obviously pleased. "I see."

I shut my eyes so they wouldn't be seen rolling, then smiled at Colton. He frowned.

"Right this way," Ginny said, swinging her hips across the high-polished black-and-white checkered floor to an empty red vinyl booth near the windows. She set the placemats, menus, and cutlery on a silver-flecked tabletop, then lanced Colton with a come-hither smile. "I'll be right back with your water."

"Jeez," I complained when she left.

"What?" he asked, still frowning. "You don't want water?"

I dragged a disbelieving gaze from Colton to Ginny's retreating form then back. "Are you kidding?"

"What?" he asked again, sounding slightly irritated now.

"Ginny was hitting on you," I said. "Right in front of me."

His features relaxed a bit. He cocked his head and let one side of his mouth tilt in a lazy half smile. "You said this wasn't a date. We're just friends who happened to run into one another."

I bit my tongue. Continuing that line of discussion could paint me as jealous or imply I wanted this to be a date. Which I wasn't and didn't.

Colton's cocky smile returned.

"I don't care that she was flirting," I said. "I was just making conversation. Clearly we should change the subject."

Colton leaned forward, resting both forearms on the table between us. "Okay. Let's talk about what you're doing in Winchester. You told me you were finished getting involved in this, and I believed you. I'm not usually wrong about people, so that irks me."

I matched his posture and body language, setting my joined hands on the table across from his. "I meant it when I said it, but now Granny's hurt, and someone needs to catch the man who did it before she winds up like Mrs. Cooper."

Colton's brows went up. "That's quite a jump. The man's focus had been on you until she came out shooting. You care to elaborate on why you think he'd target her now? Unconscious and hospitalized?"

"It could be about her land —" I said, cutting myself off when the waitress reappeared.

Ginny delivered two glasses of water then poised a pen over her little green-striped notepad. "Y'all ready to order?"

We hadn't even looked at the menus, but Colton ordered a burger, fries, and chocolate malt.

"Just fries and a malt," I said quickly, unwilling to ask her to come back again.

"Okay." Ginny jotted the orders onto her notepad, then winked at Colton and left.

"Surely you see she's flirting," I said.

"She's being nice. She's a waitress."

I rolled my eyes but regretted it immediately.

"Let's circle back to the land theory. Why don't you finish telling me what you were doing at Dr. Davis's office?"

I assumed this conversation would be like most unpleasant things, and the best way through it would be headfirst. "I found Mrs. Cooper's connection to Dr. Davis online when I noticed all the hashtags she put on her photos. Then, I remembered her hiking group's trail master saying he'd heard her break up with one man for another, and I realized those men might've been doctors, not boyfriends. So, I drove out here to ask him about Mrs. Cooper and the Million Dollar Mama hashtag. Once I was here, I wondered how mad he might've been about one of his success stories leaving him."

Colton's frown was back. "You thought he might be the killer."

"Maybe."

"Maybe?" Colton asked. "See, that bothers me. You put on a hat and some sunglasses then marched right into a potential murderer's office. A man you thought might be stalking you and who'd hurt your grandmother. Do you see the problem there?"

I narrowed my eyes on him. "It's not like he was my prime suspect. I'm just working through some theories."

"You have others?" he asked, pleasantly,

though his expression wasn't pleasant at all. "Do tell."

I filled him in on what I'd learned about the gas company and the rumors about Farmer Bentley's multiple recent property purchases. Then, it was my turn to ask the questions. "Do you know which pieces of land he bought?" I asked. "Because if Farmer Bentley killed Mrs. Cooper because she wouldn't sell, he could be coming for Granny next."

"That's why you think the killer would go after your grandmother? For her land?"

"Granny's property borders Mrs. Cooper's land. I don't know which properties Farmer Bentley has already purchased, but if they're all connected over one big area, it would make sense that Granny's would be next. Think about it. Someone poisoned the trees, and I think someone's trying to keep me from getting my cider shop open. Each time the banker comes out, there's a travesty to deal with. Makes me look like a bad investment."

Colton sat back. "Any other suspects?"

"Sure. I've considered the fact Oscar might be lying about the content of his argument with Mrs. Cooper, or that her son, a Nashville land developer, might've wanted her property for some nefarious

314

reason, or that someone at Extra Mobil is behind her death. I suppose it could even be somebody I haven't considered yet, but right now I'm leaning toward Farmer Bentley as my main person of interest."

"How did you know Timothy Cooper was in town?" Colton asked. "Have you spoken with him?"

"No." My jaw dropped and my heart rate spiked. "He's in town? How long has he been here?" According to the Facebook updates, he'd planned to fly her home for a funeral in Nashville.

"He says he drove all night after I called."

I raised my brows, sensing a *but*.

"But I'd only left a message for him on an answering machine. I asked him to return the call, but instead, he'd shown up at the station the next morning. Said he'd assumed the worst when he couldn't reach his mama." Skepticism was thick in Colton's tone and heavy on his brow.

"You don't believe him."

He rolled his shoulders back and swept his gaze around the room before returning his attention to me. "I might've panicked if I'd come home to a vague message like I'd left him, too, but you can bet I would've been calling as I drove. The police. My mama's neighbors. Hell, he could've dialed the diner and gotten the whole scoop, but he didn't make one call."

"You think he could've been here when you left that message." *That he could've killed his mother.* "I don't suppose he drives a big, dark-colored pickup truck?"

Colton gave a stiff dip of his chin. "He does, but they're not so uncommon. Oscar drives one, too, and so does that ex of yours."

I pressed a palm against my suddenly queasy stomach. He was right. I'd seen Oscar with his truck before and after the hike. "Oscar was outside Doc Austin's office a few minutes before I found the threatening note on my windshield," I said breathlessly, "and I saw him at Sip N Sup while I was there talking with Farmer Bentley. I'd blown it off as coincidence, but what if it was something more?"

A vein at Colton's temple throbbed, and he pressed a fingertip against it. "But you came here to see Dr. Davis."

I hiked my shoulders to my ears. "I don't know what I'm doing. I'm just gathering information and hoping that eventually the truth will come out."

Colton's eyes narrowed to slits.

"You asked," I reminded him. Something else came to mind. "Hank drives a BMW sedan, by the way. Not a pickup."

"You sure about that?" Colton asked.

I made a crazy face. "I've known him all my life and we dated for nearly five years, so yeah. Hank always picks a flashy car. Usually a BMW, though I suppose he might've changed to an Audi or Lexus."

"Wrong," Colton said. "He's driving a midnight blue Chevy. I ran into him at his interview with Extra Mobil earlier this week."

I opened my mouth, but nothing came out.

Ginny wiggled back into view, delivered our meals, and proved to be an extremely attentive waitress. I concentrated on my malt and fries while Colton settled down. When it was time for our checks, she left them on the table. Mine arrived face up, the total circled with a smile face. Colton's bill was folded neatly down the middle into a little tent. "I never charge a lawman for his supper," she said before sauntering away.

I made a goofy face. "So why leave the bill?" I muttered in her absence.

"She didn't." He dug into his wallet without opening the tent.

I put my napkin on the table with an intentional flourish, and the breeze flipped Colton's paper tent onto its side. My mouth fell open. "It's just her phone number."

"It happens," he said, tucking the paper into his wallet and leaving more than enough money on the table to cover both meals and a fat tip. "It's on me. I invited you, so it's my treat."

I didn't argue. I sipped the remains of my melting malt and tried not to think too much about how often women bought Colton's meals or left him their phone numbers. *It happens.* What did that mean? Where did it happen? Who were these women exactly? Were they from Blossom Valley? Were they friends of mine? I released the straw and stared at the handsome man across from me. Why had he never crossed my path or mind until tragedy struck?

"Why are you looking at me like that?" he asked. "I only take the numbers because I think it would be rude to leave them behind, if that's what you're wondering. I don't want to ruin her day by making her feel rejected."

I sighed. "That's actually kind of sweet," I admitted. Assuming it was true, and he really didn't plan to call her later. "I was wondering why we never met before all this started."

He eased back in his seat, stretching long legs beneath the table and cocking his head over one shoulder. "We met," he said. "You just don't remember me."

"What? When?" That couldn't be true." I would have remembered him. *Wouldn't I?*

Colton's phone buzzed and he frowned at the screen.

I craned my neck for a look at the screen. *Clarksburg PD.*

He rejected the call, stood, and zipped his coat. There was fresh strain in his eyes as he waited for me to join him.

I couldn't help wondering if this call was related to the one he'd received the other night in my barn, and why the sight of the numbers seemed to hurt him.

"I used to see you around plenty," he said, falling back into our conversation. "We met a couple times in passing."

I wasn't sure how that was possible. "When?"

"Last year, I guess. Summer and fall, then you kind of vanished."

"Oh." I fixed my eyes on the door. I'd become a temporary hermit after my breakup with Hank, but I didn't want to talk about that.

Colton tipped his hat at Ginny on our way out. "Have a good day."

He stopped on the sidewalk in front of our cars in the lot. "You want to lead the way back home, or should I?"

"I'll go first," I said, sliding easily behind the wheel of my red Mustang and feeling the tension I hadn't realized was gathered between my shoulders release.

He went to his cruiser and dropped inside.

I took a minute to send him a text before pulling out. I'd forgotten my manners inside.

Thanks for dinner

His response arrived before I'd gotten the shifter into reverse.

Next time, we'll eat local.

I smiled at the little screen, then into my rearview before pulling into traffic with him on my tail.

The sun was low in the sky before we crossed the river back to West Virginia. I eased my foot off the gas as we wound along the darkened country roads outside Blossom Valley. Deer were often thick along the roadsides at dusk in December. I didn't want to think of the damage a collision would cause to one of those sweet creatures. Or my Mustang. The sheriff let his cruiser fall back a few yards, probably thinking the same thing.

A moment later, the emergency lights flashed to life on top of his car.

I frowned at the sight of them in my

rearview mirror. The cruiser's siren barked to life, and I coasted onto the shoulder.

Colton's engine roared as he zoomed past me. I stared, baffled by his disappearing tail-lights. A moment later, a bevy of siren sounds rang through the night. *Oh no.*

I pressed hard on the Mustang's gas pedal and jumped back onto the road, racing toward whatever horrible thing had happened this time. I tried to keep my imagination in check, but an onslaught of awful possibilities was already circling in my mind. Had the man on the four-wheeler come back to burn down the orchard? Had he lashed out at someone else I loved? Hurt the kittens? Harmed Dot? I pressed the pedal with purpose and rocketed back through town. I caught up to the line of emergency vehicles and stuck close, drafting easily along in their wakes.

Soon the convoy slowed in the road's center, and I debated what to do.

Cars and trucks lined the shoulders. Their passengers spilled onto the lawns and fields around them, gathering to watch as first responders piled out of the emergency vehicles. I pulled off the road, sliding into line behind a rusty red pickup and searching the scene for an indication of what had happened. I could only assume there had been a traffic accident, and I prayed deeply that it had nothing to do with a killer's revenge on me.

I left the Mustang and followed the by-standers' gazes on foot, past the ambulance and fire truck I'd followed to the scene. Down the center of the darkened road. Through a sea of floodlights.

Fear and anxiety mixed with the worry I'd find Dot on the other side of this mess, and my feet kicked into a jog. Colton stood outside his cruiser, parked at an angle across the yellow lines. His head was bowed before a familiar tan and cream pickup truck that had been overturned beside a broken tree.

Farmer Bentley lay motionless in the grass several yards away.

CHAPTER SEVENTEEN

My head swam, and the earth tilted.

"Ma'am." A man in full firefighter gear stepped into view, blocking the ghastly crash from my sight.

I forced my eyes to meet his gaze while my mind struggled to process the nightmarish scene behind him. "There's only one vehicle," I rasped, my throat too thick to sound sensitive or human. Had something happened to Farmer Bentley as he drove? A stroke? Heart failure? Had he swerved to miss a deer? *Was he run off the road?*

"I'm going to need you to stand with the crowd," the fireman explained.

I nodded but couldn't find my legs to move me.

He frowned, concern altering the expression on his serious face. "Are you okay? You look like you need to sit down."

I worked to swallow the growing lump of emotion in my throat as a cacophony of sounds roared around us. The drone of voices. Onlookers speaking to one another and into cell phones. First responders passing orders and information among themselves and through walkie-talkies. The hum of the fire truck's ever running engine. The rattle and slam of vehicle doors.

My stomach heaved and jolted. My ears rang. "Is he dead?" I asked, locating my voice before my limbs. It was abrupt and insensitive, but I had to know.

The fireman offered a remorseful smile and opened his arms, corralling me away. "I need you to step back. Off the road. Take a seat and breathe."

I stumbled away, following his orders, onto the sidelines. Colton was gone. His cruiser hadn't moved, but he was invisible to me among the floodlights, flashing lights, and crowd.

I watched with bated breath as paramedics loaded Farmer Bentley onto a gurney. It was last night all over again. It was Granny in the grass, unmoving. My eyes, nose, and throat stung with panic as I waited to see what would happen next. Would they cover him with a sheet? Had he died on impact? Were the paramedics too late?

An EMT strapped an oxygen mask over his face and hoisted an IV bag into the air.

She grabbed the gurney with her free hand, and a man in a matching uniform clutched the opposite side. Together they raced Farmer Bentley to the ambulance.

He was alive.

I rolled tear-blurred eyes skyward and thanked the stars for this miracle.

"Winnie?" The sound of Colton's now familiar voice turned me around. He strode toward me from the busy street, cutting through the clutch of uniforms as a tow truck arrived for Farmer Bentley's pickup. "Are you okay?"

I nodded. My mouth was parched and my thoughts were fuzzy, but I was okay. I wet my lips and tested my voice. "He lived."

"Yeah." Colton set a tentative hand on my arm. "Maybe you should sit for a minute. You're flushed and you don't look too steady. I got worried when one of the firemen said a little brunette nearly collapsed out there. I had a feeling he was talking about you."

"There are a lot of brunettes," I said, feeling slightly better than I had a few moments before.

"How many would walk into the middle of an accident scene when every other civilian is clearly standing aside?"

"I thought it might be Dot."

Colton pursed his lips and sighed. "Come on."

I followed his lead to a massive boulder at the end of a nearby driveway and let him help me onto it. The homeowner had stenciled their last name and street number across the center. My feet dangled over the paint. Seated on the stone, I was eye level with Colton.

He angled himself to block my view of the wreckage. "How are you doing?"

"Better than Farmer Bentley," I said softly. "There's only one vehicle. What does that mean?"

Colton lowered his gaze to his boot for a long silent beat before answering. "We've got a witness who claims a big black truck ran Mr. Bentley off the road."

I covered my mouth to stave off the slap of nausea reverberating through me. "A truck like the one that ran me off the road?"

Like the one Mrs. Cooper's son drove, I thought. *And Hank.*

My stomach clenched with the residual pangs of betrayal left over from our breakup. Hank had kept secrets from me then and he was still doing it now. We'd spent hours together at his sister's birthday party, but he'd never mentioned losing his job in Ohio or applying for one closer to Blossom Valley. When I'd mentioned Extra Mobil, he'd said that was his competitor. Why was he always lying to me? And where did it stop? Suddenly his suggestions about why Farmer Bentley might've bought those properties felt as contrived as our entire relationship had been. Bile clawed up my throat, and my stinging eyes lifted to the ambulance visible beyond Colton's left shoulder. I'd told Hank it was Farmer Bentley buying up the land.

Colton's jaw locked and popped as his eyes searched mine. "I'll call the lab in the morning and try to rush a match on the paint from your bumper."

"I'm sorry," I whispered. "I told you Farmer Bentley was my number one suspect, and I was wrong. I shouldn't have said that about him." Emotion choked me to silence. It was silly and irrational, but I wondered if the accident was somehow my fault. Maybe the killer had seen me speaking privately with Farmer Bentley at the Sip N Sup. Maybe he'd overheard me asking about him. Maybe I'd painted a target on him and now he was clinging to his life. Unbidden tears slid over my cheeks, and Colton opened his arms to me.

I slid off the rock and wrapped my arms around him.

Colton's posture was stiff. His hands were fists against my back. Nothing like the embrace he'd offered as I'd cried for Granny. "This is not your fault," he said.

I shuddered at the ice in his voice and pulled away. "You're upset with me."

He shook his head. "I'm upset because that could have been you."

By six o'clock, I was at the hospital and desperate for good news. The minute I was steady enough to drive, I'd headed straight for Granny. Even if she wasn't awake yet, I needed to see her. I wanted to hold her hand and kiss her cheeks.

Visiting hours were in full swing when I arrived, and the elevator was packed as I squeezed on board. The car stopped at every floor, dropping off and picking up passengers in a painfully slow ascent. Thankfully, Granny's room was on the fourth floor and not the twelfth or I wouldn't have made it to her before midnight.

"Excuse me," I said as the number four illuminated. "This is me."

I edged my way free of the tiny crowded vessel, then hurried in the direction of Granny's ward. Scents of bleach and bandages peppered the air. The halls teemed with folks carrying balloons and flowers in every direction. Some giddy and chipper, others solemn and grave. I wished I would have brought something for Granny. I hadn't even thought to buy her flowers before I left this morning. My heart sank at the image of her alone in the silent stark white room.

I picked up the pace, doubly eager to see her and tell her about my strange emotional day. I hated what had happened to Farmer Bentley, but I couldn't help thinking that the accident removed him as a suspect for Mrs. Cooper's killer and my current stalker. That was a relief. I didn't know him well, but Farmer Bentley was a staple in the community. He was loved, and it was nice to know he wasn't a secret psychopath in farmer's clothing.

The door to Granny's room was closed when I arrived, and for one brief moment I worried about what I might find inside. Then, I heard the unexpected hum of laughter. I reached for the knob, but the door opened before I could turn it.

"See y'all tomorrow," a woman I recognized from Granny's quilting club stepped out. The man behind her had a palm on her back. "Oh!" she started before pulling me into a hug. "Winona Mae," she cooed. "Don't you worry, sweetie. Your granny is a tough old nut, and she'll be just fine. You'll see." She released me and gave my cheek a pat. "You've got plenty on your plate now, so don't stay here too long. You go home and rest. The ladies and I will be around at dawn to fix breakfast and help out at the orchard." With that, she headed toward the elevator. The man nodded at me as he passed, hurrying along behind her.

"Thank you," I said a moment too late.

I stepped across the threshold of Granny's room and paused as another rush of emotion blew through me. Granny was unconscious, but she wasn't alone, and the room wasn't stark white or silent as I'd expected. The space was packed full of colors and people. Friends gathered in the corners and along the walls, talking and laughing. Some traded stories about my grandparents or the orchard. Others shared snacks from a makeshift buffet. Pizzas, fried chicken, and potatoes had been delivered from Granny's favorite joint and set up on the empty bed across from Granny. Helium balloons skated over the ceiling, caught in a current of heat from the overhead vents. Dozens of brightly colored messages like GET WELL SOON! and FEEL BETTER FAST! were taped to the wall above her bed and signed by dozens of well-wishers. The nightstand and windowsill were heavy with flowers. My heart was heavy with thanks.

I swallowed the lump in my throat as pride and appreciation for my community stung my eyes.

"Winnie!" Dot called and the crowd turned, open-armed, toward me.

I was passed around the room, swaddled in an overindulgence of hugs and vows to assist me at the orchard any way I needed in Granny's absence. Everyone volunteered to man a game, station, or booth at the winter festival, which they insisted simply had to go on. For Granny.

Dot handed me a plastic cup of soda, then tapped hers to mine. "I came right over after work. Figured you'd already be here. Everyone else started showing up after that."

I gave her another hug, then filled her in on the accident that had kept me from arriving sooner.

"Goodness." She pressed a palm to her heart. "That's awful about Farmer Bentley. That could've been you."

I rubbed my suddenly tired eyes and sipped the soda. "That's what Colton said." And it wasn't any less nauseating to hear the second time.

Dot lifted a brow.

"I ran into him in Winchester." I rested a

hip against the foot of the spare bed and unloaded everything that had been weighing on my heart and mind for a week. I retold the story of my trip to see Dr. Davis, the motivation behind it, my lunch with Colton, Ginny the flirty waitress, and the fact Mrs. Cooper's son was in town and no one knew exactly when he'd arrived. Then, for no logical reason, I told her about Colton's hugs.

She mouthed the words, "Shut. Up."

"It wasn't a big deal," I backpedaled. "I was pretty shaken both times, and I'm sure he was just being kind."

"He bought you lunch," she countered. "He didn't have to do that."

"He was being friendly." *Besides,* I thought wryly, *his lunch had been free, thanks to Ginny who "never charges a man in uniform."*

"You know he isn't friendly, right?" Dot asked. "Polite, yes. Friendly, no. Rumor has it he keeps his distance for work purposes. I guess you never know when you might have to arrest your friends if you're the sheriff. Better not to get too close."

"He has friends. Everyone has friends."

"Yeah, hunting friends. Fishing buddies. A tailgating crew. But those are all the same handful of guys. All men he grew up with, served in the military with, or met some-where else. He doesn't keep a local circle. Some folks think he got burned back in Clarksburg, and he's being more careful this time. I think it's probably tough being the new guy in a small town and the sheriff on top of that."

I thought of the call he'd rejected from Clarksburg PD today. Had that been one of his friends who'd hurt him? And what about the detective who'd called the other night?

I watched Dot watching me. "Did you vote for him?" I asked. I hadn't, but then again, I'd barely looked at the competition. I'd liked Sheriff Hatcher just fine, and he'd been in the position all my life. It seemed almost rude that anyone had run against him.

"Sure," Dot said. "I voted for Wise."

"Why?"

"Sheriff Hatcher wanted to retire, and my mama said Colton Wise was a good man. Seemed like the right thing to do."

"I didn't know Sheriff Hatcher wanted to retire. Why did he run again?"

Dot shrugged. "I think it's hard for some folks to let go. They think retiring means admitting their purpose is gone. They get their identity so wrapped up in the job title that they don't know who they are without

333

it. Like when moms have a breakdown because the last kid leaves home."

"You're very wise, Dorothy Summers," I said, admiring the way she so easily saw past people's actions to their intentions.

"Sheriffing was Sheriff Hatcher's purpose for more than thirty years. It's no wonder he had a hard time letting that go."

"Sheriffing?" I teased.

"It means 'to sheriff.' "

I laughed.

"You want some pizza?" she offered. "Or are you still full from lunch with the mysterious and hunky Sheriff Wise?"

I lifted my plastic cup. "This Coke is plenty, thank you." Together, Dot and I welcomed incoming guests, promised nurses we'd keep it down, and hugged folks good-bye as they left.

Eventually, it was time to go home.

I dug in my pocket for my keys, a fresh question on my tongue. I considered saving it for later, but I was beginning to realize some things about myself. For one, I wasn't as long on patience as I'd always imagined myself, and for another, my curiosity rivaled the proverbial cat. "Dot?"

"Yeah," she asked as she quietly packed up the leftover food.

"Colton said he knew who I was before

Mrs. Cooper died. He says we met, informally and more than once last year, but I have no memory of it. Do you think that's strange?" I carried a stack of empty cups to the tiny, overstuffed trashcan and piled them carefully on top.

Dot gave a sad smile. "Which part? It's a small town, and you work at a popular diner. You go to school at the local college. You're out and about a lot, especially last year when you had Hank, who was a needy handful. He's probably the reason Sheriff Wise never registered on your radar. You missed a lot back then, but you were in love and that's to be expected."

"It shouldn't be that way. Having a significant other should make us better versions of ourselves, not worse."

Dot didn't argue.

"I didn't call you enough," I said, remembering how much of my time Hank had consumed. When I wasn't at work, in school, or studying, I was with him, and he liked to do things alone. Just the two of us. No couples' dates or group events. Just lots of appearances at local parties and hoopla, and even more quiet nights at home. Sometimes I was even with him while I studied. "I was a bad friend."

"You were busy," she allowed, generously.

"It's fine. It happens. Sometimes with guys like Hank, you don't realize you've fallen into a black hole until you climb back out. For the record, I'm glad you're out."

"I learned something about Hank tonight," I said, the words coming slowly to my tongue. "He drives a truck now and it matches the description of the truck that chased me and caused Farmer Bentley's accident." I suddenly understood why I hadn't seen his BMW in the diner parking lot or outside his sister's party.

Dot stilled. Her bright eyes filled with some mix of emotions I couldn't quite name. "Are you sure?"

I blew out a little breath to steady my nerves. "I know that's not exactly a smoking gun in a town like ours, or anywhere maybe, but it's weird, right? And he had an interview with Extra Mobil."

Dot paled. She turned to take a seat on the bed.

Tension weighted the air around us, and I lowered myself into the empty chair at Granny's bedside. "I told Hank about Farmer Bentley buying up all the land, and now Farmer Bentley might die. What if that's not a coincidence?"

My phone buzzed in my pocket, and I jumped. The world seemed to spin back into motion as I looked at the screen. "It's the bank!"

I swiped the screen to take the call. "Hello?"

"Miss Montgomery?" Mr. Sherman asked. "Is this a bad time?"

"No, Mr. Sherman." I said, smiling like a lunatic at Dot and pointing wildly at the phone. "I was just visiting my granny. Is everything okay?"

"Yes. Very well, thank you. I'm calling about your loan application."

I listened carefully as papers shuffled across the line.

"I'm trying to close as many files as possible before the holiday break, and yours seems to be in limbo. I have everything I need except record of a completed interview."

"Would you like to reschedule your tour of the Mail Pouch barn?" I asked, obnoxiously overeager. "I'd love to tell you more about my plans. I hear the third time is a charm," I said.

Dot's eyebrows had vanished beneath her bangs.

"I don't think so. It's been a long day for me," Mr. Sherman answered, "but like I say, I'd really like to complete this file and make a decision so we can move on. Maybe you'd like to stop into the bank tomorrow."

"Or," I said, "you could stop by Winterfest on your way home tomorrow night. You might be surprised by what you find." I crossed my fingers, hoping all those volunteers made good on their offers. "Festival begins at five sharp," I said, forcing a big smile into my voice.

He sighed. "Oh, all right. I'll run home to change and have dinner first, then come out to see what all the hoopla is about. How's seven?"

"Tomorrow at seven," I repeated. "I won't keep you long, and you won't regret it."

"See you then, Miss Montgomery."

I disconnected the call, then grabbed Dot's hands. "I need the names and numbers of everyone who said they'd help out at Winterfest tomorrow. Mr. Sherman is coming!"

CHAPTER EIGHTEEN

A bundle of Granny's friends arrived with the sun and began setting up the various booths and activities. They came with open hearts, willing hands, and a ton of donations from extra food and holiday decorations to things I hadn't known I needed until I saw them. Birdie Wilks had even borrowed her husband's coffee truck and decked it out in holiday lights for the occasion. Volunteers were scheduled to come in waves all day to execute the plans I'd made several nights ago and photocopied today for quick reference. More folks were signed up to man the games and stations throughout the night once the gates opened. Winterfest was shaping up to be ten times the event I'd imagined Granny and I handling together, and I wished more than anything that she could be there to see it.

I spent the first portion of my day in town picking up supplies. The lists I'd made under extreme sleep deprivation were surprisingly handy since I couldn't hold a thought in my head beyond the mental countdown to Winterfest. More specifically, the countdown to my meeting with Mr. Sherman, aka the man holding a golden ticket to my dreams.

I handed out fliers and candy canes on the street as I shuffled through the newly fallen snow, packing purchases into Sally's back seat and trunk. An unexpected overnight snowfall had blanketed the town in sled tracks, snowmen, and enthusiasm. It was the perfect day for Winterfest. "Hope to see you tonight!" I called to everyone willing to take my brightly colored promotions. If even a third of the folks who'd received a flier or saw the ad in the paper came out for the event, Winterfest would be a rousing success.

I slid behind the wheel after my last stop and cranked Sally's heater. I pointed the vents toward my face and kneaded my frozen hands in front of them. My leather driving gloves were stylish and kept me from touching the icy wheel directly, but they were useless for warmth. After a morning of walking around Blossom Valley, carrying packages, and delivering the goods to Sally, my fingertips were numb.

My phone buzzed with an incoming text from Dot, and I had to peel my gloves off to check the message. She and some fellow park rangers had arranged to come by at lunchtime and transform ten dozen Granny Smith apples into caramel-covered delights. All I had to do was pick up the bags of caramel and various toppings.

I sent a quick reply.

Done!

The toppings were already in my trunk with the other supplies.

I scrolled through my missed messages while I waited for Sally's engine to warm up, then played the voicemails. My phone hadn't stopped ringing with offered donations of time and supplies since I'd announced I needed help. As it turned out, my community didn't only want to attend Winterfest, they wanted to be a part of it too. By the end of my final voice message, I had a dozen more volunteers for everything from ticket taking to late night cleanup. I returned every call and accepted every offer with gratitude. Normally, my pride would have interfered. I would have insisted everyone just have a good time, make memories, and let me handle the labor, but I couldn't afford to be prideful tonight. Not when the success of the festival could change my life.

I needed Mr. Sherman to see that Smythe Orchard mattered to Blossom Valley, and Granny's business was something folks could get behind.

Dot sent another text.

See you in 20!

I double-checked the time and felt my first real strike of panic. Time had gotten away from me.

On my way!

I tucked my phone into my purse and eased onto the freshly salted road, then headed home with care because not everyone else did. A flurry of mental to-do lists flipped and scrolled in my mind. Sally was stuffed to the gills with supplies, holiday décor, and goodies. I just hoped I'd have time to complete all my personal tasks before the festival began because my first priority tonight was to blow Mr. Sherman's mind.

I'd spent the night locked inside the Mail Pouch barn preparing. I'd cleaned, decorated, and spruced everything I could. Then I'd rearranged what was left of the crates, pallets, and giant wooden spools, careful to hide the threat in the floorboards. Tonight, my future cider shop would be off-limits to festivalgoers. I couldn't risk anyone making a mess, intentional or otherwise, before my private meeting. To be sure the barn stayed in the condition I wanted, I'd roped off a perimeter for the festival, limiting festivities to the large flat acre of land between the parking lot and first rows of trees. Designating and controlling the space would make it easier to find the games and food stations, mingle with friends, and keep track of children, not to mention improve the speed and ease of cleanup.

My big fancy plans at the barn were exclusively for the banker's benefit.

According to the list I'd written nights ago, I needed the basics for a festive table setting so I could give Mr. Sherman the full cider shop experience, *if* he ever came back. Now that he was definitely returning I'd gotten overexcited and significantly carried away.

I'd started my morning in search of a nice table cover and place setting at the general store and wound up at the hardware store pursuing an open box sale on light fixtures. I fell in love with several coordinating pieces and on my way to the register, I bought a mass of assorted shiplap for forty percent off. It wasn't like me to shop at all, but happening upon the sales felt serendipitous, and who was I to argue with fate?

Sally and I crawled up the gravel lane

nearly an hour later, careful not to bottom out or lose her load. My heart sped as I took in the massive visual changes to our property. I'd only been gone four hours, but it was an utter transformation. The crew of enthusiastic volunteers had added blue lights to the white perimeter fence and giant red bows to the posts, then saturated every horizontal object in sight with garland and twinkle lights. Helpers waved from all over the property, welcoming me home.

I felt my chest tighten with gratitude. Enormous sparkling ornaments hung on the snow-dusted limbs of our most visible trees. More lights wrapped their trunks and illuminated key paths from station to station throughout the designated festival zone. A small sled ramp had been arranged near the fruit stand, populated with a hodgepodge of borrowed sleds and mounds of snow likely removed from the fully cleared parking area. I kept driving until I made it to the Mail Pouch barn to unload my impromptu purchases.

I'd fully intended to meet Dot in twenty minutes after our texts, but I saw an estate sale on the way and had to stop. The darling table and chairs set supporting the sale sign near the road was perfect for my night's agenda, and I knew it would be gone if I waited. When I stopped to make an offer, the seller gave me an unbelievable deal, a second set to go with the first, and even offered to deliver them both. By the time I left with all my newfound treasures, Sally was bursting at the seams. I'd had to bust out the bungee cords to keep her trunk from spilling my things all over the road.

I moved at double speed, getting the barn doors so I could apologize to Dot before she killed me. She'd only had an hour for lunch, and it had been that long since I'd said I was on my way.

"What's all this?" Dot's voice cracked on the crisp winter air.

I spun around, busted, and guilt wrinkled my nose. "I'm so sorry. I never shop, and I couldn't stop. I got carried away. Are you mad? Please don't be mad."

She shook her head. "I went through Granny's pantry and found everything we needed to finish seven dozen apples. The other rangers went back to work about ten minutes ago. They're covering me the rest of the day so I can stay and help."

My shoulders sank. "I'm sorry I missed them. What an awful impression."

"Don't worry about it," she said. "At least you made time to buy all this old dusty junk, am I right?" She eyeballed my overflowing car suspiciously. "You've got a real *The Beverly Hillbillies* situation going on here."

She was right. All I needed was a rocker and a granny on Sally's roof and the vision would be complete.

"Help me carry it all inside?" I asked.

Together, we moved boxes of milk glass teacups, saucers, and bowls. Bags of hand-made aprons, table runners, and placemats. Vintage serving trays, pitchers, horseshoes, and more. I'd even found a box of framed photos from Blossom Valley older than the barn. The estate sale had been a very successful stop for me. In the end, I had a hand-selected hodgepodge of pieces that coordinated just enough to be quirky and endearing. Kind of like me.

The tables were delivered before we finished unloading Sally. I thanked the man enthusiastically and invited him to return for the festival. Warm cider on the house.

I wouldn't have been happy with new overpriced items from a major manufacturer or department store. That had been my original plan, but it was one of many in my life that I was thankful, in hindsight, hadn't worked out. My newfound décor was unique to my shop, filled with history and charm, like the barn and the orchard. That the items had once belonged to a family from our community made them all the more special. I just wished I knew where I was going to put them.

Dot arranged the final box under one of my new tables and looked to me for instructions. "Is that everything that goes in here?"

"Yeah. I'll come back and decorate after we take the rest of the supplies over to the house."

"Let's do it." Dot smacked her gloved hands together and headed for Sally's passenger side.

A few minutes later, we'd finished hauling the remaining bags and boxes into Granny's kitchen, and Dot was back to work rolling apples in caramel and cookie bits. I headed to my place to get the kittens and change.

Kenny and Dolly met me at the door, mewling as if they hadn't seen me in a week instead of earlier that morning. "Hello, pumpkins," I cooed, scooping them into my arms. "What's the matter, huh? Did you miss me?"

I refilled their food and water bowls, then set them on the floor while I went to change.

I couldn't wait to see Granny at the hospital tonight and tell her about the overwhelming response to our festival. Thankfully her floor didn't have official visiting hours, and I knew the nurse on shift tonight, because I had a feeling it would be late by the time I got there. She still hadn't opened her eyes, but maybe details from Smythe Orchard's debut Winterfest and my, hopefully successful, meeting with Mr. Sherman would be the motivation she needed to wake up.

I slid into my softest jeans, warmer socks and boots, then layered a flannel button-up and hooded sweatshirt over my T-shirt. I pulled my coat on over that. It would be cold inside the barn until I got my blood pumping. I made a mental note to get some space heaters out there before Mr. Sherman arrived.

I shooed Kenny and Dolly out the door and locked up behind us. Silly as it was, the idea of visiting the barn with Mr. Sherman after dark again had plagued me with chills all day, and having the kittens with me lightened the frightening thoughts.

The sky was a bright brilliant blue as we made the trip across the orchard. Kenny and Dolly dove and rolled over one another on the snowy dirt path before me. I did my best not to step on them or slip on icy stones beneath the snow. People called out to us in greeting as we passed. I waved enthusiastically back, yelling, "Thank you so much!" and "Merry Christmas!" a dozen times before reaching my destination. I hadn't seen so many people on the farm since before Grampy died, and my heart was warm with the possibilities of a comeback.

Inside, I set my phone to play my favorite Christmas tunes and hummed along as I surveyed the work ahead. It came down to two distinct jobs. First, I needed to find somewhere to store all the things I couldn't use tonight, like the flooring and light fixtures I'd picked up at the hardware store, then I could decorate with all the beautiful pieces I'd collected from the estate sale. The second job would be fun and easy. The first would require some serious creative thinking because we were fresh out of storage on the orchard. Twenty-five acres and every nook, cubby, and outbuilding was already bursting with forty plus years of accumulated treasures. Granny's home was so full that the attic and basement had run out of space long ago, and newer items were being stored in her former sewing room and my old bedroom. My little house had the same problem on a smaller scale. I'd only lived there three years, but the few semi-adequate closets were already crammed full of very important things.

I pulled the string on the light bulb dangling at the room's center, then let the doors fall shut behind me. No need to let half the town see me struggling to hide a bunch of purchases I had no room for. Folks might start thinking I had a problem.

Since I had no idea where to put the boxes, I pushed them into a corner and got busy arranging the new dinette sets instead. I dropped gorgeous evergreen and scarlet cloths over each table to give the sets an inviting and festive feel. Then, I filled an antique porcelain pitcher with red poinsettias as a centerpiece for the first table and arranged a wreath of pine green with a flameless candle at the center of the second. Golden place mats with mismatched bone china place settings and modern silverware finished out the look. Next, I posed one half sheet of cardstock on each tabletop. The pages had a holly leaf border and scarlet curlicue lettering that listed a few potential Christmas menu selections.

Menu
Tomato and onion tartlet
Diced brie and apple ribbon sandwich
Orange cranberry biscuits with assorted
Smythe Orchard preserves
Frosted cranberries

Gingerbread cake with fresh whipped
nutmeg cream

Seasonal Ciders
Mulled Christmas cider
Honeyed vanilla cider
Cinnamon stick cider
Apple, cranberry, and ginger punch

I'd mocked up a number of possible menus weeks ago while daydreaming about the future, and I'd been thrilled to come across them again last night.

I lined the makeshift service counter with clear glass bowls and jars, then filled them with piles of holiday candies. Gumdrops and peppermints, candy canes, and butter mints. I ripped open a four-pack of vanilla and apple pie scented room diffusers and tucked them out of sight for good measure. The space was delightful to behold, but there was no reason it had to smell like dust and wood.

I turned in a slow circle to evaluate and prioritize the remaining work. The kittens tumbled past in a blur of orange fur and low adorable growls. I suspected they believed themselves to be dangerous jungle cats instead of what they were. Fluffy ginger cuddle bugs.

"Now, where to stow the boxes?" I asked

them, but they weren't any help.

There weren't any hiding places in the barn. No closets or storage rooms. Not even a horse stall to block the boxes from view. I tried to think of something brilliant and innovative before Mr. Sherman arrived and decided I was either a hoarder or a shopaholic. Neither would make a great impression.

I spotted a row of plywood boards overhead. Grampy had suspended them between the rafters years ago for storage. He'd wanted Granny to keep her bins of seasonal décor up there during the off seasons, but she'd said it was too inconvenient. I hadn't disagreed. We rarely came to this barn for anything back then. Eventually, he'd switched gears and suggested the space be used for long-term storage, like the things in their attic, but Granny panicked. The attic things were important, irreplaceable keepsakes. What if the barn collapsed, was vandalized, or washed away in a flood? Where would her memories be then? Granny liked her things where she could get to them anytime and without a ladder. I shared the sentiment about the ladder, and I preferred both feet on the ground whenever possible. Today, however, it looked like

I'd have to put on my big girl pants and climb.

I dragged a ladder from the supply barn halfway across the property and positioned it under the suspended platforms. Once I'd recovered physically from hauling the ladder, I said a prayer I wouldn't fall off and break anything, like my head. I took my time moving all the storage I'd piled against the wall and restacking it around the base of the ladder, avoiding the actual climbing portion as long as possible. Finally, I chose a box and headed up.

I wrestled the first box to the top on sheer determination. It was heavy, large, and hard to maneuver with my short, weakling arms, but I couldn't leave storage on the floor looking like clutter. My muscles screamed in protest of the weight with every step, and the ladder rocked slightly as I moved rung to rung. My tummy twisted and ached as I imagined my imminent fall. Eventually, I got the box in place with only a handful of painful scrapes and bruises to show for it. I found a few boxes of Granny's knickknacks, figurines, and collectibles already seated at the back of the board. Grampy must've ferried some of Granny's attic storage away when she wasn't looking. I smiled as I picked through the memories she'd kept, feeling inexplicably close to her despite our current geographical distance. Then, I pushed myself back to work and repeated the moving process until my muscles felt like wet noodles and I took a seat three rungs up to rest. The next box, only halfway to its destination, balanced precariously in my grip.

Above me, the plywood sagged alarmingly toward the floor.

"Uh-oh," I said, eyes trained upward. The tilt of my head caused a moment of vertigo and my fingers slipped.

The box crashed to the floor, and I screamed as its contents spilled everywhere. It wasn't a word I said often, and I was thankful not to have had an audience.

"Winnie!" The barn doors sprang open and a blast of icy wind shot through me, blowing my long-discarded coat across the floor. Colton stood, frozen in a shaft of mid-day sun. His chest rose and fell in sharp sprinter's breaths. His gaze darted over me, then the scene before him. "You're okay?"

"I dropped a box," I said lamely, turning on the ladder to make my way down. "I hate heights, and I don't normally talk like a trucker."

Colton pressed the doors shut behind him and grinned. "You screamed, 'horse spit.'

Why were you on a ladder?"

I hadn't actually screamed horse *spit,* but I wasn't going to correct him. Instead, I explained my dire storage and time limit situation, and he stripped off his sheriff's jacket and hat to help. "I'll climb," he said. "You pass the boxes."

I gathered the spilled items and checked for damage before arranging them back inside the box. "I appreciate the muscle, but I didn't expect you until the sun set."

"Just checking in," he said. "It's been a crazy day at work, but this place looks fantastic."

"Thanks," I wiped my forearm over my brow. "I'm glad you're here," I said, passing him the refilled box.

"It's no trouble. Besides, I wouldn't want you cussing again." He winked. "The property looks amazing out there."

"It wasn't me. I've barely done anything except shop." Though, I did generously tip the man delivering my tables, and I considered it my second act of kindness. I couldn't imagine what it would be like to sell my family's things, and I knew the memories they carried were priceless. Worth far more than any of the little price stickers on the boxes. So I'd promised to give the things a place where they could live on together.

Colton hefted the box overhead with ease and arranged it neatly with the others as if it had been filled with pillows instead of metal serving trays, horseshoes, and historic West Virginia license plates. "Not according to everyone I spoke to on my way over here. To hear them tell it, you planned all of this on your own while helping at the orchard and working at the diner. Not to mention the risky and unnecessary amateur sleuthing." He shot me a pointed look for emphasis on the last part. "Those folks are proud of you. They said all they had to do was follow the plans you'd already set. I think most of those folks would support you and your granny on just about anything. In fact," he continued, "several of them wanted to know when I was going to catch the man who's been harassing you. Turns out they all know what's been going on, and they don't like it. Apparently when a criminal is at large and putting a beloved member of the community in danger, it tends to make someone very specific look shamefully bad at his job."

"The sheriff?" I guessed with a grin.

He opened his palms for the next box. "Keep them coming."

I complied. "Have you gotten any new leads?"

"What'd you hear?"

"I was just asking, but do you?"

"Maybe. I'll let you know when I know."

I let it go at that. There was plenty of other things to keep me busy today.

A few boxes later, we were done.

I stared up at the dipping support boards. "Does that look safe to you?" I asked.

"Nope."

Dolly rushed my leg and leaped against my calf, clinging by her tiny talons.

"Ah!" I hopped back, falling over my feet and trying not to step on her as she leaped off. "Jeez!"

Colton chuckled. "Looks like you've got an attack kitty there."

"Yeah." I rubbed a heavy palm over the site of my injury. "I just wish she'd stop attacking *me.*"

Colton turned and climbed into the rafters.

"What are you doing?"

He fed a two-by-four down to me. "There's quite a bit of lumber and building supplies up here. We can probably use this as a support beam for the storage platform."

"Good idea." I hadn't thought of using the extra lumber for anything at all. I wasn't even sure why Grampy had bought it, but I'd have to keep those supplies in mind when it came time for renovations. Using them first could save me a lot of money down the road.

Colton returned to the floor and positioned the beam beneath the storage. With a little elbow grease, he managed to wedge one end against the sagging plywood and the other against the floorboards to stop the scary droop. "That ought to do it."

I smiled. "My hero."

"I'd better get back to work and leave you to it," he said, scooping his coat off the floor and threading his arms through the sleeves. "Need anything else, give me a call."

My ridiculous mind slid to the mistletoe I'd hung above the door as decoration, and I forced my gaze not to follow. "Thanks again for letting me borrow a little of that brawn," I said. Then, casting a look at the impromptu support beam beside me. "And brains," I added.

He pulled his gaze off the mistletoe he'd stopped beneath and nodded. "I'll see you later."

I flopped onto a chair when the doors shut behind him and considered taking the mistletoe down to avoid any future embarrassments.

Ultimately, I decided against it. In the name of Christmas.

CHAPTER NINETEEN

I didn't love the look of a random piece of lumber in the center of my holiday scene, but I wasn't willing to bring the boxes down and try to re-hide them either. So, I decided to hide the pole instead, or at least disguise it.

The familiar zing of creativity began to stir, and I was back on my feet with a shot of adrenaline. I wrapped the makeshift support post in twinkle lights and pine green, then arranged fresh pine cones and branches on the interior and exterior windowsills. I fetched a mess of icicle lights and draped them from the exposed rafters and repurposed a pair of potted poinsettias from the fruit stand to either side of the doorway. The finalized look was a Christmas miracle after all I'd been through in a week.

I locked up at the barn at three and went to help wherever I could until it was time to cross my fingers for the big show.

My tummy growled around four thirty as I emerged fresh and clean from my second shower of the day, sporting a serious blow-out and peppermint lip gloss. I scooted over to Granny's house for a bite to eat, desperate to feel near her even if I couldn't be with her just yet. The orchard was eerily silent as I crossed the field between houses. The lights and decorations felt ominous against the backdrop of a fast-setting sun. Shades of crimson bled over the snow and crept around the Mail Pouch barn in the distance. I hurried my pace, shaken by the tangible feeling of foreboding as I took Granny's steps two at a time.

Everyone had gone home to change and make dinner around four, and now, all there was to do was wait. Thirty minutes until the gates opened. Thirty minutes until I knew if my hope had been misplaced. Then two long hours until the meeting with Mr. Sherman that could change my life forever.

I let myself inside and took a minute to breathe. The house smelled like Granny; apples, cinnamon, and black coffee. The scents clung to the curtains and upholstery, burrowed deep in the carpets and walls. I flipped the lights on and swallowed the pain of knowing she wasn't there because she was hurt. Probably because of me.

My appetite waned with the thought. Still, I hadn't eaten since breakfast, and I didn't want to collapse from nerves and hunger when Mr. Sherman finally arrived. I poured a tall glass of apple cranberry cider and fixed a toasted cheese sandwich. I heated a cup of tomato soup for dunking and felt my nerves settle with my first bite.

Fifteen minutes until I opened the gates.

I munched and thought about the events of the past week, desperate not to wonder what would happen if no one came tonight and Mr. Sherman saw the decked-out orchard without a single soul but me. I thought about who I was now and who I'd been before I found Mrs. Cooper in the cider press. The week had changed me, I realized, or maybe just helped me get to know myself a little better. Yes, I was a hard worker. A waitress, a dreamer, a student. An unwavering friend, granddaughter, and member of my community. But beneath all the characteristics I worked on, I'd discovered some things that came naturally, like my curiosity and thirst for knowledge. My fierce loyalty and near-debilitating empathy. Mostly, I felt the need for answers deep in my bones, and I hadn't known that before. I'd also realized that dreaming of the cider shop wasn't enough anymore. I'd been making excuses about getting started on it for far too long, and it had taken a crisis for me to make it happen. I'd probably dragged out college graduation, at least partially, for the same reason. Not to avoid student loan debt, though that was certainly a benefit, but to avoid having to move forward when I finished because *what if I failed?*

Maybe fear of failure even had a hand in my breakup with Hank. What if I'd taken a leap, married a man and moved to Ohio, only to wind up divorced like my mother? It was a silly, childish fear, but it was real nonetheless. *And,* I thought remorsefully, *what if Hank was never who he'd seemed.*

I checked the time and pulled in a steadying breath.

Photos of my life were everywhere inside Granny's kitchen, on the walls and shelves, stuck to the refrigerator with magnets and taped to the window above the sink. A chronicle of my life. After all my grandparents had done for me, it was my turn to do something for them. I would make tonight a success if I had to go door to door hauling people to the party. I'd turn the financial situation around here if it killed me, and I *would* save their orchard.

I stuffed the last bite of sandwich between my lips and headed for the door.

It was time to open the gates.

My phone rang on the way across the field, and Dot's photo appeared on the screen. I smiled at the sight of her. "Hello?" I answered.

"I'm on my way over, but I just finished having coffee in town," she said, foregoing a greeting. "Guess who I was with." Her words poured into one another, a contagious blend of enthusiasm.

"Jake?" I guessed. I couldn't imagine who else would get her so worked up. She saw her friends and family almost every day. I glanced over my shoulder as I moved toward the fruit stand and orchard gates. The air was different than when I'd gone inside. Charged somehow. I concentrated on Dot's enthusiasm instead of the silence. "Does this mean you finally got brave enough to answer his call?"

"No." She laughed. "I ran into him in town, and he asked me out in person. It would've been rude to say no, so I agreed and he bought me a latte at that new place by the bank!"

I smiled. "I'd ask you how it went, but clearly it was awful."

"He's just as sweet and kind as I remembered. Smart too. Loves his family. Loves nature. Loves this town. He's going to meet me at the festival later, but he went to help Mr. Sherman look for something first." Dot sighed. "I just wish he wasn't so young. It's creepy, right? I mean, I could've been his babysitter ten years ago."

"You're four years older than him, not forty," I reminded her. "This is hardly a cradle robbery." A strange sound caught my ear and lifted my intuition. I turned in search of it. Was I being watched? Followed? I listened hard as the wind whistled through the trees and giant ornaments creaked on barren branches. "I hope you're almost here because I'm starting to freak out."

"Almost," she said, "and I know you're about to be swamped, but do you want to ride over to the hospital together later and visit your granny? We can talk about Jake then. Analyze the conversations for dual meanings. Interpret his body language and the subtle nuances in his speech. I won't dare say a word at the festival. Too many listening ears."

"I hate to break it to you, but if you had coffee with him in public, half the folks here are already going to be talking about it."

She groaned because I was right.

"Did you say I'm about to be swamped?" I asked, turning back to look for the kittens who'd been under my feet a moment before.

A car door shut on her end of the line. "Yeah. Assuming you're planning on letting all of us in."

"What?" I spun back to face the fruit stand and orchard gates, then jogged a few more paces for a clear view of the crowded parking lot and mass of smiling faces on the other side of the wide steel barrier.

"Oh my gosh." I pressed a hand to my heart as folks began to wave.

"Well, don't cry," she said, her voice echoing through the night and phone speaker at once.

Dot unlatched the gates and dragged them wide open.

And the crowd came pouring in.

Two hours later, my cheeks stung from icy wind and ached from a perpetual smile. Everyone I knew had come out to support Granny and me. They came on dates and in groups, as families and friends. Every table and chair was full. Every game had a line of players and plenty of helpers. People were absolutely everywhere.

Pride swelled in my chest. If nothing else, all these people would now know Smythe Orchard was open all year long. And that was priceless.

I just had to convince Mr. Sherman to fund me.

I sipped a hot cider and bopped my head to Loretta Lynn's "Good Old Country Christmas" piping through outdoor speakers near a makeshift dance floor. I hadn't planned for dancing, but there were apparently quite a few local couples who couldn't be stopped, and they knew a line dance for every song. The only thing that would make the moment more satisfying would be if Colton finally showed up. I couldn't reach him by phone, and none of the deputies I'd seen tonight knew where he could be. Everyone thought he was already here. They were certain of it.

So, where was he? Hopefully not like Farmer Bentley or Granny.

Dot and Jake appeared, strolling along chummily until I caught Dot's eye. I waved. She would know if it was too soon to call the hospital and see if something had happened to him. She pivoted in my direction. "What are you doing?" she asked.

"Have you seen Colton?"

Jake frowned. "Who?"

"Sheriff Wise," I corrected. "He was supposed to be here. All his deputies say he was on his way, but his cruiser isn't in the lot and there's no sign of him."

"Maybe he drove his truck," Jake said, "and there are a lot of people here. You've probably just missed him."

I looked to Dot for an opinion.

She didn't look convinced. "I'll see if I can find the sheriff, but you know who else you're missing, right?"

"Who?" I'd barely voiced the question when the proverbial light bulb snapped on, and I nearly swallowed my tongue. "Mr. Sherman!" I burst into a jog in the direction of the barn, and my phone rang. Dot's face was on the screen.

"What?" I asked, feeling the panic squeeze my lungs. How could I have let myself get so distracted that I forgot about the most important meeting of my life?

"I just didn't want you to walk alone. It's dark, so I'll stay on the line until you get there. And just in case Mr. Sherman's been there and gone, I'll keep my eyes out for him in the crowd too. Jake says we can tell him you were caught up with all these customers because you're so in demand."

"Bless you."

The sun had lost its battle against twilight, changing the sky into gorgeous shades of periwinkle and mauve where blinding orange and gold had hovered on the horizon. Overhead there was nothing but an inky dome filled with winter stars.

I stared in awe at the barn on the horizon

as I ran. The regal structure had stood tall and strong for more than one hundred years. It had been part of so many lives. Part of history. The walls had seen more than I could imagine, and thanks to its future cider shop, the beloved Mail Pouch barn would see so much more.

"Aren't you nervous walking alone at night now?" Dot asked.

"I hadn't been, but thanks for bringing that up," I said.

"Sorry, I've just been thinking about all your threats. The things you've seen and experienced lately," she said. "I hate them, but I admire you for your fortitude. I always have."

"My fortitude?" I asked. "Because I haven't locked myself in a fortress until this is over? Believe me, if I could find a fortress, I'd be setting up my cot."

She chuckled. "No. It's not just this. You always take everything in stride and you overcome the bad stuff. You're steadfast. I can't even follow through with giving a guy my number and then answering the phone."

I heard a low chuckle in the background on her line, presumably Jake.

"Yeah, well, I recently came to the conclusion I have a problem." I laughed. "I can't seem to leave anything unfinished. It's more like something to be medicated than admired."

"Perspective," she said.

"I guess, but you know what bugs me?" I asked while we were on the subject of my inability to let things go. "Why did someone vandalize the barn? It's separate from everything else, and we never use it. The trees, I get. Circling my house with lighter fluid, I get. But why mess with the Mail Pouch barn? How did the vandal even know I'd see the fire before the fire burned out by itself in the can? And why not just light the whole place up?"

"Wow. Count your blessings," Dot said. "If you overthink it, you could jinx yourself."

That was true, but I couldn't stop pulling the thread. "How many people really knew about my cider shop plans? And how many of them knew I was meeting with Mr. Sherman that night?"

"Well, you are being stalked," she said. "It's probably reasonable to assume the location for the shop and the meeting time could have been overheard."

I stopped outside the closed barn door and looked back at the lights and merriment of the festival. "Mr. Sherman called me to set the meeting up that night. I was in Granny's kitchen. No one overheard me, and it was almost closing time at the bank."

"What are you saying?" Dot asked

"I'm not sure."

"Maybe you should come back here and wait for him tonight, or I can come to you."

A set of headlights flashed over me as I reached for the barn door. A bolt of panic lanced through me in response. "Someone just pulled onto the access lane behind the barn." I fixed my attention on the large truck, heart tightening with each breath. "What does Mr. Sherman drive?'

"He's got a big truck," she said. "I'm sure you've seen him out hauling his four-wheelers or Jet Skis."

A shadowy figure slid down from the cab and headed my way, one hand lifted over-head in greeting. "Sorry I'm late," he called.

I sighed in relief, pushing my paranoia aside. "It's okay," I said. "It's him."

"Thank goodness," Dot said. "Tell him Jake and I say hello, and call me as soon as you're done."

I disconnected hesitantly, instinct prickling over my skin.

Mr. Sherman had known about our meet-ing the night of the fire. He'd been the one to make the arrangements and set the time. He'd also been late.

He drove a truck like the one that ran me off the road. Like the one that had nearly killed Farmer Bentley. Dot said he used it to haul his four-wheelers.

I shivered as the pieces of my puzzle fell soundly into place. *Lots of people had trucks and ATVs,* I reminded myself. Except . . . who else knew about our meeting?

My phone rang, and I answered in instant relief. "Colton?"

"Winnie!" He barked. "Where are you?"

"I'm at the orchard —" The words lodged in my throat as Mr. Sherman came clearly into view. Gun raised to my chest.

"Good. Find one of my deputies and stick tight until I get there," Colton said. "I'm on my way, but, Winnie, I know who's been doing all this, and I can't find him."

The banker opened a palm, a silent request for my phone.

"Winnie?" Colton pressed. "Did you hear me?"

Fiery tears burned paths across my cheeks. "It's Mr. Sherman," I croaked.

The banker took my phone and crushed it under his boot.

CHAPTER TWENTY

"Inside," he said, flicking his wrist to indicate I should enter the barn.

I obeyed, praying I wouldn't die in the place where I'd planned to start my future. "You said you were running late from work the night someone trashed the barn, but you were the one out here messing it all up, weren't you?" I turned to face him, hoping Colton was close, or that he'd call a deputy who'd look for me. Dot knew where I was, someone just had to ask.

Mr. Sherman shut the door behind us.

Everything I'd been missing slammed nauseatingly into place. Mr. Sherman was the one who'd been threatening me. The same man who'd hurt Granny, ran me off the road, and nearly killed Farmer Bentley. He worked at the bank. He knew about my plans for the cider shop, the dates and times of our scheduled meetings, and all the properties Farmer Bentley was buying. I'd had all the right clues, but I'd been putting them together wrong.

"Sit down," he said, stalking forward.

I moved backward on instinct.

He spun one of my new chairs around and set it in front of the makeshift support beam. Sweat dripped over his temples and beaded on his lip despite the aching cold. "Sit."

I flinched at the urgency in his voice. "You don't want to do this," I said. "You don't have to do this."

"Shut up." He pulled a length of rope from his pocket. "I'm out of choices."

"Not true," I said, shaking my head erratically. "You always have choices." *Don't kill me, for example.* "You can still get back in your truck and run. Leave town. Start over on a pretty island somewhere."

"Sit!" he bellowed, and my knees somehow bent.

I fell into the chair and planted my feet to keep from rocking against the newly erected support beam. I wanted to talk him out of shooting me, not be squashed to death by hundreds of pounds of tchotchkes and café décor. "Everyone knows I'm meeting you here tonight," I said. "If anything happens to me, they'll know it was you."

"I didn't put it on my calendar," he said.

"It'll be your word against mine, and you'll be dead."

"Doesn't matter. You'll still be caught. You have to know that, and you don't want to go to jail," I guessed.

He rubbed his face, pointing the gun away from my chest long enough for me to catch a full breath. His watch came into view. It hadn't been there the last time we'd spoken.

Another truth registered. "Jake was late meeting Dot tonight because he was helping you look for something," I said. "You were looking for your watch. You thought you'd lost it while you were killing Mrs. Cooper. That was why you came back to the press building that night. You were the one who knocked me down the stairs."

He lowered the gun again, aiming for my chest. "I had to try to find it," he said. "If it was here, and one of those CSI guys found it, they would've linked it to me by some random miniscule little thing, and then I'd be in prison. I couldn't have that. Lucky me, it had fallen off in my truck. Now, put your hands behind your back."

"No."

He frowned. "Yes."

I debated my chances of escape by running past him. If I could get outside, I could get help.

Mr. Sherman's hands shook. He wiped sweat from his upper lip. "Do it. I need to get out of here."

Kenny and Dolly squeezed their tiny bodies between the slightly open barn doors and trotted inside. My heart seized. I wanted to shoo them back to safety, but it was too late.

Mr. Sherman caught my gaze and swung his gun toward my babies.

"Don't!" I shouted, pushing my wrists behind my back. "Fine. Here."

"Smart girl," he said, moving around to stand behind me. He worked the ropes confidently over my icy skin in long complicated patterns while the kittens rolled end over end at my feet, enthralled in their game. I wondered briefly if the gunshot or sound of my body crashing onto the floorboards would distract them.

"That ought to hold you," Mr. Sherman said, stepping back to face me.

I wiggled my wrists and felt the scratchy texture of plastic garland between them.

He'd tied me to the pole.

I gave the heavy burden overhead a cautious look and tried to keep still. If he shot me, at least my collapsing body had a chance of knocking all the storage down on him. I tested the binds gently. They didn't give. "Why are you doing this?" I asked. "Why did you kill Mrs. Cooper? Why did you try to kill Farmer Bentley?"

Mr. Sherman stepped back, a look of genuine shock on his brow. "You mean, you don't even know?"

I waited, assuming the answer was obvious.

He ground out a hearty string of curses.

"I told you that you didn't have to do this. I don't even know why any of it is happening."

"Well, it's too late now." He pulled the hammer back on the gun.

I held my breath. No one would hear the gunshot over the festival music and crowd. Dot would be the one to find me. She was the only one who'd come looking for me when I didn't show up later with details about my special one-on-one meeting with the banker. I stared at him. The man who'd taken so much from me. The one who planned to take so much more. "At least help me understand why I have to die. Are you working for Extra Mobil? You're what? A killer for hire now?"

"No," he said. "Extra Mobil paid me to buy land at below market value from owners I knew were in financial trouble. I'm a banker. A good one. Not some hired gun."

I hiked an eyebrow. "You sure about that?"

He groaned and rubbed his face again. "Everything was fine at first, then Bentley figured out what I was up to. He started approaching failing farm owners before I could get to them, and he offered fair market price for the parcels. I couldn't compete with that."

My stomach dropped. "Extra Mobil is coming to Blossom Valley," I said. And Farmer Bentley was buying the properties, not to sell mineral rights to the oil company, but to protect us from what was coming by making sure Extra Mobil never got their hands on enough land to make a move.

"That stupid farmer drained his entire life savings buying up properties to keep me from them."

I shook my head, horrified by what Mr. Sherman had done in response. "He got in your way, so you tried to kill him."

"He figured out my deal with Extra Mobil and threatened to go public. I couldn't let that happen, but I couldn't break my deal with Extra Mobil either because they brought me in on retainer."

I stalled the efforts to free my wrists so I could think about that. "Like a lawyer?"

"Like they covered my gambling debts so I didn't lose my house. Or a kneecap," he muttered, beginning to pace before me. "All I had to do was purchase enough adjoining properties under the name they provided. It should have been easy money. Half this town's broke."

"Was Mrs. Cooper broke?" I asked, resuming the efforts on my binds. I supposed it was possible. All those plastic surgery costs had to add up. "Did she freak out when you made the offer?"

"I never made her an offer," he snarled. "Bentley had started warning people about me. When he told her, she threatened to make a big stink. I stopped by her place to talk her down, but she was already worked up when I got there. She kept yelling and I couldn't think."

The world seemed to still around me. This was what I'd been waiting to know. This was what had started it all. And suddenly, it made sense. "She came to tell Granny about you," I realized. "She wanted to warn us the way Farmer Bentley had warned her." My eyes stung and blurred as a wave of emotion threatened to pull me under. "And you killed her! What is wrong with you? How could you do that? For what? For some oil company? For your gambling debts?" An ugly sob wrenched from my chest and the tears fell in a hot deluge. How had I been so stupid as to think her son or Hank would have done this? I should've known to follow the money trail.

Mr. Sherman turned for me, striding into my personal space and looking as if he might like to kill me after all. "I didn't mean it," he demanded, eyes cold and hard with warning. "She wouldn't listen, and she ran. I followed her to your place, hoping to talk some sense into her. To try to calm her down." His Adam's apple bobbed long and slow. "I chased her into that little building, and she slapped me. I caught her arm before she did it again, but she struggled, and she fell on those stupid platform heels. She hit her head on the metal press and didn't get back up. I didn't know what to do. It was an accident."

"So you ran. You showed up for our meeting later that day as if nothing had happened, and you were going to let my granny take the fall for your crime."

"This orchard was already in financial distress," he said matter-of-factly. "With your granny in jail, she would have been forced to sell. She'd need the money for her attorneys. I'd buy the property for the oil company as planned, and she'd eventually be set free because she didn't do it. Things could have worked out. It could have been a win-win, if you hadn't started poking around."

"Yeah, a real win-win," I scoffed. "Tell that to Mrs. Cooper and her family." I imagined the scenario he'd described. Following her to our orchard. Lurking, waiting for a chance to make her see what he wanted. I pictured him hidden in the trees, and another puzzle piece fell in line. "You're the one who poisoned our trees. You wanted to convince Granny they were sick or dying so she'd be more discouraged and likely to sell. You probably assumed Granny would be an easy target since the orchard was struggling financially already. You thought the dying trees would seal the deal."

His face went red. "Close your eyes. You've got your answers. Now you're out of time."

I desperately scanned the room, taking in my last sights, remembering my life's details so vividly I was sure I could take them with me. "Please don't do this."

A small orange kitten crouched beside him.

A very stupid idea came to mind, but it was the only idea I had. I braced my feet against the floor and hunkered in my seat.

Dolly launched.

Mr. Sherman screamed as she climbed

wildly up his pant leg with razor sharp claws.

I threw myself backward, slamming my chair and head against the makeshift support beam with every bit of force I could muster.

The thunderous creek of weight on wood rumbled overhead and in my chest as the support beam gave way. My head jerked forward, ricocheting from the impact. My vision blurred. A bone-rattling *crack!* exploded through the barn, and Mr. Sherman's gaze went high as my chair toppled over, and an avalanche of plywood and storage crashed over us.

The earsplitting blast of a gunshot registered and my world went black.

CHAPTER TWENTY-ONE

"Winnie!" A muddle of muffled sounds and panicked voices pricked my ears, drawing them back to life. I begged my scratchy eyes to open, but there was only dust and darkness when I did.

"Winnie!" The word came again and again on a thousand voices now, high and low, screeching panic and booming demands.

I couldn't breathe. I willed my lungs to work, but the effort resulted in excruciating pain and a cough.

"Here!" A familiar voice rose above the rest. Dot's voice. "Help! She's here!"

The earth rumbled beneath me, and the choir of voices grew louder.

The pressure on my chest began to lift.

"Winnie?" Dot asked, falling onto her knees and into clear view.

I gurgled an ugly sound, so thankful she was there.

"Stay with me," Dot said, tears streaming

as she reached for my cheeks. "Open your eyes!"

I cracked my lids open against the light, surprised that I'd shut them. A carousel of emergency lights swept over the tightly packed room in waves, showcasing dozens of fearful expressions.

"Mr. Sherman," I said.

"I know."

EMTs cut through the crowd to my side and ducked into position with Dot. They exchanged ominous looks.

"She's going to be fine," Dot announced, a little too firmly.

They nodded and got to work poking and probing my body.

Dot swung her fierce expression back to me. "You're going to be okay."

I nodded.

"Winnie!" Colton's voice startled my eyes open once more. *When did I close them?* He stopped short, eyes wide and cheeks pale as he took in the four of us on the ground.

Dot rose to clasp his hand in hers, and he jerked away. Her pretty white coat was ruined, streaked and smeared in crimson. "She's going to be fine," she repeated in an ugly growl.

My heart gave a strangled thud as I recognized the substance on her coat. Blood.

Ice climbed my veins. The result of an IV. The air grew crisp in my lungs. The effects of an oxygen mask. I focused my hazy thoughts on Dot as my gurney began to roll.

"Not my blood," she said. "Colton, Winnie was shot."

Christmas in Blossom Valley is something not to miss, which was probably why Granny opened her eyes on December 20. Dot drove me to pick her up on Christmas Eve, the day of her official release, the tenth day in a row of subzero windchill and endless snow. The swelling in her brain that had kept her asleep was finally gone, healed by time, careful medical attention, and an abundance of fervent prayers.

I'd shared her room for two nights following Winterfest, mostly for observation. The doctors eventually released me with a bevy of stitches and plenty of prescription pain-killers for my multitude of injuries. My main instruction had been to rest. The concussion had guaranteed that. For days, every time I'd moved my eyes or any inch of my body, I'd regretted it. I'd cracked a rib, busted my head, and suffered numerous lacerations and contusions from the fallen storage boxes and their contents. Mr. Sherman's bullet had also grazed my side, but that had turned out to be less problematic than the head injury I'd given myself while knocking the support beam out from under the storage platform. It was a wild but successful act of bravery or stupidity depending on who told the story. Either way, it had saved my life.

Mr. Sherman was knocked out long enough for the deputies to arrive in response to the gunshot.

The kitties escaped without injury.

And Dot was right. I was going to be okay.

Granny touched the passenger side window with her fingertips as the orchard came into sight. The view was postcard perfect with a fresh foot of snow on the ground and flurries blustering in the air. "Home," she said in one small whisper.

I patted her shoulder over the back of her seat. "Home for Christmas," I said. "That might be my new favorite saying."

Granny set her hand on mine, holding it in place a few beats longer. "I'm so glad you're okay, baby girl."

"Back at ya," I said. "Thanks for waking up and not ruining my holiday."

Granny smiled.

Dot clucked her tongue. "You two need to knock it right off. No more facing off with bad guys."

Granny released my hand to drag a finger-tip across her heart in a little X. "Deal," she said. I think I'm going to accept the Knitwits' invitation to attend their convention. I think it's time I start doing a lot of new things. I'm not going to live forever, so I'd better get started now."

Dot nodded in approval, then locked me in her knowing gaze via the rearview mirror. "What about you? How are you going to occupy your time?"

I beamed. "I have an idea or two."

She winked as she turned up the long gravel drive, past a parking lot already tight with vehicles.

"What on earth?" Granny asked. "Who's running the orchard in this weather?"

"Orchard's closed," I said, but a few folks we know helped me put something else together.

Dot parked outside the Mail Pouch barn and honked her horn.

The little access door popped open, and Colton rushed out to greet us, hunched over in the driving snow. He helped Granny inside, and Dot ushered me. I turned immediately back to see Granny's face as she crossed the threshold.

Roughly seventy-five of our dearest friends had worked in teams, occasionally around the clock for the two weeks following my final meeting with Mr. Sherman. Once word had spread, there was no stopping the offers of aid and assistance. After I'd quit puking at the sound of anything louder than my own heartbeat, thanks to that concussion, I began making lists. And I commissioned one phone call. Dot reached out to Doc Austin for me.

I sold Grampy's red Mustang to the man who'd helped him find and restore it. Then, he'd made an offer on the third car as well. I cried as I signed the titles over to him, but I knew the cars would be in good hands. I knew Grampy would approve, and I knew it was his way of still helping me reach my dreams, even after three long years in heaven.

The money had covered the contractor costs for renovations, electrical, heating, and plumbing. Then I'd flattened my chubby savings account to put up walls and finish the interior.

Granny's friends stood behind the newly erected bar. Dispensers of my cider lined the surface before them, along with neighbors on every bar stool. The place had been well appointed in donations, memorabilia from the area, and general farmhouse chic décor. I'd liberally layered Christmas over all that until everything in sight had a twinkle light, holly berry, or reference to the man in red. Like me in my favorite sweater, the barn was dressed for a good old country Christmas. There was even a tree in the corner, covered in tinsel and faux apple garlands. Two small kittens were no doubt hiding in there as well.

Granny leaned against Colton in shock and immense pleasure. Her eyes brimmed with unshed tears. Her cheeks rose high in the widest smile I'd ever seen. "My stars!" She looked at me in awe. "I can't believe you did all this! It's amazing!"

"I didn't do it," I said, feeling the lump rise in my throat. "They did." I drifted my gaze over the humble and smiling faces throughout my new cider shop. "And Grampy," I added. Without him, the fate of my dream would have remained in the hands of a banker, and I didn't want that anymore.

Colton gave her a hearty hug, then passed her into the crowd.

I watched raptly as the man I'd grown to know as a friend, strode confidently to my side. "How are you feeling?"

"Better now," I said.

"Oh, yeah?" His eyes twinkled with mischief. "Any particular reason?"

"Well, I've been given a ton of pain medications."

Colton laughed. He stuffed long fingers into the front pockets of his suit pants and smiled, looking instantly ten years younger. "Granny looks like she's doing okay."

"She is," I said. "How'd it go in court?" I gave his dark suit an appreciative look. It wasn't something I'd imagine him choosing without a judge involved, but he wore it very well.

"We've got Sherman against a wall," he said. "My team matched the four-wheeler's tracks on your land to a vehicle registered to him. A bystander at Mr. Bentley's accident gave a partial license plate and full truck description that matched Sherman's truck. Once Bentley was able, he gave a full statement outlining what he'd been up to with the properties and why. We found a fifty-thousand-dollar deposit made to Sherman's bank account the day before the first property was purchased in the name of a dummy corporation belonging to Extra Mobil.

"With all that on his shoulders, Sherman broke down and admitted to stalking and threatening you. He copped to running Bentley off the road and injuring your granny. He's holding out on pleading guilty to murder, but the things he told you are helping us build a case that puts him at Nadine Cooper's house the day she died. I think we'll get it done from there. Extra Mobil will be scrambling to recover from this for a while. They've been ordered to pay fines and undergo an investigation. Plus it's generally bad for business to have so many criminal acts committed in your name. The only thing that never panned out was the paint I collected from your bumper. I wasn't able to get a good enough sample for the lab to work with. Luckily, we won't even need it."

"Were you the one who had it buffed out while I was laid up with the concussion?"

Colton smiled. "I don't know what you're talking about."

"Uh-huh." So far that was the same thing everyone said.

I caught his gaze lingering on my torso, specifically the side where I'd been shot, and I poked his chest in warning. "Hey. It wasn't your fault, so knock it off."

Colton still blamed himself for what had happened to me, but he'd done everything he could. When he received news that Farmer Bentley was awake, he made a trip to the hospital on his way to Winterfest. Once Farmer Bentley told him what Mr.

Sherman had done, Colton went to the bank to arrest him, but he was gone. And he wasn't at home. Colton came for me next, but Mr. Sherman was already here.

"It doesn't look like I'm the only one feeling guilty," Colton said, cocking his head for a better look into my averted eyes.

"I can't stop thinking of what I could have done differently to change all of this," I said. Not being able to move around or keep my eyes open for long periods while my concussion healed had given me a lot of time to think. Mostly, I'd just wished I could go back to the day Mrs. Cooper had come looking for Granny and I'd sent her away. "I should have tried to coax the problem out of her. I could have invited her to wait with me while Granny finished the hayride or offered her a glass of cider and tried to get to know her. She was my neighbor after all, and I hadn't even known she had a son."

Colton gave my hand a reassuring squeeze. "You can't think like that. You had no way of knowing what would come, and there are some things that just can't be changed." A flash of pain burned across his face, and I wondered if he spoke from experience. "We have to try to live for the moment and be thankful for what we have," he said. "Look." He let his gaze trail pointedly over the crowd inside my barn. "Your granny's well. The cider shop is open. You helped bring a killer to justice and gave Mrs. Cooper's family closure. Not to mention saving Blossom Valley from the big bad, very crooked, oil company and its henchman. I'd say you did all right."

I grinned, unreasonably proud of his compliments.

The flicker of pain returned to Colton's brow and he dropped his gaze back to meet mine. "I wish you hadn't been hurt in the process."

"I'm fine," I promised, gripping his fingers a little tighter in mine.

"Now, sure, but when I saw you laying there . . ." He stepped closer, expression fathomless. "I realized something."

"What?"

"Winnie! Sheriff!" Hank glided into view, cutting through the crowd with a tall glass of cider and stopped at my side. "Great party! I can't believe this place. You always talked about it, but I never thought you'd really do it. Some things just take a near death experience, I guess." He laughed at his joke, unaffected by the zigzagging chemistry he'd plowed through like a blind mule.

Colton frowned. He released my hand, then braced both palms onto his hips.

Hank wrapped an arm around my back and tugged me against the lean length of his side. "We make a great team, huh?" He smiled at me, then at Colton's frowning face. "That information I gave you really paid off, I guess. I couldn't believe it when I heard what happened. I've been trying to call you for days, but I haven't been able to get through. Goes straight to voice mail."

Colton's expression wavered slightly. His gaze slid to meet mine.

"I've been resting," I said. "Healing up."

Hank patted my back. "No worries. I'll just share my good news now. I'm staying."

"Staying where?" Colton and I asked in near unison.

"Here." Hank beamed. "I applied for the open public relations position with Extra Mobil, and I got the job! I didn't want to mention it until I heard back, but after the corruption scandal, they've got a big need for a man like me. I put people at ease."

Colton's mouth twitched. I rolled my eyes.

"Best part," Hank continued, "is that the facility is only thirty minutes away. I can commute!"

"From here?"

"That's right, Winona Mae. I'm coming home!"

I patted my pockets with a groan. "I think

it's time for more pain pills."

Colton snorted.

Hank rushed away. "I'll get you a water," he called.

I dropped my head forward in defeat. "Horse spit."

Colton grinned. "Indeed." He watched Hank hurry away. "Go easy on the pills. You could become an addict with your ex moving back to town."

I wasn't really taking them. I liked my head clear. Just rest and ibuprofen for me. "I still can't believe I suspected him as a murderer."

"He does seem more like a well-dressed golden retriever than a cold-blooded killer," Colton said.

"Don't tell him you think he's well-dressed unless you want a friend for life."

The volume on my radio increased, and Granny appeared near the Christmas tree. She belted the opening lines to "Let It Snow!" and slowly the crowd began to chime in. The chorus of raised voices sent joyful shivers across my skin and plastered a fresh smile on my lips. This was Blossom Valley. This was the enduring spirit of community and friendship that I never wanted to let go.

Colton set a palm on my shoulder and

stepped in close behind me.

"It's pretty great, huh?" I said, turning in the small space.

He moved his palm to the small of my back, stabilizing me as I arched for a better look into his eyes. "I think you're amazing."

Funny how Colton Wise had been a stranger at Thanksgiving, but on Christmas Eve, he felt a lot like home. "Is that right?"

"Mm-hmm." He dipped his head in my direction and whispered into my ear. "I have to make a call. I won't be long."

"Okay." I stepped back, slightly disappointed and clearly unable to read the man's signals. I blamed my head injury. And the abundance of presumptuous mistletoes. "Everything okay?" I asked, pulling his attention from the phone.

"Yeah." He forced a tight smile. "Everything's good." He stepped outside, and a pile of snow blew in to replace him.

I watched his path outside the window, talking on his phone in a snowstorm. Another man with secrets.

"Merry Christmas," Dot said, sidling up to me with two steaming mugs of cider. She passed one to me, and I wrapped my palms around its warmth.

"Merry Christmas."

We stood shoulder to shoulder, watching

the snow fly beyond the glass.

"You doing okay?" she asked, inhaling the fragrant steam with a smile.

"Yep. I've been thinking about the acts of kindness I told Farmer Bentley I was performing, and I know how I want to fulfill the last one."

"Oh yeah?" She slid a sly smile my way. "Do tell."

"I will foster the next injured or abandoned animal you bring me until I can find it a forever home. Goat, squirrel, turtle, whatever. My last act of kindness is for you, or rather for the things I know are most important to you."

Dot tipped her head against my shoulder. "That's perfect! Thank you."

"You're welcome."

A soft chorus of "Silent Night" began, and we turned away from the window, focusing instead on the beautiful moment at hand. Inside the old Mail Pouch barn, my cider shop dream come true was filled to the rafters with music and laughter, good friends, and gourmet cider.

It was the beginning of my new adventure, and I couldn't wait to get started.

RECIPES

WINNIE'S SLOW COOKIN' CIDER

Everyone loves homemade apple cider, so why not brew up a batch for your next party or get-together? Better yet, make a pot for yourself. Garnish with a handful of chopped green apple and a cinnamon stick for fun. You can serve this simple recipe hot or cold, but you can't go wrong with cider.

1 dozen apples in a variety of flavors.
2 large oranges
1 lemon
4 cinnamon sticks
3 teaspoons whole cloves
2 teaspoons vanilla extract
1/2 cup brown sugar
1/2 cup white sugar

Wash your apples thoroughly, then slice them before adding them to your slow cooker.

Peel and quarter your oranges and lemon. Drop the pieces into the slow cooker with your apple slices.

Add cinnamon sticks and cloves.

Fill the cooker with water.

Cover and cook on low all day or even overnight! Keep cooking until the apple slices are soft and tender.

Mash the ingredients in the cooker, then continue to cook another 1 to 2 hours.

Cover a large pot with cheesecloth and slowly pour the apple mixture in. Repeat the process several times as needed to catch large pieces.

Strain once more with a fine-mesh strainer to eliminate smaller bits. Repeat until the cider is smooth.

Add vanilla extract and sugars while your cider is warm. Stir.

Pour and enjoy hot or cold! Refrigerate or freeze leftover cider.

HUNK OF HEAVEN TATER SALAD

Got a potluck coming up? Not sure what to bring? Knock 'em dead with some tasty tater salad, a long-held country tradition sure to make folks smile. Just remember, *tater salad is personal.* Take your time with the measurements and keep at it until the flavor is just right for you.

6 large or 8 medium-size potatoes
4–6 hardboiled eggs
1 1/2 cups real mayonnaise
2 tablespoons cider vinegar
3 tablespoons sugar
2 tablespoons yellow mustard
1/2 teaspoon salt
1/2 teaspoon pepper
1 teaspoon garlic powder
1 cup onion, chopped
Paprika as garnish

Peel and boil potatoes. Cool. Dice.
Peel and chop eggs.
In a medium bowl, blend mayonnaise, vinegar, sugar, mustard, salt, pepper, and garlic powder until smooth.
Add potatoes and coat well.
Mix in onions and eggs.
Dash with paprika for pizzazz.

HANK'S MAMA'S DUMP CAKE

There isn't anything simpler than dump cake, and it's guaranteed to bring folks running. So, next time you're in a hurry to whip up something sweet, grab these four ingredients from the kitchen, and you'll be the hit of the party.

Note: You can use any combination of pie fillings and cake flavors to suit your fancy.

Granny loves cherries and chocolate cake. Dot prefers peaches and yellow cake. Winnie likes pineapples and cherries. The recipe's so simple you might as well try all three!

1 21-ounce can of cherry pie filling
1 16-ounce can of crushed pineapple
1 boxed white cake mix
1 1/2 sticks of butter

Preheat oven to 350 degrees.

Mix cherry pie filling and pineapple together in a medium bowl.

Pour into a 9-by-13-inch baking dish.

Sprinkle cake mix over fruit.

Add pats of butter evenly across the top.

Bake 45 to 60 minutes, until top is brown and bubbly.

Serve with vanilla ice cream or whipped topping.

Happy eating, y'all!

ACKNOWLEDGMENTS

Thank you, dear reader, for picking up this book and for giving Winnie and Granny's story a chance. You might not realize it, but you make my dream possible. I can't thank you enough for that.

Thank you, Martin Biro, and the entire, amazing Kensington team for seeing merit in my work and for making it better. I will never stop celebrating that win. Thank you, Jill Marsal, my agent extraordinaire, the beautiful magician who never stops believing in me and always keeps me busy.

Thank you, Jennifer Anderson, for reading all my words. I owe you so many hugs and coffees and glasses of wine. I hope you're running a tab. Thank you, Darlene Lindsey, my blessed mother-in-law and dear friend. I couldn't do this without you, and I can never repay you. Thank you, Mama, for making me believe I can move mountains, and Daddy, for teaching me to climb them.

Your love of West Virginia inspired this series, and I hope I can do it justice.

Last but not least, Bryan, kids, what can I say? I forget things and talk to myself and sometimes wear pajamas for weeks on end, but I love you all with every ounce of myself, and I know that one day you will change the world. You've already changed mine irrevocably.

ABOUT THE AUTHOR

Julie Anne Lindsey is a multi-genre author who writes the stories that keep her up at night. When she's not creating new worlds and organizing the epic adventures of fictional characters, Julie can be found carpooling her three kids around Northeastern Ohio and plotting with her shamelessly enabling friends. Today, she hopes to make someone smile. One day she plans to change the world. Julie is a member of the International Thriller Writers, Romance Writers of America, and Sisters in Crime. Visit her online at www.JulieAnneLindsey.com.

CPSIA information can be obtained
at www.ICGtesting.com
Printed in the USA
BVHW071929081020
590579BV00003BA/11

9 781432 880989